THE
SAINT
PETER'S
PLOT

THE SAINT PETER'S PLOT

Derek Lambert

Arlington Books
Clifford Street Mayfair
London

THE SAINT PETER'S PLOT
first published October 1978
Arlington Books (Publishers) Ltd
3 Clifford Street Mayfair
London W1
Second impression December 1978

© *Derek Lambert 1978*

Typeset by Inforum Ltd Portsmouth
Printed and bound in England by
A. Wheaton and Company Ltd Exeter

ISBN 85140 289 5

For Mike and Sybil Keats,
Natasha, my god-daughter, and Alexia.

PART I

I

The Commanding Officer of Adolf Hitler's crack SS regiment took his leave of the Pope at 11.33 am on July 29th, 1943, unaware that he was closer to death than at any time during the bloody campaigns he had fought in Europe and Russia.

By 11.40 am Josef 'Sepp' Dietrich was walking briskly — a marching step almost — across St. Peter's Square towards the line of white travertine stones that links the embracing arms of Bernini's colonnade and marks the boundary of Vatican territory inside the city of Rome.

Behind Dietrich, former butcher and Munich bully-boy, a young man with the face of a saint and a 9 mm Walther pistol concealed beneath his jacket signalled to an older man stationed on the boundary line.

The older man, his bald patch as neat as a skull-cap, signalled back with the current edition of L'Osservatore Romano, The Vatican newspaper.

As Dietrich passed the Egyptian obelisk a sudden gust of wind disturbed the sultry day blowing plumes of spray from the two fountains, dislodging a prelate's hat and startling a flock of pigeons into flight.

Dietrich, pugnaciously built, big-eared and cold-eyed, noticed none of this: he was too preoccupied with the speed of recent events. The Allied Invasion of Sicily; the withdrawal of his own regiment, Die Leibstandarte Adolf Hitler, from the Russian front to Italy; the dismissal and arrest on July 25 of Benito Mussolini by his own people.

9

The next event, Dietrich brooded, would be the capitulation of Italy to the Allies. So? Germany would be better off without them!

By the time Dietrich reached the black Mercedes-Benz waiting for him near the boundary line, the man with the bald patch had climbed into the driving seat of a Fiat 500 fuelled earlier that morning with Black Market petrol.

Dietrich paused beside the Mercedes, drumming his fingers on the bonnet. Beside him stood a plain-clothes driver, rigidly to attention waiting to dive for the door-handle.

But perhaps a walk. It had been a long time since Dietrich, founder in the early '30s of a unit of shock troops that were the forerunners of the SS, had walked for pleasure. You didn't walk for pleasure in Russia; you didn't do anything for pleasure in Russia — except kill Russians.

He turned to the driver. "I'm going to walk back." The driver displayed no surprise. "Follow me at a discreet distance."

Dietrich set off towards the Tiber, sweating inside the double-breasted grey suit that he had last worn at a meeting with Hitler at the Eagle's Nest in the Bavarian mountains.

The suit hung loosely on him. Small wonder after the deprivations of Russia; the battle for Rostov — the Leibstandarte's first defeat — the Arctic winter of '42-'43, the Pyrrhic victory at Kharkov.

But in any case, Dietrich felt uneasy in civilian clothes. He was born for uniforms, swaggering uniforms with a silver death's head badge on the cap, the double runic 'S' on a steel helmet, leather belts with *My Honour is my Loyalty* inscribed on the buckle.

But in Rome the Germans wore civilian clothes. They were not an occupying army. Not yet.

Dietrich observed with contempt the Italians walking the streets of their capital. In particular the men. They couldn't wait to get out of uniform, and despite the shortages of war they still managed to groom themselves as beautifully as Berlin fairies.

When Dietrich reached the great rounded bulk of Castel Sant' Angelo, once the military bastion of Rome, he toyed with the idea of recommending that all Italian deserters be thrown into its mediaeval dungeons. And the Jews, of course. As he crossed the Ponte S. Angelo, spanning the khaki-coloured waters of the Tiber, he smiled for the first time that morning.

Behind him, a hundred yards between them, two cars followed — the black Mercedes and the little Fiat. The man with the bald patch had now been joined in the passenger seat by the young man with the Walther. They were arguing.

*　　*　　*

The plan had been simple but conceived in haste.

Word had reached the partisans from The Vatican — next to Switzerland the biggest nest of spies in Europe — that Hitler's most feared and fearless soldier, Sepp Dietrich, had been granted an audience with the Pope.

The core of the partisani was comprised of Italian officers and troops who had seen their fellow countrymen executed by the SS on the Russian front for lack of enthusiasm for what was, to them, an insane and suicidal campaign. Dietrich, the embodiment of SS fanaticism, was an irresistible target in Rome.

But the partisani, busy deploying themselves for the inevitable German occupation, were not yet organised. Dietrich might only stay in Rome for a few hours: the assassination plot had been devised in less than thirty minutes.

According to The Vatican source, Dietrich would, after his audience with the Pope, visit the Most Rev. Alois Hudal, the German bishop renowned for his Nazi sympathies, at his church, S. Maria dell' Anima.

The site of the church was ideal for the assassination. A stolen German stick-grenade tossed as Dietrich climbed out of the Mercedes, a maze of escape routes through the old, cobbled streets.

11

The young man with the saintly features had served on the Russian front, and he had been posted outside The Vatican because he could immediately identify the SS Commander. He would signal to the older man who knew Rome as intimately as a cab driver. As soon as Dietrich took off in his Mercedes the older man would drive his Fiat through the short-cuts and tell the assassin to take up his position.

And it all might have gone smoothly enough if Sepp Dietrich hadn't decided to take a walk in the sun.

In the Fiat the young man said: "We should kill him now."

The older man gripped his arm. "Patience, my friend."

"Patience!" Hysteria played tricks with his vocal chords. "The biggest bastard unhung strolls in front of us and you talk about patience!"

"He will go to the church. Then we will have him."

"Supposing he doesn't. Supposing he changes his mind. Supposing he decides to fill his guts with pasta instead of seeing a priest."

The older man shrugged. He was a Sicilian, said to be a relative of the legendary Mafia leader, Don Vito Cascio Ferro, and his violence was controlled and reasoned. He wished it was he who had the Walther in the belt of his trousers.

He tried to reason with the younger man whose brain had been touched by the Russian winter. "If you tried to shoot him now there would be no escape. And in any case you might miss. What is the range of a Walther P. 38? The same as a Colt .45, forty-five metres, no more. And even as you pulled the gun he" — pointing at the driver of the Mercedes — "would kill you."

And, thought the Sicilian, *under torture you would blow everything*.

The hand of the younger man strayed inside his jacket. "You didn't see what he and his sort did in Russia. You didn't see them beat men to death with the buckles of their belts."

"The SS?" Unsolicited, a note of admiration crept into the Sicilian's voice. "Ruthless, perhaps," shrugging, "but certainly the best troops in the world. Possibly the best the world

12

has ever known."

The younger man stared at him. "You admire them?"

"I'm merely saying they're good soldiers.'

The younger man tightened his grip on the butt of the Walther. "Are you sure you are fighting on the right side?"

"Oh yes," said the Sicilian, "I'm sure of that. You see I'm a Sicilian," as if that explained everything. "But it doesn't prevent me from admiring an enemy. Even before I kill him," he added.

They were across the Tiber now, turning left in the direction of the Piazza Navona. The Sicilian sensed that their private crisis was over: if the trigger-happy novice at his side had made a move he would have done it on the bridge.

The young man sulked. "You know something?"

"What?" braking when the Mercedes slowed down as Dietrich stopped to take off his jacket and drape it over one arm.

"I think you were scared back there."

"Of course I was."

"I could have killed him."

"Of course you could," the Sicilian said, taking one hand from the wheel and feeling the bald patch as though he wanted to doff it.

"I'll tell the others about this," said the young man and the Sicilian thought: "Not if I cut out your tongue, you won't."

Now Dietrich was crossing the road, gesturing to the driver of the Mercedes to stop.

"Now what?" said the younger man.

"Wait and see," the Sicilian said.

As they passed the stationary Mercedes they saw Dietrich sit down at a white-painted table outside a trattoria. Immediately a waiter with a black bow-tie and a white apron was at his side.

"You see," the young man said, "he's going to stuff himself with pasta."

"I hope he doesn't expect meat sauce," the Sicilian said. "Times are hard."

"What are we going to do?"

"What can we do but wait?"

13

The Sicilian parked the Fiat beside the flaking trunk of a plane tree. "I suggest," he said to the younger man, "that you take a stroll. Two men waiting in a car are always suspicious. Believe me, I know."

*　　*　　*

Dietrich didn't order pasta. He didn't seem to have the same stomach for food these days. He ordered a bottle of Peroni beer, put his feet on the chair opposite and tried to relax. But it was difficult. There was too much on his mind, not the least of which was his audience with the Pope.

Dietrich had determined not to be overawed. After all he had but one God — Hitler. And Hitler had responded to his worship to the extent of admonishing Heinrich Himmler Reichsführer of the SS: "Dietrich is master in his own house which, I would remind you, is mine."

Dietrich had anticipated a measure of servility from the Pope. After all, The Holy See was in peril: the German 3rd Panzergrenadier Division lurked threateningly outside Rome and Hitler was reported to have stated: "I'll go right into The Vatican. Do you think The Vatican embarrasses me?"

Certainly not. Nor would Pius XII embarrass Sepp Dietrich.

And yet when he entered the audience chamber and saw the Pope in his white and gold robe seated on a throne on a small platform, he had immediately felt intimidated. It was all stage management, he told himself. All the old tricks of assertion — the enforced wait outside the chamber, the dominant positioning of the throne, the lighting.

But it was more. Dietrich found himself not only in the presence of the Pontiff but of a consummate diplomat who, speaking fluent German — he had been Papal Nuncio in Germany for many years — committed himself with gentle authority to absolutely nothing.

But, Dietrich comforted himself as the cool beer coursed down his throat, I did make my point. Perhaps I didn't extract

14

a promise but my request was not denied.

He ordered another beer from the waiter who was probably a deserter or a conscientious objector. God, how he loathed Italians.

This time he gulped the beer. Attacked it in the way he satisfied all his appetites. But, when all the beer was gone, he finally acknowledged the root of his unease which he had been concealing from himself ever since he had left The Vatican: for the first time in his life he had admitted the possibility of ultimate defeat; for the first time in his life he had admitted the fallibility of the Führer. And to the leader of the Catholic Church!

Sepp Dietrich flung some money onto the table, swung his legs off the chair and strode across the road to the Mercedes.

To the driver he snapped: "Now take me to this other crow."

*   *   *

The grey Fiat beat the Mercedes by thirty-eight seconds to the Vicolo della Pace where, at No. 20, visitors were admitted to S. Maria dell' Anima.

The young man who had rejoined the Sicilian dashed into a doorway and spoke urgently to a partisan named Angelo Peruzzi, who was waiting with the German stick-grenade hidden in a worn leather brief-case.

Peruzzi nodded, gesturing impatiently to the young man to get out of the way, and slipped the leather tongue of the brief-case. He slid one hand into the briefcase and grasped the hollow wooden handle of the grenade. An observer might have assumed that he was fingering a Bible because he was dressed as that most inconspicuous of Roman inhabitants — a priest.

He walked swiftly up the cobbled side-street, arriving outside No. 20 just twenty seconds before the black Mercedes arrived.

And then the course of Italian history, of world history, might have been changed if it had not been for a beautiful Jewish girl named Maria Reubeni.

II

Maria Reubeni had awoken that morning in her apartment in the old Jewish quarter of Rome near the Bridge of the Four Heads at 5.30.

These days she always awoke early, sometimes with problems of the previous night processed and solved, always with her mind turbulent with ideas.

Maria was a fervent Jew but not an Orthodox one. Her fervour was directed towards salvation rather than religious observation. She was sure that one day she would be a Zionist, but at the moment she was more concerned with saving Jews than rehabilitating them.

She rose from the bed and stood naked at the open window of her bedroom and peered round the yellow curtains for her daily glimpse of the river — the advertisement for the apartment had said simply 'overlooking Tiber' without mentioning that you could break your neck looking for it. She saw a swirl of water and withdrew from the window satisfied. It had become a ritual this daily peek at the river: not for any aesthetic reason: merely to remind her each day that the Tiber had once regularly flooded the ghetto into which Pope Paul IV had thrown the Jews in the sixteenth century. To Maria Reubeni the flow of the Tiber was the flow of Jewish persecution ever since.

But Maria was not a Jew who dolefully studied anti-Semite history while awaiting the next blow. She could not understand why the Jews of Europe were allowing themselves to be

16

exterminated by the Germans. My God there were enough of them. Now she was determined to save the Jews of Rome.

She left the window open so that she could smell the first breaths of freshly-baked bread and coffee from the street below and turned on the shower in the bathroom. The cold water drumming on her shower-cap and sluicing down her body cooled her thoughts and gave them direction.

It was now a critical time for Italian Jewry. She and the other members of DELASEM, Delegazione Assistenza Emigranti (Jewish Emigrant Association), had known this ever since the war had started to go badly for the Axis powers. Italy would crumble. The Germans would move in. The Jews would suffer.

Now Mussolini had been ousted and it was just a matter of time ... First DELASEM had to persuade the Allies and Italy's new government under Pietro Badoglio to postpone an announcement of an armistice until they had got the Jews out of Italian-occupied France — and organised sanctuaries for the Roman Jews.

Maria dried herself, glanced briefly at her fine, heavy-breasted body in a wall mirror, dressed herself in a lime-green skirt and blouse and began to brush her long hair, so black that it seemed to have bluish lights in it.

Then she went to a cafe near the Theatre of Marcellus and ordered black coffee, the ersatz variety which tasted more like gravy, and a slice of pizza with a filling no thicker than a post-age stamp.

The waiter with the anaemic moustache served her with a traditional flourish.

"Have you heard the news today?" he asked.

She shook her head, mouth full of pizza.

"Palermo has fallen," the waiter told her.

"It fell on the twenty-second," said Maria.

"Ah, you have better information than me."

"I listen to the BBC."

"Soon they will be on the mainland. Soon, perhaps, in Rome?" He looked at her hopefully. This goddess who had brains as well as beautiful bosoms.

"Perhaps," said Maria.

The waiter pointed at the pizza and coffee. "Now every Italian knows we should never have gone to war. It is hurting us where it hurts most," prodding his stomach. And then sadly: "We Italians are not fighters."

She looked at him steadily. The waiter smiled uncertainly. She stood up, at least three inches taller than him. "Never let me hear you say that," she said, searching for money in her handbag.

"You think we are fighters?" Astonished.

"You are implying that Italians are cowards," Maria said. "Have you ever heard of Suda Bay?"

Miserably the waiter shook his head and began to clear the table to avoid her gaze.

"The Italians sank the British cruiser, *York*, and three supply ships. And how did they do it?" waiting until he was forced to look up. "With human torpedos, that's how. And the pilots only ejected when the explosives were on target."

"I didn't mean — " the waiter began.

"The Italians are as brave as anyone. It is merely that we" — *What am I, Jewish or Italian?* — "are not stupid enough to sacrifice our way of life — that is what we have more than any other nation, a way of life — for an empty cause. But we are ruled by our hearts and not our minds, and that is why we allowed ourselves to be led to disaster by the Fascists."

Her speech finished she strode from the cafe.

"Ah, she's got guts, that one," said a workman in blue dungarees sipping his coffee.

"Six months ago she would have been thrown into jail," observed another.

"Perhaps she will be very soon," said the first workman. "When the Germans come."

The waiter said: "Why? The Germans have no love for Mussolini. Why should they throw her into jail for insulting him?"

"Because," said the second workman, "she's a Jew. That's why, my friend."

Outside the cafe Maria turned on her heel and headed

towards the Corso. She was surprised at her pro-Italian outburst; after all, the Italians had introduced racial laws aimed at the Jews — even the Jewish artichoke had been renamed; but, Maria comforted herself, that had been the doing of the Fascists. But why had she wasted words on the waiter? Perhaps, she thought, because I know no man of character and strength in whom to confide; a man, that is, to whom I am physically attracted. Not even Angelo Peruzzi whose strength is a sham.

She didn't take one of the green trams this morning. She wanted to smell the scents of Rome as it finally climbed from its bed after its drowsy awakening. The sky was misty blue and the streets rang with the clip-clop of horses' hooves — more horses around these days than cars. But today Maria sensed a fresh nuance to the summer morning; a new expectancy as the Romans awaited the Germans, a razor-blade of cruelty; and when a pneumatic drill started up she jumped as though it were gunfire.

*　　*　　*

At the Fountain of Trevi Maria met by appointment a man she did admire. Although admiration was the limit of their relationship because the man was forty-eight — and a priest.

His name was Father Marie-Benoit, known in Rome as Maria Benedetto. He was a French Capuchin friar who had dedicated himself to rescuing Jews from their oppressors.

From the outset his career had been unorthodox. In the First World War he had served with the 44th Infantry Regiment as a stretcher-bearer and rifleman and had been awarded the *Croix de Guerre* with five citations and the *Medaille Militaire*. He was being trained as a machine-gunner when the Armistice was signed and was then transferred to the 15th Algerian Rifle Regiment in Morocco. After that he became Professor of Theology at the College International de St. Laurent.

At the outset of the present war he served first as an Italian interpreter with the French South-east Army Group. When France surrendered he went to Vichy, France, to Marseilles, sorting house of gangsters and refugees from German-occupied Europe. There he organised escape routes for the Jews.

Subsequently he was recalled by his Father Superior to Rome, where he had previously served, and was installed in the Capuchin Monastery at 159 Via Sicilia.

Currently he was working on plans to evacuate Jews from the area of southern France occupied by the Italians because, as soon as the Italian surrender to the Allies was announced, the Germans would move in and implement Hitler's Final Solution.

Seeing him standing beside the fountain Maria Reubeni thought: "Now there's a man."

She walked up to him. "Good morning, Father."

He smiled at her. "Good morning, my child." His features were serene and yet it seemed to Maria that the serenity was a mask beneath which any extreme was possible.

He pointed at the fountain's rocks set against the wall of the palace, at the statues of gods and goddesses and tritons, and the cascades of water spilling into the great bowl. "That water," he said, "comes from Agrippa's aqueduct, the Aqua Vergine, probably the sweetest water in all Rome. And do you know what the English used to do with it?"

She shook her head.

"Make tea."

She laughed.

"Great people the English. A pity they never colonised Rome. If they had we might spend the rest of the day waiting for the sun to go down over the yard-arm instead —"

"Of waiting for the Germans to come."

Father Benedetto sighed. "And come they will. Already the German Army is preparing to take over. We have a lot to do," he said taking her arm. "Papers to forge, food to hide, escape hatches to oil."

"But first," she said, "the Jews in France, in Nice. How is it going, Father?"

"Slowly," said the priest. "As you know, I've seen the Holy Father and sought his help. So far nothing's happened but that was only thirteen days ago. These things take time. And the Holy Father is in a very difficult position," he added.

"Very," the girl said drily. "He finds it very difficult to acknowledge the existence of Jews. Particularly dead ones."

"Now that," said the Capuchin friar, "is not quite so. There are many factors involved. But this is no time for a debate about Papal diplomacy." He led her from the little square in the direction of the Corso, gesturing with his free hand. "Palaces, basilicas, villas . . . We live in a museum. And there must be many dusty hiding places in a museum."

"But will you be able to get the Jews out of France?" Maria asked.

"We hope to get in touch with London and Washington through the British and American representatives at The Holy See. The prisoners in The Vatican," he said smiling. "Which reminds me," tightening his grip on her arm, "I understand there was a very important visitor to The Holy See today."

They reached the Corso, the windows of its elegant facades covered with dark-blue paper as an air-raid precaution. There were a few people around heading for the food queues; a kiosk opposite the Piazza Colunna displayed newspapers bearing nebulous headlines because editors were no longer sure what constituted good and bad news.

"Who was that?" Maria asked. "The Chief Rabbi?"

"On the contrary," Father Benedetto said. "He was a German."

"That doesn't surprise me."

"His name might."

"Who was it, Hitler?"

"Not quite." Benedetto bought a newspaper with a map of Sicily on the front page. The arrows on it seemed to indicate that the Enemy was winning. Or were they now the Allies? "His name is Dietrich."

"Not Sepp Dietrich?"

"So it seems."

"But what —"

"That is what we'd like to know," the priest interrupted.

21

"Why was Hitler's favourite soldier-boy seeing the Holy Father?"

"Or why," said the girl, "did the Pope grant an audience to a swine like that?"

"Whichever way you like to put it," Father Benedetto said mildly. "Apparently it isn't generally known that the audience took place."

"How do you know?" She plunged her hands deep into the pockets of her skirt and began to walk slowly down the sidewalk, head bowed in thought.

"From our contact" — he corrected himself —"*your* contact in The Vatican. It seems," tapping her on the shoulder with the rolled-up newspaper, "that you have a way with priests."

"But why didn't he contact me?"

"Apparently you were out of touch last night."

"I suppose I was. I was having dinner with my father." She took a pack of cigarettes from her handbag, then put it back because you didn't smoke in the presence of a priest, certainly not walking in the street. "Who did he contact?"

"Angelo Peruzzi," the priest told her and, because of her startled reaction, asked: "Why, does it matter?"

She said abruptly: "It might."

"Well, you'd better go and see him," said Father Benedetto uncertainly. "He's a good man, isn't he?"

"A good man, yes. But a weak man who disguises his weakness with bravado. If you'll excuse me, Father, I'd better go to him now."

"Very well, my child." He touched her arm. "God be with you."

Yes, she thought as she boarded a tram, Angelo was a good man. A brave man? Possibly. But bravery wasn't necessarily strength, bravery didn't embrace wisdom. How many acts of bravery had been committed for facile motives? Would Angelo kill just to prove himself to the rest of the partisani?

*　　*　　*

22

From the tram, jammed with rich and poor united by lack of gasoline, Maria gazed at churches and palaces opening their pores to the sun; at the sand-coloured walls of the Palazzo Venezia and its balcony from which Mussolini had declared war: at the white wedding cake across the square, the Vittorio Emanuele Monument.

In this square, when the overthrow of Mussolini had been announced, Maria had seen black-shirts flee for their lives as the crowd spat on a bronze bust of Mussolini. The euphoria had been sustained by the rumour that Hitler was dead.

Now the celebrants had retired and the Fascists were showing their noses again. Mussolini was still alive, the Germans would soon be here, and already in the streets you could see young men with bright blue eyes wearing combat clothes beneath civilian jackets.

Maria turned her attention to the stumps and roots of ancient Rome. The Allies had already bombed the city, wrecking the Basilica di San Lorenzo. How many more noble buildings would join the ruins of the Coliseum and the Forum before the war was finished? And who would destroy them — the Germans or the Allies? If only, Maria thought, the Italians could decide which *was* the enemy.

She alighted from the tram under a Fascist slogan, *Many Enemies, Much Honour* and made her way up the Via Cavour, a long and dreary street leading away from the sunlit ruins.

Here, in a small square reached by a flight of worn steps, Angelo Peruzzi had a one-roomed apartment. The tapestries of the square were underclothes and faded blouses hanging from the balconies. The only inhabitants at this time were starved cats that had escaped the stewpot.

Maria mounted the hollowed stairs and knocked on the door. No reply. She took the key to the room from her purse. Angelo had given her the key in the hope that she would join him in bed, but she had laughed at him and he had sulked for a week.

He was handsome enough with his brigand's face and polished black hair; but he wasn't a Jew, and in any case she had no respect for him.

The room smelled of stale tobacco smoke. On one side was an unmade camp bed. *And he wanted me to share that!* Opposite the bed a bookcase filled with innocuous volumes — these days you didn't display either Fascist or Communist literature — and, on the walls, photographs of the Peruzzi family grouped round proud Papa who looked like an old-time Chicago barber.

Maria glanced at the papers lying on the table, one of its legs supported by a manual on firearms. She picked up an unlabelled bottle of red wine and smelled it. She grimaced. Gutrot! Angelo Peruzzi, aged twenty-eight, drank too much. It saddened her that she had to work with such men. But these days every willing hand was valuable, and Angelo was in contact with the most influential partisani, each group prepared to fight for its own rights in post-war Italy.

At first Maria had wondered why the more level-headed partisani bothered with Angelo. Then she had discovered that they used him because he liked to kill.

She was replacing the bottle when she noticed the sheaf of paper on which it had been resting. On the first sheet were scrawled three words in Angelo's childish hand-writing: DIETRICH VATICAN HUDAL.

Slowly Maria lowered the bottle to the table. She glanced at her wrist-watch. It was 11.30 am. If Dietrich had been granted an audience with the Pope, then it would be over by now.

In two strides she was across the room, pulling back the bed, grimacing at the smell of unwashed sheets, pulling an old oak wedding chest from underneath. She tossed aside old magazines until she reached Angelo's private armoury. A dismantled Thompson sub-machine gun, a Luger pistol and a stiletto with an elaborately carved handle.

All present and correct — except a German stick-grenade.

Maria ran out of the house into the square where the cats spat and arched their backs. Then she was in the Via Cavour running towards the centre of the city.

An old Lancia passed her, the driver — a fat man with a few

strands of hair greased across his scalp — glanced at her over his shoulder. She waved and he smiled, winked and stopped the car.

"What's the hurry, my pretty one?"

She jumped in beside him and told him to take her to the Piazza Navona as though she were addressing a taxi driver.

He shrugged, smiled, patted her knee and drove away.

"Urgent business?"

"Very."

"Perhaps after this, ah, urgent business, we could meet and have a little drink. Perhaps in the sunshine on the Via Veneto..."

"Perhaps," thinking: "If Angelo has ruined everything I'll kill him."

"What is the, ah, nature of this urgent business? It isn't usual to see beautiful girls running on a hot day in Rome." He glanced sideways at her. "You looked as though you were running for your life."

"I'll tell you about it later," she said. "When we're having that drink. And maybe after that..." managing a smile at the fat Fascist black-marketeer beside her. "Could we go a little quicker?"

"Nothing easier." He stamped on the accelerator. "There's no traffic on the roads. Not many of us are lucky enough to have cars these days. I have lots of beautiful things I could show you."

As they neared the Piazza Navona Maria told him to stop.

"But I thought —"

"This will do," she snapped.

As she climbed out she turned on him. "I know your face now, you fat pig. You'd better watch out."

She lifted her skirts and ran through the narrow streets arriving at S. Maria dell' Anima just as a black Mercedes was pulling up outside.

She saw Angelo Peruzzi in his clerical clothes as he was reaching into the leather briefcase. She threw herself at him, grabbing his hand inside the briefcase.

He swore and tried to push her away. She pressed her body against him, trapping the briefcase between them.

He pushed again with his free hand but she clung to him. He thrust his hand under her chin: "Get away from me or I'll break your neck."

She could feel his strength overcoming her; all she needed was a few moments more.

"Get away . . ."

Her head was bending backwards. Another fraction of an inch and the bones of her neck would snap. She gave way and fell to the ground, just as the door closed behind the bulky figure in the ill-fitting grey suit.

Angelo's lips were trembling. With shaking hands he slipped home the tongue of the strap over the spring-clip on the case.

"You bitch," he said.

III

The inquiry into the Dietrich episode was held in a cellar in the Borgo — a grenade's throw from The Vatican, as Angelo Peruzzi had once put it.

But this evening Angelo Peruzzi was not in joking mood. He was trying desperately to maintain his prestige which is difficult when you have been all but overpowered by a woman.

Angelo's prestige had been based on his willingness, and proven ability, to kill. And it owed its strength to the smallness of the group at a time when the partisani were an inchoate force of splinter groups which would only become a unified resistance movement when the Germans occupied Rome, and the British and Americans invaded the Italian mainland.

Angelo also drew his strength from Maria which had not been fully realised by the other members of the group. Until now.

The cellar was lit by a naked bulb hanging from the ceiling. The three men — the two who had stalked Dietrich, and Angelo Peruzzi — sat on packing cases sharing a bottle of grappa while Maria sat on the table swinging her long legs as her agitation increased.

Angelo's only possible ally was the younger man with the frost-bitten brain, but he was no match for Maria's passionate eloquence or the menacing presence of the Sicilian.

Angelo was saying: "I still think I should have killed him."

Carlo, the younger man, said: "What kind of partisani are we if we fail to kill a big fish like Dietrich when he's handed to

27

us on a plate?" By now he was asking questions instead of making statements. He looked at the Sicilian who shrugged. "If you had seen men like that in Russia . . ." Carlo always produced Russia and they forgave him a lot because of what he had been through.

The Sicilian drank from the bottle of grappa and handed it to Angelo Peruzzi. "And what about the things the Russians did to the Germans? What about the story of the gold?"

"What gold?" Angelo asked, happy for any diversion.

"It seems the SS were searching for gold in some village. They threatened to arrest the entire population — and by arrest they meant murder — if the gold wasn't produced. They left four men in charge. Next day they returned and in one of the buildings they found a box marked GOLD." The Sicilian paused for effect. "When they opened it they found it contained the heads of the four men they had left behind."

"Sometimes," Carlo said, "I wonder whose side you're on."

The Sicilian gave a gold-toothed smile. "Mine," he said.

"You should be in Sicily fighting the Germans."

The Sicilian closed his smile, took a knife from his belt and tested its blade with his thumb. "My place is here in Rome. Here I have contacts. Family contacts," he emphasised. "Sicily will fall within a month. And when the Germans march into Rome there will be much work to do," throwing the knife at a photograph of Mussolini on the wall.

Maria lit a cigarette, blowing the smoke into the aureole of light around the naked bulb. "If Angelo had killed Dietrich we wouldn't be in any position to fight the Germans."

Angelo started to speak but she held up her hand.

"If Angelo had thrown that grenade the Germans would be here now. They would be in The Vatican. We would have been finished before we started. They would have slaughtered hundreds of innocent men, women and children. Our movement would have been obliterated."

"*Our* movement?" The Sicilian retrieved the knife from the Duce's face, already slitted with many wounds. "What exactly are your priorities?" His parents had sent him to Rome

28

to be educated and he spoke Italian like a Roman.

She swung her heart-breaking legs a little quicker. "Very well, it's obvious that I am concerned with the Jews. But that doesn't mean we cannot work together."

"That is true," the Sicilian agreed. He held up the bottle to determine how much grappa Angelo Peruzzi had swallowed. "And I tell you now that I agree that it was a mistake to try and kill Dietrich."

It was then that Maria realised the strength of the Sicilian. To be strong you had to admit your mistakes; beside the Sicilian, Carlo and Angelo were actors, cowboys.

The Sicilian said to Angelo: "But don't despair, my friend. You did what you thought was right," and Maria realised that the Sicilian was taking over. *I would never have said such a thing to Angelo.*

And to the three of them the Sicilian said: "We must stop fighting among ourselves. We must make decisions and keep to them." *Your* decisions, Maria thought. "And if anyone doesn't . . ." He spoke with his hands. "In Sicily we have always had a way of dealing with such people." He threw the knife which this time embedded itself in Mussolini's throat.

The two younger men remained sulkily silent.

"You see," the Sicilian said to Maria, "I thought it was you who had ordered the killing of Dietrich."

And now, she thought, he has all of us.

"You think I'm such a fool?"

He shook his head, smiling. "But you are a woman. A woman is ruled by her heart."

Anger flared. She stubbed out the cigarette in a saucer. "I am not a Sicilian woman."

"You are a beautiful woman."

The anger expanded, although she was pleased by the blatant flattery.

"You're out of date. Times have changed. This isn't just a man's war. Perhaps," she said more calmly, "things have changed forever. Maybe the war has given us that."

"Maybe," the Sicilian said, emptying the last of the grappa

down his throat.

"So what do we do now?" Carlo asked.

The Sicilian said: "We have to get guns. We have to meet the other partisani. We have to get organised. But first," he said to Maria, "there is something you must do — find out why Dietrich is here."

"Perhaps he's looking for Mussolini," Maria said tentatively.

"Possibly. But I doubt it. Otto Skorzeny's been put in charge of that. And Hitler wouldn't risk a clash of personalities like that — Skorzeny and Dietrich. Christ, what a couple!" the Sicilian exclaimed, admiration in his tone. "But in any case, they're all wasting their time in Rome. Mussolini was taken to Gaeta and then to the Pontine Islands."

"It's not just Mussolini they're after," said Angelo. "They want to get Badoglio, his ministers, the King, every one of the shit-heads," said Angelo, whose hatred embraced all authority.

"Even Skorzeny will have his work cut out," the Sicilian said. "They're all nicely tucked away, a lot of them at the Macao barracks surrounded by half the Italian army."

"Perhaps Dietrich brought a message from Hitler," Maria ventured.

The Sicilian brushed aside the suggestion. "The German ambassador to The Holy See could have delivered that. Any number of Germans could have delivered it. The Führer," sarcastically, "could have telephoned The Vatican himself. "No," he said thoughtfully, "there was something more to it than that. I think Dietrich was on personal business. SS business."

He stood up, one hand feeling the bald patch. He was not a tall man, but his muscles pushed against his open-necked white shirt. The undiscerning would have likened his face to that of a peasant, but there was authority there — *family* authority — and small refinements in the set of his brown eyes, the sensitivity of the line from nose to mouth. None of which diminished the overall impression of implacable brutality.

He turned to Maria. "Now you must get to work. After all, you have the best spy in The Vatican." He took her arm. "Come, I'll see you home. By the way," he said as they reached the foot of the stone steps, "did you know it's Mussolini's sixtieth birthday today?"

IV

Maria Reubeni's Vatican contact was praying. As usual his prayers were tortured.

Kneeling beside his bed in his Vatican quarters he pressed his hands together and shut his eyes as he had done when he prayed as a child in the Bronx.

"Please, God, forgive me for my devious ways." *Consorting with the Nazi bishop and at the same time betraying his confidences.*

"And for doubting the Holy Father." *Wondering why, despite his financial help to the Jews, the Pope had not been more outspoken in his condemnation of their persecutors.*

"And" — bowing his head lower — "for the times I have doubted *Your* infinite wisdom." *For permitting this terrible war irrespective of whether its victims found ultimate salvation.*

Here he paused, because he was about to seek forgiveness for a carnal sin that he knew he would repeat since he was powerless to prevent it.

"And forgive me for failing to sublimate desires of the flesh." *Maria Reubeni.*

Father Liam Doyle, twenty-five years old, grey-eyed with wavy brown hair and keen, Celtic features already stamped with the conflict of innocence and knowledge, prayed a little longer before rising and going to the window of his frugally-furnished room, and staring bleakly across the shaven lawns of The Vatican gardens where children played and fountains splashed in the dusk.

He had felt confused ever since his arrival at The Vatican

two years ago from the small church in New York. There his principles and his volition had seemed inviolate: to help the poor — there were enough of them in the Bronx — and to guide the congregation, mostly Irish like himself, in the ways of God.

But Liam Doyle, son of a policeman and a seamstress, one of eight children, had been blessed, or cursed, by a facility with languages. First he had become fluent in Latin and then he had mopped up Spanish and Italian so that he was much in demand in the ghettos. Word of his linguistic abilities reached St. Patrick's Cathedral and he was dispatched to Rome as a young seminarian.

The honour frightened him, but delighted those who worshipped in his grimy little church with its anti-Papal graffiti on the outside walls. "Patrick Doyle's boy going to join the Vicar of Christ. Now there's a thing." Their delight was heightened by the fact that he would take with him the sins to which they had confessed — he was much preferred in the Confessional to the Bible-faced Father O'Riley — those sins, that is, that had escaped the wrath of Patrolman Patrick Doyle.

Liam Doyle's fear had been well justified. He could not equate the splendid isolation of The Holy See with Christian charity. When he explored its treasure troves he remembered the pawn shop across the street from his old church where women hocked their wedding rings for a dollar.

Nor could he understand the arrogance of some of the monsignori in a world addled with poverty, starvation and suffering. *Blessed are the meek* ...

And he never felt at ease in this state within a city. These blessed one hundred and nine or so neutral acres bounded by St. Peter's Square, The Vatican walls and the walls of the Palace of The Holy See, constituted by the Lateran Treaty in 1929, where less than one thousand people lived tax-free lives of privilege.

Was this the way Jesus, the son of a humble carpenter, would have wished it?

But perhaps the fault lies in myself, Father Doyle brooded as the dusk thickened and settled on the courtyards, chapels and museum; on the grocery, pharmacy and radio station of the minute state from which the spiritual lives of three hundred and seventy-five million Catholics were ruled. There has to be authority and it has to be garbed with spendour: it *is* a throne. And there has to be immunity from outside pressures: a regal purity, perhaps.

Liam Doyle sighed. My trouble, he decided, as a plump cardinal strode past in the lamplight beneath like a galleon in full sail, is that I see every side of an argument. I lack decision.

He decided to brew a pot of tea on the gas-ring beneath a Crucifix on the wall. And while he waited for the kettle to boil he read the worn Bible that his mother had given him twenty years ago, seeking as always answers to his confusion. From the testaments he found solace, but it was only temporary, and when he awoke in the morning the doubts were still there, fortified by sleep.

The war had not helped Liam's state of mind. It wasn't merely the mindless slaughter vented on the world by an insane dictator: it was the effect of the war on The Vatican. It seethed with rumour. It was haunted with fear that the Germans would occupy it — they wouldn't be the first to sack Holy Rome — and there was even a story that Hitler planned to kidnap the Pope.

But it was the politics of the place that particularly unsettled Liam. The uneasy suspicion that the Papal diplomats were more concerned with stemming the tide of Communism than with condemning Nazi Germany. But how could you condemn a nation that was locked in battle with Bolshevism, the greatest threat to Christianity the world had ever known?

And there I go, Liam thought as he poured water into his dented aluminium teapot, seeing both sides of the argument again.

He poured himself a cup of tea and took a bourbon biscuit from a tin on top of the bookcase. Sitting on the edge of the bed, nibbling the biscuit and sipping the scalding tea, he tried to channel his thoughts in other directions — to his work for the Pontificia Commissione Assistenze (PCA), the Papal charity organisation for which he worked as an interpreter. But this time the Bible had failed him: his tortured train of thought continued its headlong progress.

Not only were Vatican officials engaged in dubious politics but many minor officials were involved in spying. They spied on the British and American representatives *imprisoned* in the Hospice Sant' Marta, and on the Pope himself. Phones were tapped, cables deciphered, Vatican broadcasts monitored.

Many of the spies operated from ecclesiastical colleges and other Papal organisations outside The Vatican in the city of Rome. What disturbed Father Liam Doyle most acutely was that he was one of them. And that night he was going to meet the woman who had recruited him, Maria Reubeni.

*   *   *

Liam had met Maria through his work as an interpreter. He had lately mastered German and she worked as a Hebrew translator. In view of the plight of German Jewry it was inevitable that they should have met.

The meeting occurred in an open-air café beneath a green awning off the Via IV Novembre, near the ruined markets and forum of the Emperor Trajan, on June 2nd. The date was imprinted on Liam's brain.

The purpose of the meeting was to question a Jewish refugee from Poland, who spoke Hebrew and Yiddish and a little German, in an effort to compile yet another dossier on Nazi atrocities, in order to provide The Vatican with the proof they continually demanded.

The refugee who had been smuggled across Europe to Marseilles and thence to Rome was so exhausted and scared that they had agreed on the telephone not to interrogate him in an office.

Instead of coffee or a glass of wine they gave him a lime-green water-ice. He was, after all, only twelve.

At first he spoke in small, shivering phrases but soon the

35

warmth, the water-ice and the mellow antiquity of the place had their effect. And it was a familiar tale that he told the priest and the Jewess.

It dated back to November 23rd, 1939, when the Jews of Warsaw, where he lived, had been ordered to wear yellow stars. Then, eleven months later, confinement to the ghetto administered by a Jewish council. Famine, cold, deaths by the thousands.

Then in 1942, *Endlosung*, the Final Solution.

Fear halted the words of the little boy in the too-long shorts, shaven hair beginning to grow into a semblance of an American crew-cut. They bought him another water-ice, and waited. The girl pointed to a lizard, watched by a hungry cat, basking on a slab of ancient brick. The boy's lips stopped trembling, he smiled.

And in a strange mixture of languages he delivered his adolescent version of the terrible facts that were leaking out from Eastern Europe. The beginning of the liquidation of the Warsaw ghetto, transportations to Treblinka death camp, gassings with carbon monoxide from diesel engines, followed by another gas (which Maria knew to be Zyklon B).

Horror froze around them in the sunshine.

Then the boy came to the revolt of the Warsaw Jews which began on April 18th, two months ago. He had been smuggled through the German lines in an empty water-cart during the fighting.

Maria leaned forward and spoke to him in Hebrew. The boy straightened his back and answered her firmly.

Liam asked Maria what she had said.

"I asked him if the Jews fought well."

"And what did he say?"

"He said they fought like tigers."

"And?"

She shrugged. "They were massacred." She sipped her glass of wine. "But at least they fought. For the first time in nearly two thousand years they fought back as a people."

Liam stared at her fascinated. When he had first seen her he

36

had been aware of an instant physical reaction. But his emotions had been swamped by the sickening catalogue of inhumanity the child had carried with him across Europe.

Now the passion in her voice reawakened the feelings. He wanted to lean across the table and touch her hand. He was appalled.

She put away her notebook and said: "Well, there you are, Father, there's your evidence. Do you believe it?"

"Of course I believe it."

"But will anyone else inside your little haven believe it?"

He ran one finger under his clerical collar. "I cannot say," lamely.

"So you, too, are a diplomat rather than a priest."

He wanted to shout: "Not true." To unburden his conscience to this beautiful, aggressive daughter of Rome.

She lit a cigarette. "Don't worry, Father. They will want more proof as always. And they will say, 'We need more than the word of a child.' As if anything more was needed," patting the boy's stubbly hair. "Another ice-cream?"

At that moment the cat pounced. But the lizard was too quick for it, disappearing in a blur of olive movement.

The boy laughed and said to Maria: "That's how I escaped."

"No more ice-cream?"

He shook his head.

"Then it's time I took you home."

"Where is he staying?" Liam asked.

"He has family here. That's why he was brought to Rome. They thought it would be safe here. But now ..." Her hands finished the sentence, Italian style.

"A Polish Jew has a family in Rome?"

"You wouldn't understand," the girl said. "He is a Jew. He has family everywhere."

Liam wondered at her hostility. He guessed — hoped — that it related only to her attitude towards The Vatican. She stood up suddenly, every movement vital, and paid the bill. Then she took the boy's hand. "Good-bye, Father, it has been pleasant meeting you," in a voice that belied her words.

Liam stood up and, to his amazement, heard himself proposing another meeting, lying to himself and to the girl, concocting a story that they needed to compare notes to enable them to present convincing evidence to the Papal authorities, knowing that this was a lie within a lie because many dossiers and petitions had been presented to The Vatican with negligible results.

She looked at him quizzically. "Very well. I'm dining in Trastevere tonight. Perhaps we could meet there for a drink. You do take a glass of wine, Father?"

"Occasionally," Liam told her.

They arranged to meet at a trattoria, and he watched her walk away holding the boy's hand and he knew that he should never see her again, that he should run after her and cancel the appointment, but he didn't move. And, as she passed out of sight, he knew, standing there among the ruins of imperial Rome, that his life, his creed, had been irrevocably changed, that he was about to embark on a struggle with temptation which would be the greatest test of his life.

They met that evening in a trattoria, in the Piazza D' Mercanti in the artists' quarter of Trastevere on the opposite bank of the Tiber.

Liam was disappointed to find that Maria had company. A young man with swaggering manners and, Liam suspected, many complexes, and a Sicilian who was never called by his name. Both men indulged in the sort of banter which many men employ to disguise their unease in the presence of clergy.

They drank from a carafe of red wine and smoked a lot, as did most of the other customers who crossed the river to find Bohemia. A musician in a grease-spotted black suit and open-necked white shirt was playing a violin, but only the occasional thin note penetrated the noise of Italians relaxing.

Liam and Maria completed the farce of comparing notes, then the swaggering young man named Angelo ordered more wine and topped up Liam's glass, and Liam thought: "You're trying to get me drunk, my young friend. What better joke than a drunken priest?"

"So, Father," the Sicilian said, lighting a thin cigar, "what do you think of the latest events?"

"The war you mean?"

"What else? Your information must be good, Father. The best in Rome, eh?"

"I doubt if I know more than you," Liam said, believing he told the truth.

"Come, Father, an American priest inside The Vatican. You must have access to much intelligence."

Liam frowned. He couldn't think of any particular intelligence that had come his way.

"Are you not in contact with Mr. Tittman, the American diplomatic representative?"

"I've met him," Liam said.

"I'm told that he is angry because he doesn't always have the same privileges as other diplomats."

"That," said Liam, "is because in the past the United States had barely recognised The Vatican diplomatically. It is only through the Holy Father's kindness that he is there at all."

"And Sir D'Arcy Osborne, the British envoy. Do you know him?"

"I've spoken to him," Liam said. He realised that the Sicilian was showing off his knowledge. "Why?"

"They're both still sending their coded messages on The Vatican radio. A lot of good that will do them — the Italian Fascists have cracked the code and passed it on to the Germans."

"You seem very well informed," Liam said, wondering where it was all leading.

A girl wearing a low-cut bodice and ankle-strap shoes passed the table and tweeked his ear. He blushed.

Maria Reubeni lit a cigarette. She smoked too much, Liam thought, noticing and averting his eyes from the thrust of her breasts against her blouse.

She said abruptly: "Do you know Bishop Alois Hudal?"

"The German bishop?"

"Nazi bishop," Angelo Peruzzi interrupted.

The Sicilian prodded his cigar towards Peruzzi. "Let the priest speak."

Liam told them he knew Hudal very well. He got the impression that they already knew this.

He had first met the diminutive, bespectacled bishop through his duties as interpreter. He had continued the association with the Austrian-born prelate for two reasons: to improve his German, and because Hudal seemed sympathetic to the Roman Jewry who might at any time suffer like the Jews all over Europe.

When he remarked on the bishop's Jewish sentiments Angelo Peruzzi broke in. "You mean you believe all that shit?" stopping when Maria rounded on him and told him to clean his mouth out.

She turned to Liam. "I must apologise, Father, for Angelo. I will buy him a bar of soap on the Black Market."

Liam smiled at her gratefully. But in the Bronx he had become accustomed to men who defiantly swore and blasphemed in the presence of a priest, especially when they had taken too much liquor.

The Sicilian examined the glowing tip of his thin cigar, somehow a sinister instrument in his thickly-furred hand. "What Angelo is saying," as though Peruzzi spoke in a foreign tongue, "is that Hudal has expressed sympathy for the Jews for his own purposes."

Laim looked puzzled.

Maria told him: "He means that Bishop Hudal doesn't want the Germans to ship us to the death camps when they come. Not that he gives a damn — sorry, Father — not that he gives a jot about the Jews. But he thinks that such action would force The Vatican into denouncing the Nazis. If there was bad blood between Berlin and The Holy See it would destroy his precious dream."

Liam wondered why they each interpreted for each other, perhaps the habit was catching. "What precious dream?" he asked, sipping the rough wine and grimacing.

The Sicilian said: "Hudal is a madman. He believes in a Holy

Roman Empire. A partnership between the Nazis and the Church. A united front against Bolshevism."

"He's never mentioned it to me," Liam said mildly.

"The bastard doesn't know what side you're on yet," Angelo Peruzzi said, while the Sicilian pointed his thin cigar like a pistol and asked: "What side *are* you on, Father? And" — smiling his gold-toothed smile — "don't say, 'On God's side'," which was exactly what Liam had been about to reply.

Liam found the conversation bewildering. He thought the Sicilian looked like one of the debt-collectors who had called so regularly at premises near his church in the Bronx. Angelo looked like a homicidal psychopath. What was Maria Reubeni doing in such company?

"I am not on any side," he said, glancing at Maria for support.

"Come now, Father," the Sicilian urged him. "Even a man of the cloth must take sides. He must recognise evil."

"But he needn't participate."

"But he always has," the Sicilian observed. "At least in the history books I've read."

Liam took another sip of wine. It didn't taste quite so bad this time. "I cannot condone what the Germans have done," he said after a while.

The violinist had moved up to their table and was playing *Come Back to Sorrento*. Liam would have liked to share the song with Maria, alone.

But the music hadn't touched Maria's heart. She asked: "Does The Vatican condone what the Germans have done, Father?"

Ah, the old, old controversy. He took another sip of wine, mustered his forces. "You mean the Holy Father?"

"That's right," Angelo Peruzzi said. "The Vicar of Christ, the boss."

"Of course he doesn't condone atrocities," Liam told them. "His attitude is quite simple. He believes that if he denounced the persecution of the Jews they would suffer even more terribly." Liam frowned, trying to put himself in the position of

41

Eugenio Pacelli, the enigmatic Pope Pius XII. And probably" — *no possibly* — "he is right. In Holland the priests spoke out. The result? Seventy-nine per cent of all the Jews there — the highest proportion of any country — were deported to concentration camps. Furthermore," Liam went on from his pulpit in the smokey trattoria, "he knows that Hitler is crazy enough to attack The Vatican if he spoke out against him. Destroy the fount of Christianity. Destroy the fount of humanitarianism. Perhaps destroy our civilisation . . ."

"I see," said Maria as though she didn't. "So Pacelli is really saving the Jews."

"He is doing what he believes to be right," Liam said.

"In other words he is doing nothing."

"He is doing a lot," Liam told her. "I know that from my work. Perhaps he is not *saying* a great deal . . ."

The Sicilian said: "Of course Pacelli was The Vatican's man in Germany for a long time. He met the Nazi bishop there."

Suddenly anger overcame Liam. "Are you suggesting there is some sort of conspiracy between Bishop Hudal and the Holy Father?"

Maria shook her head. "In fact we know that Papa Pacelli disapproves of Hudal."

Liam smote the table. "I tell you that the Holy Father is doing what he believes to be right. I tell you that he has protested privately to Hitler. All he wants is peace."

"And goodwill to all men including the Krauts," said the Sicilian. He glanced at the heavy gold watch on his hairy wrist. "Time for us to go," motioning to Angelo. "We'll leave you together to discuss the fate of the Jews."

"Aren't you seeing me home?" Maria asked the Sicilian, and Liam heard himself saying: "Don't worry, I'll escort you," like a college boy on his first date.

"Are you sure?"

"Quite sure."

As the two men departed, Liam was overcome by a glow of pleasure untainted by physical desire. But for how long?

The torment of Father Liam Doyle was just beginning.

42

* * *

As Liam made his way to his assignation with Maria Reubeni
on that July night six weeks later he noticed a group of tourists
wandering past the columns of the Bernini colonnade. But
they walked not as tourists, aimlessly and wonderingly; they
walked stiffly with fists clenched and Liam, with his newly-
found knowledge of intrigue, knew that they were Germans
staking out The Vatican in case Benito Mussolini was hidden
inside its walls.

Liam walked briskly over a bridge spanning the moonlit
waters of the Tiber, absorbing the atmosphere of war-time
Rome at night. Blacked-out windows, the ring of horses'
hooves on cobblestones and the tap of women's high heels on
the sidewalk. A woman smoking a cigarette approached him
from a doorway on the opposite bank of the river, but withdrew smiling when she noticed his soutane.

As he walked Liam brooded about his relationship with
Maria. For a while he had pretended that she merely wanted
his help because, through the Papal charities, he could assist the
Jews. And, deliciously and guiltily, he had considered the
notion that perhaps she liked him for himself.

But soon logic asserted itself. The interest of the girl — and
her unwholesome friends — was centred on his association
with Bishop Hudal. They had known about the association
from the beginning.

After their first meetings Maria had contented herself by asking apparently aimless questions. Then she had actively encouraged Liam's friendship with Hudal "as you say he is so
concerned about the Jews."

When Liam was finally and hopelessly involved with her,
she had made it clear that she wanted him to extract information from the German bishop. To spy.

But, being an intelligent girl, she had provided him with an
escape route for his guilt: the information he provided was
only being used in the interests of Roman Jewry if the Germans
occupied Rome.

43

But Liam, now aware of the plotting within The Eternal City and The Vatican City, knew that far more was involved. He was being used by Maria's friends, partisani, who were mustering their forces into an organised resistance movement. When the time came they would shoot, bomb, kill. Aided and abetted by Father Liam Doyle! Liam groaned aloud as he hurried towards his clandestine rendezvous with Maria. They met in a side street off the Largo Tassoni. The moonlight was in her hair and he could smell her perfume and he thought: "This is the last time," but he knew it wasn't.

"I'm glad you could come, Father," she said.

Did she have any feeling for him at all? Or was he just a weakling to be exploited, a clerical courier to be used as she doubtless used other men.

"It is a fine night for a walk."

"I have something important to ask you," as they strolled beneath the stars.

"And what is that?" No longer *my child*.

"Sepp Dietrich visited the Pope yesterday."

"Sepp Dietrich?"

She told him about the SS Commander.

"But why would a man like that seek an audience with the Pope?"

"That, Father, is what I would like you to find out."

"From Bishop Hudal?"

"From the Nazi bishop," she said, stopping and standing very close to him. "Will you do that for me?"

"I'll try," Liam said. And, hoping that she wouldn't lie: "What has this to do with helping the Jews in Rome?"

Maria said: "The SS Special Action Units are responsible for massacring Jews. In Russia they've been killing 100,000 a month."

But, from what she had told him, Liam had gathered that Dietrich was primarily a soldier. "You think he might organise a Special Action Unit in Rome?"

She nodded. "I do, Father."

He knew she lied and it pained him.

V

But Liam Doyle was not destined to discover the reason for Sepp Dietrich's visit to The Vatican from the German bishop, because the SS officer didn't confide it to Hudal.

Dietrich distrusted priests. In particular eccentric priests trying to confuse pure National-Socialism with Christian doctrinaire.

But one day Hudal and the other pro-Nazi clergy with Vatican connections — men like SS officer George Elling, a priest, ostensibly studying the life of St. Francis of Assisi — would be vital links in the plan code-worded Grey Fox.

At the moment Dietrich wasn't telling. His visit to S. Maria dell' Anima was merely a preliminary move.

As he dismounted from the black Mercedes-Benz on the morning of the 29th July he vaguely noticed a priest and a girl struggling across the street and dismissed the scene as yet another example of Italian hysteria.

In the presbytery flanked by the tomb of the last non-Italian Pope, Hadrian VI, adorned with figures representing Justice, Prudence, Force and Temperance, he was greeted enthusiastically by the little prelate.

"It is indeed a pleasure to meet you," Hudal said holding out his hand.

"The pleasure is mine," Dietrich said without enthusiasm.

They went into a book-lined room where Dietrich noticed a painting of the Crucifix and photographs of Pius XII and Adolf Hitler on the walls.

On May 1st, 1933, Dietrich recalled, Hudal had entertained seven hundred guests, including top Nazis, on the premises and the place had rung with the cry: 'German unity is my strength, my strength is German might.'

Hudal handed Dietrich a glass of wine. "And what brings you to the Holy City?" he asked.

"Pleasure," Dietrich told him. He sat down on a threadbare easy-chair and crossed his stocky legs. "My unit has been transferred from the Russian Front. I've always liked Rome," he lied.

He had visited the city once before. On May 2nd, 1938, in company with his beloved Führer, Von Ribbentrop, Josef Goebbels and the imbecile Rudolph Hess who had flown to Britain in 1941. He had detested the place then — its climate, its monuments, the instability of its people and its soldiery. Dietrich had even been forced to witness the Italian troops' ludicrous imitation of the Nazi marching step known as the *passo Romano*.

"I am always pleased to receive a friend of the Führer," Hudal said. He clasped his hands. "How are things on the Russian Front?"

"Not good," Dietrich told him.

Hudal looked anxious. "But only temporary set-backs, I trust."

Dietrich shrugged. It was only that morning that he himself had admitted the possibility of defeat. "We fought well in the Belgorod-Kursk sector.

Hudal leaned forward expectantly. "And?"

Dietrich said heavily: "General Model ordered a withdrawal. A strategic withdrawal, of course! The Ivans are marching on Orel at the moment."

"But ultimate victory will be ours," Hudal said, "It is God's will. The Bolsheviks must be crushed. They are our principal enemies."

"*Our* enemies? Do you mean enemies of the Church or enemies of Germany?"

The Vatican, Dietrich thought, was obsessed with the threat

46

of Communism. From the Pope downwards. Thank God! He smiled thinly: it was an appropriate setting to mark his appreciation. And one of the leaders of the anti-Marxist movement was the fanatical little priest sitting opposite him.

Now Dietrich put the bishop to the test. "What if Germany were defeated?"

"Unthinkable," Hudal snapped.

"But just supposing."

"Then we would fight on."

"We?"

"All of us loyal to the cause of National-Socialism. And Christianity," he added as an afterthought. "After all, we rose from the ashes of the First World War."

"The Americans and British wouldn't let that happen again," Dietrich said.

"They couldn't stop us."

"I think," Dietrich said carefully, "that if we were to rise again it would have to be somewhere else."

"You mean in Italy?"

The last place on God's earth! "No, not Italy. The British and Americans would keep a tight rein on the Black Shirts here."

Hudal looked at him suspiciously. "You seem very fatalistic, Gruppenführer."

"Merely anticipating every eventuality."

"Where then, Spain?"

"I hardly think so," Dietrich said. "Franco has refused to cooperate with the Führer." He paused, staring at the photograph of Hitler. "No, I think it would have to be farther away than that. Brazil maybe, one of the South American countries."

"That seems rather far-fetched."

But Hudal was out of touch. He hadn't seen the slaughters in Russia. He didn't seem to realise that the Allies would soon be on the mainland of Italy. That soon they would be landing in France. Above all he couldn't comprehend the atmosphere in Berlin where already some of Hitler's trusted lieutenants were planning their escape routes.

Patiently, Dietrich nosed his way through the little cleric's dogma and blind fanaticism. "If — let us just say if — some of the top men wanted to escape when there was no longer any possibility of victory, would you help them?"

"If they weren't escaping purely because of cowardice."

Well put, Dietrich decided, regarding Hudal with new respect. "If they were escaping to form a new order elsewhere. The cream of Aryan manhood. To form an alliance between the Church and National-Socialism," Dietrich suggested slyly.

Hudal's eyes gleamed. "Then of course I would help."

"And you have many followers here who would help?"

"Of course."

"Inside The Vatican?"

"I have many friends inside The Vatican. The Teutonic College itself is on neutral territory."

Dietrich stood up. He stuck out his hand. "Then let us hope we never have to make use of them."

Hudal stood up. "Are things really as bad as you make out?"

"They're not good," Dietrich said.

*   *   *

That night as he lay between the soft sheets of a bed in the luxurious Excelsior Hotel where many German officers stayed, Dietrich, unaware that he had escaped death by a couple of seconds, reappraised his day. A bad one.

Soon he would be back fighting in Russia — the Führer couldn't afford to keep the Leibstandarte "slummocking" (as Field-Marshall Günther von Kluge had put it) in Italy much longer — and today he had finally acknowledged to himself that only defeat lay ahead. So much for those shining dreams of the '30's, for the glorious victories of the Leibstandarte as they swept through Europe.

Dietrich, hands behind his head, staring at the ceiling, knew that he would fight to the last tank, the last man. And he would execute the Führer's every order even if he had lost that intuitive touch of genius of the early days. Hitler had resurrected the pride of Germany: had shown its men that they still had balls. Elevated me from a nonentity to the commander of the most feared military machine in the world.

Dietrich reached for the suitcase beside his bed. Underneath a copy of *Mein Kampf* was a well-thumbed sheet of paper, a copy of Hitler's remarks at the birthday celebrations for Hermann Göring on January 12th, 1942.

The role of Sepp Dietrich is unique. I have always given him the opportunity to intervene at sore spots. (Sore, well that was a bit of an understatement). *He is a man who is simultaneously cunning, energetic and brutal. Under his swash-buckling appearance Dietrich is a serious, conscientious and scrupulous character. And what care he takes of his troops. He is a phenomenon . . . someone irreplaceable. For the German people Sepp Dietrich is a national institution. For me personally there is also the fact that he is one of my oldest companions in the struggle.*

And I would die for him, Dietrich thought. Or, more practically, save him from the vengeance of the enemy.

Which was precisely what Dietrich proposed to do.

This was the plan known only to a handful of other top-ranking SS officers. To snatch Hitler from the muzzles of the enemy guns when Germany was finally on the brink of defeat. Regardless of the Führer's wishes. Dietrich smiled fondly as he imagined Hitler's ferocious reaction if he heard of Grey Fox.

And it was Grey Fox — Dietrich's description of the Pontiff — that had prompted Dietrich to seek an audience with the Pope. How could Pius XII refuse with the 3rd Panzergrenadier camped on his doorstep?

Dietrich had proposed to sound out the Pope's true feelings towards the Nazis. To test his reactions to any proposal to spirit top Nazis to freedom via The Holy See. To threaten, in the vaguest terms, retribution if he didn't agree to collaborate. To extract a promise from the one man who couldn't break his word.

But it hadn't worked out like that. Dietrich had lost his motivation in the presence of the Pontiff with his long eloquent fingers, pallor of sanctity, aescetic features and gaze of total understanding.

The Pope had promised nothing, given no hint of his sympathies. He had handled the exchange with the practised ease of the career diplomat.

And finally Dietrich had kissed his ring a chastened man. Out-smarted by a priest!

But still, Dietrich comforted himself in his hotel room, the Pope had not denied any of his faltering proposals. Cold comfort.

Dietrich swore tersely and, thrusting aside the memory of the humiliating experience, took a green folder from the suitcase. On the first page was a list of eight names. The possible candidates to implement Grey Fox. Not Dietrich himself, nor the other SS conspirators, because they were all soldiers, nothing more, and they intended to fight to the last.

The chosen candidate had to have exceptional qualifications to carry out the most daunting mission of World War II. Bravery obviously — if he was Leibstandarte that went without saying. Authority. Resourcefulness. Unquestioning loyalty to the Führer.

But he had to have more even than these qualities. Much more. He had to be a man whose moral fibre had not been corrupted by the brutality of war. Untouched by cynicism. A man who still *believed*.

Inside the green folder were reports on the eight candidates. All good men. The finest examples of the Waffen-SS. But only one man had those additional qualities that Dietrich sought.

Now he would have to be put through the tests that the Committee of SS officers had devised. Tests far more exacting than the gruelling training of the SS.

With a thick-leaded pencil Dietrich scored out seven names on the list. The eighth name was Kurt Wolff.

VI

The Russian T-34 tank seemed to have lost its way. It stopped 150 yards from the German foxhole, its 75 mm gun swivelling slowly like the proboscis of some prehistoric animal scenting danger.

The young officer seconded to the 5th SS Panzer, the Viking, raised his head over the lip of the foxhole and cautiously surveyed it.

He turned to the Sergeant crouched beside him. "Do you think they know we're here?"

"I don't know, Hauptsturmführer."

"Then it's time we let them know."

"If you say so, Hauptsturmführer."

The blond Captain with the startling blue eyes looked at the T-34 — perhaps one of the survivors of Kursk, the greatest tank battle in history — through a pair of captured Russian binoculars. No movement except the slowly rotating gun.

"A pity to lose a fine specimen like this, Unterscharführer."

"You are not suggesting we capture it?" the Sergeant asked. He hadn't yet made up his mind about this laconic young officer, the embodiment of the Teutonic dream, who had so mysteriously arrived in the midst of the exhausted Viking, now in full retreat towards the Dnieper, the last natural barrier before the Polish border.

Ordinarily he would have assumed that he was a fanatic; dispatched from headquarters to bolster morale. My God it needed bolstering! The Viking had been fighting since the inva-

51

sion was launched over the River Bug on June 22nd, 1941. More than two years in this bastard wilderness that the Ivans called Mother Russia!

But no, this man was no instrument of discipline, instructed by generals skulking far behind the sound of gunfire. This man was a soldier, albeit a rash one. There was the Knight's Cross at the throat of his tunic, open at the neck, and a Silver Wound Medal, and a scar on his cheek which the Sergeant recognised as the furrow from a bullet.

Nevertheless he was an enigma. The scar long healed, the tunic miraculously well-preserved, standing out like a spare prick on a honeymoon among the crumpled, lousy, blood-stained clothing of the old soldiers.

The Sergeant glanced curiously at the captain as he surveyed the tank through the field-glasses. He noticed a muscle moving in the Captain's jaw-bone, the needles of his close-clipped hair, the small cleft in his chin. Not a man to argue with, this one.

But who are you? Where have you come from?

The Captain lowered the field glasses: "You're right, Sergeant."

What had he said?

"We can't capture it. We'll have to destroy it," he remarked conversationally, apparently overlooking the fact that all they possessed between them was a Schmeisser machine-pistol and a 9 mm Walther pistol.

The Captain pointed and the Sergeant raised his head to follow the line of his finger.

A Panzerfaust, a grenade launcher, lay on the wheat-coloured grass fifty yards from the foxhole.

He wants me to go and get that? No, my friend, those days are long past. We fight only to survive. Wait till you've been two years on the *steppe*.

"Cover me," the Captain snapped.

The Sergeant was ashamed of his suspicion. "With a machine pistol, Hauptsturmführer?"

"At least it's better than the Walther," the Captain said.

God in heaven, he was making jokes!

"But they'll spot you. One burst and they'll have you."

"There's some cover over there," the Captain said. Some scrub on which the first frost of autumn was just beginning to melt.

And then he was up and over the edge of the foxhole, wriggling flat-bellied over the grass.

The turret of the T-34 swung round.

You'll dirty that precious uniform, the Sergeant thought inconsequentially. But they hadn't spotted him. Not yet. The Sergeant raised the Schmeisser. Did the idiot want a bullet scar on the other cheek? Or through his chest?

The Captain was ten yards from the grenade-launcher when a machine-gun opened up from a belt of woods to his left. He flung himself to the ground and stayed there until the burst spent itself.

The Captain raised his head — *For Christ's sake keep down!* — then his shoulders. As the machine-gun opened up again he scuttled behind a boulder.

Instinctively the Sergeant aimed the machine-pistol in the direction of the machine-gun. But what was the point? They were well out of range. Vaguely the Sergeant wondered what they were doing there. How they had got there. Had the Ivans secretly mounted yet another attack? Had the tank lumbered up merely to give the machine-gunners some target practice? Usually, the Sergeant thought grimly, they preferred prisoners for target practice. But what fighters. Even the Waffen-SS had to admit that.

The barrel of the gun on the tank swung lazily in the direction of the Captain hidden behind the boulder. One shell and both boulder and brave Captain would be no more. But they didn't fire. Giving the machine-gunners some sport, the Sergeant decided. And after the Captain, me ... Why in God's name had this crazy two-man reconnaissance mission been mounted in the first place?

An aircraft with gull-shaped wings and a silver belly flew overhead. A Stuka. Perhaps one burst from its cannon might change the situation. But the Stuka flew away across the *steppe* — the infinite *steppe* — in the direction of the Dnieper.

Their only chance was if the Captain could make it back to the fox-hole. Then, if the machine-gunners are fool enough to move nearer, I'll have them with the Schmeisser.

If . . . Peering over the top of the fox-hole the Sergeant realised that the Captain was indeed on the move. In the opposite direction. Towards the grenade-launcher.

And had reached it!

As bullets whipped over his head the Captain rolled into a hollow.

Now the tank must finish him off.

The Sergeant saw the snout of the Panzerfaust protruding from the hollow. Its grenade was said to be capable of punching a hole through eight inches of armour-plate. But the tank was beyond its effective range. Still, it was worth a try.

Machine-gun bullets plucked viciously at the ground around the hollow.

Then the Captain fired the grenade-launcher.

The Sergeant had no doubt of this because he heard the grenade clang against the tank's armour. The hollowest clang of them all. A dud.

So this is how I am to die, the Sergeant thought. After two years of battle, after glorious victories and a few defeats, I am to die here in a foxhole.

For what? he wondered, failing at first to hear another sound on the crisp autumn air. But when the machine-gun stopped firing he heard it. The Stuka had returned. And was diving as only a Stuka can dive. It opened up with machine-gun and cannon.

The shells and bullets fell short but when the Sergeant again peered over the edge of the foxhole the T-34 was on the move heading for the cover of the woods. And the machine-gun was silent.

The Stuka climbed, wheeled, prepared for another attack. But as it came into a screaming dive the tank had reached the woods.

Inside the Russian tank the two German SS officers, instructed by Sepp Dietrich to put Kurt Wolff's courage and initiative to the test, nodded at each other before abandoning it for their own armoured car.

When they reached the German machine-gunner he stood up and said: "Excuse me, Gruppenführer, I know I shouldn't question an order but what was that all about?"

He never found out because one of the officers blew out his brains with a Luger pistol.

* * *

Kurt Wolff's principal regret in his youth — he was only twenty-two now — was that he hadn't been born early enough to be a fully-fledged member of the SS in those exciting, formative years of the struggle.

But he was old enough to remember the Congress of Victory, the Nazi rally at Nuremberg, in September, 1933. He was twelve years old then and he was wearing a black vest and shorts, marching in the Zeppelinwiese, with sixty thousand members of the Hitler Youth, in intricate formations that spelled out in black, red and white slogans, BLOOD AND HONOUR or GERMANY AWAKE.

In the centre of the formations was a swastika.

Military bands thumped out Lehar and Beethoven, flags fluttered in the late summer breeze. Then the finale: Sixty thousand knives simultaneously drawn like a flash of summer lightning.

Wolff was not an emotional man but he was still deeply moved when he gazed at the photograph of the rally, saw the child-like trust on the faces of the boys. Ten years later, how many of those boys had died for the cause?

He remembered the scene in the Luitpoldhalle after the display. At the back of the stage the German eagle clasping a swastika; at the sides of the hall a hundred or so SS resplendent in the black and silver uniforms.

One day, the twelve year-old Wolff had thought, I will

wear that uniform. And I will fight the Führer's enemies. I will die, if need be, for the man who has made my country great again. I will die for my God!

A fanfare of trumpets had heralded the arrival of Hitler. Beside him were two men whom Kurt hadn't recognised. (They were Reichsführer Heinrich Himmler and Reinhard Heydrich, chief of the Central Security Office.) But he was to know them well in the years to come.

Then all the lights had been switched off. Snap. Total darkness. And a single beam of light picking out the figure of Adolf Hitler. And spotlights finding the SS men in silver and black as they lowered their drawn swords.

Kurt didn't understand a lot of what the Führer said — perhaps he shouldn't even have been in the hall — but it was more exciting than anything he had heard anywhere else. A super breed of men was emerging; one day he might be one of them. They would dominate the world, they would eradicate weakness and treachery, Bolshevism (whatever that was), and the rich capitalists (whatever that meant) who stole the hardearned monies of the ordinary German. Forget Versailles (wherever that was). Germany would be great again.

Tears formed in Kurt Wolff's eyes as he witnessed what was in fact the official recognition of the Leibstandarte SS Adolf Hitler.

From then on it was the only unit to which Kurt Wolff ever wanted to belong.

*   *   *

The Leibstandarte first came into being on March 17th, 1933 as a personal bodyguard to Hitler before his power was absolute, when the brown-shirted SA and the black-shirted SS — derived from Schutzstaffeln, meaning Protection Squads — were competing, and the Communists and Nationalists were still to be reckoned with.

One of the first duties of the Leibstandarte under the command of Sepp Dietrich was to shoot the leaders of the SA rounded up by the SS, now a unified force under the leadership of Himmler, in the summer of 1934. The purge became known as the Night of the Long Knives.

The SS became an independent unit within the Nazi Party and the cream of them, the Leibstandarte, were honoured with a special oath of allegiance: "I swear to you, Adolf Hitler, as Führer, and Reich Chancellor, loyalty and bravery. I vow to you, and to those you have named to command me, obedience unto death, so help me God."

When the German Army reoccupied the Rhineland in March, 1936 — Hitler had announced conscription a year earlier — it was spear-headed by the Leibstandarte. Hitler's dream of a Thousand Year Reich was under way; and he had made it clear that the elite of his dream was the ideological SS, and that the kernel of the elite was the Leibstandarte.

At the time of the Rhineland occupation Kurt Wolff was fifteen. And, like the other boys at his school, he was intoxicated with the deeds of these fair-haired heroes, the embodiment of Himmler's schemes for racial purity, these supermen in their black overcoats and breeches adorned with silver, their boots as bright as mirrors. Had they not cowered the French Army by their very presence in Saarbrucken?

By the time the Leibstandarte, attached to the 2nd Panzer Division of the 16th Corps, had moved into Austria two years later, and the Czech Sudentenland eight months after that, Kurt was approaching call-up age.

But two factors stood in the way of Kurt's enrolment into the Leibstandarte. In the first place his father, a Major in the German Cavalry in the First World War, wanted him to join the Fourth Cavalry Regiment. To become a 'real soldier' instead of an 'asphalt soldier' as the Wehrmacht, the copventional armed forces, termed the SS which was now a fully-fledged force of police troops. 'Asphalt' because they spent so much time stamping the parade ground.

Kurt loved his father, a prosperous landowner with extensive vineyards in the Main valley of north-east Bavaria, but he could not understand his father's attitude towards the SS.

57

"What do you have against them?" he would ask as they sat at dinner in the great yellow-bricked house overlooking the ranks of vines heavy with fat green grapes. "They're the best soldiers in the world."

His father, grey-haired, monocled, a widower, would sip a goblet of white wine and reply: "They're not soldiers, Kurt, they're policemen."

"Then why did Hitler send them into the Sudetenland before the soldiers?"

His father never had much of an answer to that. Instead he would evade the issue by describing the SS as the guinea pigs of Himmler's racial theories. "Aryan manhood! We were good enough to fight in 1914-18 without such experiments. And we nearly won," he would say waving his cigar at Kurt. "Never forget that. If the Americans hadn't come in we *would* have won."

But the First World War was merely history to Kurt. "But the Führer has stated that one day the SS will fight on the battlefields."

Wearily his father asked: "What battlefields? Haven't there been enough battlefields already?"

"The battlefields in The Struggle," his son replied. *Of course there would be battlefields. They had been told so in their history lessons which encompassed the future as much as the past.*

Usually his father left it at that and Kurt was relieved, because one of his friends had once repeated a remark made by his father derogatory to Hitler and next day his friend's father had been arrested by two civilians in long leather coats. Not, of course, that he would sneak on his own father.

Once in their town house in Munich, the seat of the Nazi party, his father said: "I want you to be a soldier, Kurt. But in an army committed to peace."

"The Führer has said that armies for the preparation of peace do not exist — they exist for triumphant exertion in war," his son quoted.

And there Kurt Wolff senior left it. But he didn't abandon his plans for his son to enter the Cavalry. Although the second factor standing between Kurt and the Leibstandarte also affected his father's ambitions for him.

Kurt was nearly six feet tall. But he was also physically weak and the knowledge embittered him.

His ribs protruded from his chest like the ridges of a washing board, his limbs lacked muscle and his lungs wheezed with asthma. However, he was never set upon because the bullies respected his flinty character. Even at seventeen Kurt Wolff had presence.

But sometimes, standing in front of the mirror in his room adorned with Nazi insignia, and gazing at his thin body, he felt like weeping. Although, of course, he never did.

When the Germans launched their *Blitzkreig* on Poland in the autumn of 1939, Kurt made a determined effort to improve his physique and his health. He took up weight-lifting, he tried to barrel out his rib-cage with chest-expanders, he devoured enormous steaks and went climbing in the mountains south of his home.

Then secretly he tried to enlist in the Leibstandarte. Because his credentials were impressive, because he was tall enough — minimum height five feet and eleven inches — he got as far as a medical. But the elite of the SS required supermen — a filling in a tooth could disqualify a candidate. And when the doctors saw his scrawny body they shook their heads.

But the ultimate humiliation was rejection by the Cavalry. Not because of his physique but because of his asthma.

The possibility of a desk job within the Wehrmacht remained.

Kurt fled to a health clinic in the Bavarian Alps.

There for six gruelling months, under the supervision of an ageing athlete named Muller, he punished himself.

He hung from wall-bars until it seemed as if his arms were being pulled from their sockets; he ran hundreds of miles along mountain paths; he exercised with the chest-expanders until the springs broke; he swam thirty lengths a day in an ice-cold pool; he boxed with professional pugilists so that his eyes were permanently blacked for the entire six months; he lifted weights so heavy that Muller warned him about the dangers of a hernia; every morning at dawn he stood on the balcony of the health centre and breathed deeply of the frosted mountain air; he climbed ropes and vaulted leather-topped boxes and he performed press-ups until he collapsed on the floor gasping with pain.

He ate steak and fish, cheese and eggs, and fresh vegetables and slept precisely eight hours a night. He walked always with his chest thrust forward and his belly pulled in. He didn't smoke, he didn't touch liquor, and he didn't visit the whores in the nearby town like some of the young men who left the health clinic with new diseases instead of cures.

And he won.

When he returned to war-time Munich — Germany was now at war with Britain and France — he was hardly recognisable as the weakling who had left six months earlier.

The bellows of his chest no longer wheezed: his back was straight, his ribs were finely muscled, his biceps bulged the arms of his old suits, his face was still pale but there was health in his lips and eyes.

He immediately reapplied to join the Leibstandarte, and kept out of his father's way for a week.

When he was accepted he went to a bar and drank a beer and a Schnapps, and angrily brushed at his eyes with the sleeve of his jacket as joy expanded inside him.

While he was being trained and crammed with Nazi doctrinaire, the Leibstandarte were blazing trails across Holland and France as the demoralised Allies fell back to the final withdrawal at Dunkirk.

At college Kurt had always shown a flare for engineering and he knew more about armoured vehicles than many a Wehrmacht general. After his initial training, the toughest in Germany, he went on a tank course and astonished his instructors with his knowledge of the Mark IV.

His expertise with armoured vehicles kept him in Germany until early in 1941 when he was commissioned. All the time he fretted for action and, after pestering superior officers with requests for a posting, he finally joined the Leibstandarte fighting in Greece.

By June 1941 Obersturmführer Kurt Wolff was in command of a Mark IV poised for the invasion of Russia. The tank was one of 3,580 on the banks of the River Bug, supplemented by 7,184 guns, 600,000 assorted vehicles, 2,000 aircraft and 750,000 horses.

At 3.15 am on June 22nd the guns opened up, the tanks rumbled forward and the bewildered Russians were overwhelmed.

The Leibstandarte captured a key bridgehead over the Dnieper and headed triumphantly towards the Black Sea, slowing down as summer storms turned roads and *steppe* into glue.

One morning in July, with the armoured column bogged down in black mud, Wolff and a party of six men were sent into a wood of silver birch to smoke out a harrassing detachment of the retreating Red Army.

Most of the men never saw the Russian detachment.

Two grenades hurled them to the ground. Then, as they tried to crawl for cover, the Russians picked them off among the skeletal, dripping trees with rifle and machine-gun fire.

One bullet ricocheted off Wolff's steel helmet, another hit him in the belly, and a third bared his cheekbone.

At first there was no pain, just a wave of shock. Wolff grabbed a stick-grenade from the outstretched hand of a dead man beside him, pulled out the china pin, counted to three and hurled it in the direction of the gunfire. A sheet of flame. Silence. Then the cries of wounded men.

With one hand pressed to his belly Wolff inspected his comrades. Only two were still alive. He began to pull one of them to the comparative safety of a pile of sawed logs — as the Russian riflemen opened up again.

Wolff, blood pouring down his cheek, dragged the first man behind the logs. Then returned for the second. On the way back he prised a Schmeisser from the fingers of a dead corporal sitting against the trunk of a birch tree as though on a picnic. Then Wolff collapsed, feigning death, which in any case didn't seem far away.

The shooting stopped.

After a few moments he heard the snap of twigs as the Soviet troops cautiously approached. There were four of them. The leader kicked the first body with his boot and put a bullet through the head just in case.

As the crack of the shot lost itself in the trees, Wolff squeezed the trigger of the Schmeisser and watched with terrible fascination as the four Russians doubled up and died. They were the first men he had killed. They were to be the last for a long time.

He was dragging the body of the other wounded German towards the pile of logs when reinforcements arrived. He collapsed at their feet.

He was transferred to a military hospital in Poland where the doctors shook their heads as they surveyed the wound in his belly. "He will never fight again," they murmured. "If he lives, that is."

But they reckoned without the singleness of purpose that had transformed a weakling destined for a desk in Berlin to a member of Hitler's elite fighting unit.

Slowly, very slowly, he recovered and was awarded the Knight's Cross 'for his courage in single-handedly wiping out a unit of enemy troops.'

Then he was posted to a training camp where he worked on the new Tiger tanks fitted with tracks 2½ feet wide, anti-magnetic armour and adaptations to enable their engines to start in sub-zero Russia.

And all the time Wolff, still deemed unfit for active service, fretted to be back with the Leibstandarte proper as he read of the exploits of his heroes, Sepp Dietrich who answered only to Hitler, Jochen Peiper, the hero of Kharkov, and his swashbuckling comrade Kurt Meyer known as Panzermeyer.

By this time the SS Panzer Divisions had been formed under the command of an SS general. They were the most feared troops in Russia and Kurt Wolff yearned to be with them.

Once again he harangued his superiors until he was finally allowed to go before a medical board. By this time the SS were desperate for manpower — they had taken volunteers from Holland, Spain, Sweden, France (even fifty British) and ethnic Germans from the Balkans.

Wolff was pronounced fit.

In the early summer of 1943 he returned to the Russian Front where the Germans were on the defensive after Stalingrad, the biggest defeat inflicted on the Germans since the Napoleonic Wars.

But Wolff, sheltered from reality by his wounds, could not conceive of defeat. He hadn't been brutalised. Nor, because of the physical defects of his teens, had he witnessed the early massacres and executions in Europe.

He was still an idealist.

He was the stuff heroes are made of.

He was the obvious choice for Grey Fox.

VII

Wolff's second test took place in a ruined farmhouse 150 miles behind the sagging German front-line.

He had been pulled back from the Viking — to which he had been seconded to patch up broken-down-tanks to an assembly camp prior to rejoining the Leibstandarte.

He was quartered in the farmhouse in one of the few rooms that still had a roof over it. (The farmhouse and the surrounding village had been razed by the Germans during the great advance.)

He shared it with two Wehrmacht officers, a Captain Steiner and a Major Wenck.

As he unpacked they remarked on the Runic flashes of lightning on his steel helmet and the death's head on his peaked cap.

"So we have a member of one of the famous Panzer divisions as our guest," remarked Wenck, unshaved, broken-nosed, a little drunk.

"Leibstandarte," Wolff said briefly, throwing a grey blanket onto the crude wooden bed.

"Ah, the Führer's bodyguard," said Steiner, tall and arrogantly handsome except for the bags under his eyes.

Wolff didn't reply. He lay on the bed, lit a Russian cigarette and stared at the ceiling.

"He's certainly going to need one soon," Wenck said. "The way things are going.

Wolff ignored him.

Steiner asked: "Been on the Eastern Front long?"

64

"Not long," Wolff replied.

"Still think we're going to win?"

"Of course," Wolff told him. "The Russians have over-extended themselves."

"You really believe that?"

"I believe in ultimate victory."

"I'm glad someone does," Steiner said. He stood up, over six feet tall; he would have made a good SS officer, Wolff noted, except for his mentality. "Hungry?"

Wolff who was starving said: "I could eat something."

"And drink something," Wenck remarked. "A little vodka will do you good," like a doctor prescribing treatment.

They went downstairs to the dining room. One corner of the roof was bared to the grey sky, now darkening. On the pine-wood table stood two flasks of vodka, two bottles of Georgian wine, three green-glass tumblers, three tins of corned beef, a bowl of beetroot soup and some hunks of black bread. A log fire burned in the grate.

They were served by two plump-breasted Ukranian girls whom the two Wehrmacht officers eyed lasciviously.

"Mine's the one with the thick legs," Steiner said. "He," pointing at Wenck, "out-ranked me. But she knows a trick or two, that one." And to Wolff: "You can give her a tumble if you like. Get the dirty water off your chest. But don't tire her out too much," he said, sitting down and pouring vodka into the three tumblers.

Steiner stood up and clicked his heels. "To the Führer."

They tossed back the vodka and Wolff felt it burn its way down his throat and drop like molten lead in his stomach. He poured himself a glass of wine to dilute it and thought: "I'll probably get drunk but what the hell."

In Poland he had drunk in moderation and had slept with a couple of girls, one of whom he had loved a little. But he had never abandoned his keep-fit regime, exercising when the hole in his belly had barely healed.

Steiner refilled the glasses while the girls, black-haired and gypsy-faced, hovered in the background.

"But don't get taken in by them," Wenck said gesturing at the girls with his glass. "When the Ivans get here they'll have our balls just like that," brandishing a carving knife.

Wolff said: "You seem very certain that the Russians will break through."

"*Will* break through? Will?" The broken-nosed officer laughed theatrically. "They're going through us like shit through a goose." He stood up. "Anyway, my idealistic young friend, another toast. To the Leibstandarte, the elite within the elite."

Wolff could hardly refuse the toast.

"What about you?" Steiner asked. "Do you have a toast?"

The vodka was slipping down easily now. Wolff stood up and raised his replenished glass. "To victory."

"Jesus Christ," murmured Wenck.

They drank.

Wenck snapped his fingers at the two girls. They opened the tins and placed the squares of meat, glistening with jelly, in front of the three officers.

At the same time Steiner slipped his hand up the skirt of one of them and said: "That's my girl. No pants. Always at the ready like a good soldier."

They ate hungrily, drinking more vodka washed down with the red wine. "Does Dietrich feed you like this?" Steiner asked, stuffing black bread into his mouth.

"He gets the best there is," Wolff replied.

"But of course," Wenck said. "Reichsführer Himmler sees to that."

"On the contrary," Wolff replied. "The Führer sees to it."

"But of course I forgot. The Leibstandarte are very special. They get cake and we get black bread."

"At least we're soldiers," Steiner said, eyeing Wolff speculatively. "Not policemen in fancy dress."

But Wolff, accustomed like all SS to the jealousy of the Wehrmacht, refused to be drawn. "Odd, isn't it," he said equably, "that the policemen are always in action where the fighting is the toughest."

Steiner and Wenck now appeared to be very drunk and Wolff was far from sober. Frosted air breathed through the gap in the roof but none of them felt it.

Wenck said: "And now for some brandy," clapping his hands.

One of the girls produced a bottle of straw-coloured-liquor and poured coffee that tasted of cardboard.

Steiner drank some of the brandy, grimaced and leaned across the table. "Have you been to Berlin lately, Kurt?"

Wolff shook his head.

"Karl was there three weeks ago, weren't you, Karl," to Wenck.

"I was. A strange city these days." His voice was slurred. "Full of rumours. And Plots ..." He stood up and walked to the fire where he stood warming his back; Steiner and Wolff sat in two easy chairs, holed by cigarette burns, on either side. "Full of plots," Wenck repeated.

"What sort of plots?" Wolff asked.

Wenck said to Steiner: "Should I tell him?"

"Why not?" Carelessly as though alcohol had dissipated all caution.

"I don't know ..."

"Out with it for God's sake, man," Wolff snapped. "We're not schoolboys."

"But an SS officer ..."

Steiner interruped. "Wenck is talking of plots against the Führer."

"I don't believe it," Wolff said immediately.

Wenck shrugged and drank some more brandy, "Some of the generals are not happy."

"They never have been," Wolff said.

"There has already been one attempt," Steiner remarked.

"Attempt at what?"

"Attempt to finish off the Führer. At Borisov in 1941. There will be others."

"And they will fail," Wolff said, standing up and stretching. The girl with the thick legs looked at him expectantly. "I think

I'll turn in. I've heard enough idiot talk for one day."

Wenck said: "It's not only Wehrmacht officers who are involved."

"If you're implying that the SS is involved .." A cold hatred was beginning to replace Wolff's indulgence. These two men were nothing more than traitors. "I think," he said to Wenck, "that you'd better take that back."

Wenck belched. "Not everyone is blind like you, Hauptsturmführer." He turned and threw his glass into the flames. "I'll wager that if you knew the end was near you'd change your tune. If you finally realised that a madman was sending men to their deaths when all was lost then you'd throw in your lot with the generals."

Wolff drove his knee into Wenck's crotch. And, as he bent forward with a thick cry of pain, raised the blade of his hand for the killer rabbit punch at the base of the neck.

Steiner intercepted the blow. "For Christ's sake, Wolff, he's drunk."

Wolff turned and hit the taller man in the solar plexus, but his fist encountered hard muscle. In the background the two girls twittered anxiously.

While Wolff and Steiner struggled, Wenck painfully straightened up. "All right," he shouted, "I apologise."

Wolff relaxed, disengaged himself from Steiner. Then he took his pistol from its holster, pointed it at Wenck who was retching into the fire and said: "I want more than an apology."

Steiner said: "For Christ's sake put that thing away."

Wolff turned the gun on Steiner. "Shut your filthy mouth." And to Wenck: "Stand up straight or you'll choke on your own vomit."

Steiner said: "You'll be court-martialled for this."

"A dead man can't give evidence."

"But I will."

"You'll be dead as well."

Wenck, his face white, sweat beading his forehead said: "What do you want?"

"I would like," Wolff said, "to hear you repeat the Leibstandarte oath of allegiance to Hitler," and turning to Steiner: "You too."

Steiner shrugged. "Very well if it pleases you."

"It does," Wolff said. "Very much."

Together the two officers intoned the oath after Wolff.

Wolff raised his arm in the Nazi salute. "Heil Hitler."

"Heil Hitler," they said.

*   *   *

When he had gone up to the bedroom Steiner said the Wenck: "He did well."

"Too well," Wenck said, putting a hand to his aching crotch.

"He passed with flying colours," the Captain said. "One more test now. The worst. Poor bastard."

"What I want to know," Wenck said, "is why I get a knee in the crotch and you only get a punch in the gut."

"A matter of rank, Sturmbannführer," Steiner told him. "A mere Captain is only worth a blow in the belly whereas a Major deserves a kick in the balls."

*   *   *

Snow was falling when Wolff's third and last test took place in the winter of '43.

Winter was the Russians' ally, the Germans' enemy. The Russians revelled in it, their white-clad troops covering phenomenal distances on skis. And they were always on the attack, Cossack cavalry suddenly materialising from behind veils of falling snow, Stalin tanks splintering the ice beneath the snow, guns lighting the dusk as shadows filled shell-holes on the desolate steppe.

One morning in late November Wolff was fed with information about a minor counter-attack aimed at rescuing a pocket of German troops cut off by the Russians.

That night, while Wolff lay sleeping in a cottage, a three-man raiding party entered the village where the Germans were camped, took him prisoner — helpless in his sleeping bag — tied him to a sled, and took him through the snow-flying night to a deserted mill ten miles from the village.

The interrogation was conducted by candlelight.

"We know there is going to be a counter attack. From what direction will it come? At what time?" All in broken German.

Wolff quoted regulations about interrogation of prisoners, gave his name and number and nothing more.

At first they roughed him up a bit. Knocking him down as, hands tied behind his back, he stood rigidly to attention as he had once stood on the parade ground of the Lichterfelde Barracks in Berlin.

When he was on the ground they kicked him.

Wolff stared up at his captors but saw only eyes gleaming in the candlelight in their woollen snow-masks.

"At what time? Where?"

Then they stripped off his outer clothing, bound his feet and dumped him outside in the snow where the temperature was —5, even lower with the Chill Factor created by the wind whining over the *steppe*.

It had stopped snowing and the moon shone through wounds in the clouds. Wolff struggled with the rope binding his wrists and ankles but soon the cold froze his limbs.

Then they carried him back into the mill and dumped him into a bath of hot water where he experienced the agony that only those who have immersed frost-bitten limbs in hot water can appreciate.

"Where? When?"

Name and number.

They shrugged. "You are being very foolish. Tell us what we want to know and we will let you go. If you don't . . ."

Wolff who knew about Russian atrocities — they had once decapitated some Germans and paraded their heads on spikes — prepared himself to die.

He thought of his father. Of the ranks of vines with their fat grapes. Of Munich. Of a girl in Poland. Of the ageing athlete,

Muller, who had made a man of him. Thank God for Muller who had given him the stamina to resist.

They then removed two fingernails from one hand with a pair of pliers.

"Where? When?"

Name and number. Fighting the cold blackness that threatened to envelop him.

They stood back and considered him, weighing the problem of all torturers: not to go too far: not to defeat the object of the interrogation.

Only two of them did the talking. The third, whose name was Wenck, stood in the background, arms folded across his chest.

"There's only one way," one of them said. "It always works."

The other nodded. "If they think they're going to lose their manhood they always talk."

"But we'll give you a last chance," the first interrogator told Wolff. "Look, we know there's a counter-attack coming. It won't make all that much difference if you give us the details. You've lost the war anyway," he added.

Wolff spat at them.

The first interrogator picked up a rusty knife. "We've given you every chance," he said. "More than the SS give their victims."

They pulled down his long woollen pants. He felt the blade on his testicles.

"Where? When?"

Wolff's body was racked by a violent spasm of shivering. He screamed silently within himself.

And then a fusilade of bullets smacked into the wall of the mill punching a line of holes and shattering a window.

The three captors froze. Looked at each other. And were gone.

Kurt Wolff had passed all his tests.

VIII

The month of September, 1943, was a desperate time in Rome.

On September 8th General Eisenhower announced the surrender of Italy over Algiers radio. For another hour Rome radio played selections from operas; finally confirmation of the armistice was broadcast.

Many Romans had expected to see British and American parachutists drop from the skies — an Allied landing on the Italian mainland was part of the Armistice agreement. Instead they saw field-grey German troops on the streets.

German paratroops were stationed on the boundaries of Vatican territory; German agents were infiltrated inside its walls. All Italian military units such as the Piave Motorised Division were disarmed.

Rome fearfully awaited the Germans' next move but the fear was at its height in two sections: The Vatican and the Jewish communities.

Already DELASEM, financed in Italy via Switzerland by JOINT, the American Jewish Distribution Committee, had received a bitter disappointment. They had understood that the Armistice, actually signed on September 3rd, would not be announced until October; this they believed would give them time to rescue the Jews on the French Riviera. But immediately the Armistice was announced the Germans moved into Italian-occupied France and nearly 50,000 Jews were trapped, fodder for the gas-chambers.

Father Benedetto, *Il Padre degli Ebrei*, now concentrated all his attentions on the Jews of Rome who would surely be persecuted and set up a committee with Settimio Sorani (the president), Aaron Kasztersztein and Stefan Schwamm.

Inside The Vatican fear fed on the German intentions to the Jews. Pope Pius XI had been outspoken in his condemnation of anti-Semitism, but since his election on March 2, 1939, the enigmatic Pius XII had been extraordinarily cautious because, it was argued, he believed that Papal intervention would exacerbate the plight of European Jewry. Would he act if the Germans started to implement the Final Solution in Rome?

Inside The Vatican walls monsignori, diplomats, humble priests and the *Sotto Vaticano* — everyone from a floor-sweeper to a plumber — heatedly discussed the possibilities.

Many asserted that Hitler would order a Jewish purge to incite the Pope to action — and then occupy The Vatican on the pretext of Papal interference. (In fact on September 12th, 1943, an SS General was ordered to 'occupy The Vatican, kidnap the Pope and bring him and the Curia north,' — to Liechtenstein. But the plan was abandoned).

There was much sympathy for the Pope.

Much hope.

And much hatred.

On September 3rd British troops had sneaked across the Straits of Messina and landed at Reggio on the toe of Italy. On September 8th-9th the major assault, Operation Avalanche, was made on the beaches of Salerno to the west, by General Mark Clark and the US Fifth Army, and at Taranto to the south-east by the British 1st Airborne Division.

On September 12th Otto Skorzeny and fifty paratroopers rescued Mussolini from the Sports Hotel at the peak of the 10,000-foot Gran Sasso mountain. He was flown to Hitler's Wolf's Lair in East Prussia. (The Leibstandarte provided the palace guard for the chastened dictator.)

The Germans in Rome were exultant. From the depressing catalogue of defeat there had suddenly arisen a phoenix of pride. The derring-do of the old days. While there were still men around like Otto Skorzeny — even if the prize had only been the pathetic Duce — then they could still win the war.

Father Liam Doyle encountered the small flame of hope as he made his rounds bringing help to the needy, not to mention intelligence to Maria Reubeni and, he feared, the partisani.

Sometimes he prayed for guidance in the great basilica of St. Peter's, the largest church in the world. But it seemed to him that his prayers were public, punctuated by the footsteps of sightseers; that the Papal Altar beneath Michelangelo's Cupola, was more of a showpiece than a seat of worship, that the chapels flanking the nave were sideshows.

And why not? Liam asked himself; this was the terrestrial throne of God. And then chided himself: There you go again, the Irish in you, seeing both sides of the question.

Nevertheless he took himself more frequently to a small chapel unaffected by the hands of Michaelangelo or Bernini. A humble place, angels' wings flaking on the skin of the dome, undisturbed by the tap-tap of high-heeled shoes on marble floors. It reminded him of his church in the Bronx.

Ridiculous, Father Doyle. You are blessed with the privilege of worshipping in St. Peter's, or any of the great temples of Rome, and you choose to kneel in a stable rather than a palace.

But, hearing again the confessions of the sad sinners of the Bronx, he was for a while at peace as he prayed and made his confessions to a Roman priest who understood the temptations of the flesh to which Liam was subjected but was confused by his other revelations.

From God there came no guidance. And Liam knew that this was because, if he truly sought the core of honesty within himself, he would know the answers.

But he didn't seek it, not truly. He continued to visit the German bishop and his cohorts at S. Maria dell' Anima, he extended his rounds to include the German College and the German Embassy to The Holy See at Villa Bonaparte on the Via Piave, and he reported everything he heard to Maria Reubeni.

Gradually Liam's fears that he was being used by the partisani towards violent ends subsided. The German invaders behaved themselves therefore there was no retaliation.

Until, that is, the events that began to unfold on September 26th, 1943.

*   *   *

Herbert Kappler was an officer in the SS in Rome. He was fair-haired, correct, attractive to women and sported a classic duelling scar on one cheek. He consorted with a Brazilian girl who spoke Italian and German.

On the afternoon of the 26th Major Kappler invited two Jewish leaders, Ugo Foa and Dante Almansi, to his office at SS headquarters on the Via Tasso.

At first the conversation was pleasant enough. The fortunes of the war, the weather, the exploits of the amazing Otto Skorzeny.

"A true son of the Fatherland," said the Major, leaning back in the chair behind his desk. On the walls were two photographs, Hitler and Himmler. The Major's hand strayed to the legacy of the sabre-slash on his cheek, his badge of courage. "Even you Jews must admit his audacity."

The two Jews were non-committal. They told the Major that although they were Jews they were also Italian citizens.

"So?" The Major shrugged. "It makes no difference. Italian Jews, German Jews, Polish Jews — you're all the enemy." In the pleasant tones of a man discussing the pruning of his roses. "However," he went on, "we have no intention of dealing with you in the normal way.".

The Jewish leaders sighed with relief.

"On the understanding," the Major continued pleasantly, "that you contribute to The Struggle."

The Jews looked at each other. "How can we do that Herr Sturmbannführer?"

"Please dispense with the Herr," the Major admonished them. "We do not use it in the SS." He got down to business. "The Jews have always been fond of gold?"

"Isn't everyone?" one of the Jews asked, puzzled.

The Major ignored him. "Fifty kilograms is a nice round figure."

The Jewish leaders waited apprehensively.

"It would do marvels for the German economy. The war-effort." His voice became brusque, but still correct. "I want fifty kilograms of gold delivered to this office within thirty-six hours." He glanced at his wrist-watch. "The deadline — giving you a little leeway — runs out at 11.00 hours on the twenty-eighth."

The two leaders protested that it wasn't long enough but, glancing at his watch again, this time to indicate the interview was over, Kappler said: "If we don't get the gold, two hundred Jews will be deported."

*   *   *

Maria Reubeni said: "So it has begun."

They sat round a table in Maria's tiny apartment with the Picasso prints on the walls, orange sofa scattered with cushions, sunlight touching a vase of fresh-cut roses and silver heirlooms on the sideboard.

They were a mixed bunch. Maria's father, his ascetic features enobled by a wonderful nose; an old Jew with a long grey beard; Fathers Liam Doyle and Maria Benedetto and the Sicilian.

On the table lay a half-eaten meal of spaghetti; they had all lost their appetite for it, all, that is except the Sicilian who ate greedily, washing down the spaghetti with draughts of Chianti.

"We must not be too hasty," said the old Jew. "It is only gold they want, not lives."

The Sicilian rolled spaghetti round his fork. "It works out at 250 American dollars a head." The Sicilian was good at figures when they represented money.

"A small price to pay," said the old Jew.

Maria rounded on him: "Are you crazy?" Checking herself

76

when her father said: "Don't speak to your elders like that, Maria."

Her father was the only man — except the Sicilian — whom she obeyed. That was why she had left her parents' house two blocks away and moved into the third floor apartment 'overlooking the Tiber.'

He was an art dealer. A quiet man of implacable will who had once been held for twenty-four hours by the Black Shirts during the Fascists' half-hearted repression of the Jews. He was also orthodox and he and his bed-ridden wife sorrowed at the rebellion of their only daughter.

Maria turned to the Sicilian: "I say we refuse to give them their gold. That is only the beginning. After that they will want more treasure, more loot. And who's to say they will keep their word? Have the Nazis ever kept their word? They will take their gold and then they will take us.. What do you say?" she appealed to the Sicilian.

He swallowed a mouthful of Chianti and said in his perfect Italian: "It is none of my business."

Liam Doyle looked at him sharply. "Why do you say that?"

The Sicilian mopped up his sauce with a hunk of coarse bread. "Because I am not a Jew."

"But we are all in this together."

"Not quite," the Sicilian said. He lit one of his thin cigars and sat back contentedly. "But if you want my opinion ..."

The old Jew smoothed his beard. "We must find the gold. It would be a crime if we didn't. Two hundred lives ..."

Maria turned to Benedetto. "What do you think, Father?" hopefully.

He said apologetically: "I think we should find the gold. They may keep their word."

"But it's blackmail."

There was a silence. In the street below they heard the sounds of shouting. Voices in phrase-book Italian. Maria went to the window. Two German soldiers were questioning an Italian — the waiter from the cafe where she breakfasted. He produced papers from inside his black, waiter's jacket. They were

77

apparently in order. The soldiers handed them back to him and shoved him so that he fell to the ground. The soldiers moved on with measured steps.

Maria returned to the table. Her father was speaking, quietly and with authority. "At the moment it is the only thing we can do." To his daughter: "It is not a defeat. For the time being we must play it their way."

"That's what the Jews all over Europe said. Look what happened to them."

"It will not happen in Rome," her father said firmly.

Maria knew she was beaten but she turned to Liam Doyle. "And what do you think, Father? Do you think we should give in to blackmail?"

"I think," Liam said carefully, "that we should do what is best for the Jews of Rome."

"And what kind of double-talk is that?" It was the first time for many weeks that she had turned on him and she saw the pain on his face but it didn't stop her. "You come here from your sanctuary, from The Vatican which has been anti-Semite since time began, and say we should do what is best for the Jews. What hypocrisy."

"I *have* been helping you," Liam said.

"And perhaps reporting back to the Holy Father. Telling all your German monks what we're up to."

Liam was silent.

Her father held up his hand. "Quiet, Maria. You have said enough."

The Sicilian wiped his mouth with the back of his hand. He stood up saying: "You did ask my opinion."

"But you didn't want to give it," Maria snapped.

"I said I would give my *opinion*. Nothing else."

"And that is?"

"That you should find Kappler's gold."

"Why, for God's sake?"

"Because you need the time," the Sicilian said. "And may I suggest a source of that gold?"

When no one answered the Sicilian pointed a finger at Liam

and said: "The Vatican."

When the Sicilian gave his verdict Maria finally accepted that she was wrong. Carried away by emotion. An Italian-Jewess in full flood.

Counsel returned. In the street outside she advised Liam not to make any approaches to The Vatican because it would make his sympathies conspicuous.

And she apologised to him for what she had said. "My tongue is a serpent, sometimes I cannot control it," smiling at the young man with the grey eyes whose masculine instincts were imprisoned in black, locked tight by his white dog-collar.

He smiled back. "Ten Our Father's and ten Hail Mary's." It was the first joke she had heard him make.

* * *

The approach to The Vatican was made through Father Borsarelli from the Convent of the Missionaries of the Holy Heart, a friend of the Jews.

And The Vatican responded.

Liam Doyle rejoiced. Perhaps at last the anti-Jew stigma attached to The Holy See would be wiped out.

The Papal authorities offered to make up the weight of gold if the Jews hadn't collected enough by the time the deadline ran out. Up to a maximum of fifteen kilograms, that is.

But perhaps Vatican gold wouldn't be needed.

All over Rome the Great Gold Rush of 1943 was under way.

Gold poured into the Synagogue. Beautiful watches, thinned by age, that chimed the hours; heirlooms hidden in dusty attics; bowls and chalices; bracelets and cigarette cases and tie-pins and earrings and old coins.

The wealthy and the poor Jews of Rome gave. So did some Catholics.

The Jews had pleaded for — and been granted — an extension of the deadline until 4 pm on the 28th.

Escorted by a friendly police officer in plain-clothes, a handful of Jews took the loot to the SS headquarters situated between the churches of S. Maria Maggiore and San Giovanni.

The Jews had added extra gold to avoid any argument. An SS officer weighed the gold and, after a brief dispute about the weight, accepted the ransom.

The gold was transported to the Sicherheitsdienst (SS Security Service) in Berlin where the giant Ernst Kaltenbrunner was now in charge, following the assassination in Czechoslovakia in 1942 of Reinhard (the Hangman) Heydrich.

The Jews received no receipt. But they relaxed. Until the SS struck again twenty-four hours later.

This time they raided the Temple on the banks of the Tiber and departed with two million lire from the safe.

The next morning more Germans returned to study old documents in the Temple; then they raided the home of the Chief Rabbi Italo Zolli who had gone to ground since the Armistice had been announced.

But still no arrests. No deportations to eternity. Was historical precedent to be confounded? Were the Jews to be left alone?

Maria Reubeni doubted it. But, with the escape hatches for the Jews now prepared, she relaxed enough to allow the Sicilian to make love to her.

*   *   *

Until now Maria, in her 21st year, had been a virgin.

She had been courted by Jew and Gentile but had sent them packing when they suggested bed. Not because her appetites were not strong — indeed she believed them to be stronger than many of the young men who sniggered about sex and boasted of their conquests — but because she had to respect a man before she slept with him.

On hot Roman nights she lay restlessly in her bed thinking about physical love. Wanting a man but despairing of ever finding one who matched up to her requirements.

He had to be dominant which, she admitted, was a challenge to any man, her personality being what it was. He had to be masculine; not necessarily a truck-driver but, even if he was a Greek god in an Italian silk shirt, he had to exude masculinity. And he had to have courage which, she agreed, could only exist alongside fear. He had to be honest, at least with himself, and he had to possess humility when required. Impossible prerequisites!

Until the Sicilian came along. Not that he measured up to all her demands — she would have preferred a cultivated lover who would choose dinner for her instead of always ordering pasta and cheap red wine — but masculine he undoubtedly was.

She had felt the attraction the evening he took over their little band in the cellar in the Borgo. She knew he would be rough and selfish with none of the preliminary love play that was apparently so essential. The knowledge excited rather than disgusted her.

There would be little tenderness, she knew. And she wondered if one day when she met a man she loved she would regret this excursion into sensuality. But this was war; all over the world women were throwing aside their inhibitions. Soon the Sicilian might be dead. Soon I might be dead. Soon the man I might one day have loved might be dead.

The one possibility that didn't occur to her was that the Sicilian might not want to make love to her.

After a long day working with Father Benedetto at 159, Via Sicilia, she met the Sicilian in a cafe in the arcade of the Piazza Colonna.

They ate pasta — of course — and then she invited him back to her apartment for coffee and brandy.

"Very well," he said non-committally. None of the sly confidence of the other men she had invited back.

They caught a taxi — there were still one or two around — which took them to the old ghetto area where Maria lived.

Maria drew the yellow curtains; rain spattered against the blacked-out windows. She lit a small gas-fire and made coffee while the Sicilian helped himself to brandy.

Then they sat opposite each other across a green-marble coffee table while Maria wondered what he would do and when he would do it. But he seemed content to drink his coffee and toss back thimblefuls of brandy.

She found herself wondering what he looked like naked but instead of sex they talked about the German occupation.

Maria thought: To hell with the war!

"We are well organised now," he was saying. "We have formed a junta, the *Comitato di Liberazione.*"

"But why you?" she said. *Was he one of those men who made violence a substitute for sex? Was he impotent?* "When people ask, you just say because you're a Sicilian. That's no kind of answer."

He shrugged and took off his black leather jacket; she could see black hairs curling at the neck of his red shirt. "I am also Italian. I think the Italians up here could use a little of our . . . expertise."

He spoke well, she thought. He was a strange mixture with his Roman speech and his peasant manners. "But you were here before the war . . ."

"Expanding our interests."

"The mafiosi?"

He spread his hands. "The Onorata Societa, if you must. Then the war came. But we still did well." He laughed. "We are still doing well. Flour, butter, cigarettes, coffee," grimacing as he sipped from the small porcelain cup in front of him, adding: "Proper coffee not chicory and dandelion roots like this."

"But you supply it at a price?"

"To those who can afford it. To the *gli amici degli amici* we give it away."

"And to us?"

The Sicilian grinned. He reached into a leather bag he had brought with him. "For you." He tossed a bag of coffee onto the table followed by a packet of butter, a slice of Gorgonzola cheese, a slab of milk chocolate and half a dozen packs of Chesterfields.

"I don't want your Black Market food," Maria snapped. "Who did you steal it from?"

He opened a pack of Chesterfields and offered it to her. She brushed it aside. "It doesn't matter where it came from. It's for us, for the partisani, for the Jews . . ."

"Not for this Jew."

"It's a fair payment," he said.

And now she understood him. She picked up the slab of chocolate and threw it at him. Then the butter. Then the cheese. "And now get out. What do you think I am, a whore?"

"A woman," the Sicilian said, standing up. He reached across the table and grabbed the collar of her blouse. She scratched his hand drawing blood.

With one foot he kicked over the table. "Do you want me to tear that beautiful blouse?"

"I'll kill you," she said, frightened now.

He dragged her into the bedroom where fragments of her childhood stood arrayed on a chest of drawers.

"You filthy bastard," she hissed. "You pig."

"Get undressed or I'll rip the clothes off you." He stretched out his hand towards her blouse. He pulled and the buttons flew off and she put her hand to her breasts sheathed in a black brassiere. "Get undressed." He was stripping off his shirt, unbuttoning his trousers.

She stared fascinated, found to her disgust that she was excited. She put her hands behind her back and undid the brassiere, watching his face as her breasts broke loose. She took off her skirt, looked up and saw that he was naked. What else was there to do but enjoy it?

And then they were on the bed together and his mouth was on hers and she was moaning although she didn't hear herself, and then with one thrust he was inside her and the pain was as she knew it would be but it fused into a rising ecstasy as he drove into her and she called out and locked her legs round his back.

And then it was over. No remorse, no disgust.

She waited till her breathing returned to normal. Then she whispered: "Maybe now I'll accept that food and those cigarettes."

*　　*　　*

It was 6 am on the Sabbath. Maria Reubeni slid from the bed where the Sicilian still lay asleep and went to the window for her early morning ritual.

The dawn was blurred with drizzle, the Tiber bleak. Rome was still asleep. Except for the men on the wet street below. Germans. Half a dozen of them in uniform, fully-armed.

One of them, an officer in a peaked cap, was battering on a door with the butt of a pistol. A man with a black beard, trousers and jacket pulled on over striped pyjamas, came to the door blinking and yawning.

The officer spoke to the man who nodded. The officer gestured to two soldiers. The bearded man began to protest but the two soldiers pushed him back in the hallway.

Maria saw the officer cock the pistol and follow the two soldiers.

She strode to the bed and shook the Sicilian. He was instantly awake, reaching for the throwing knife on the bedside table. "What is it?" as though he had been awake for hours.

"Germans. Outside."

He threw aside the bedclothes and peered through the open window. "What happened?"

She told him.

They knelt peering over the window-sill while the remaining four Germans armed with Schmeisser machine-pistols waited outside the open doorway keeping watch down the deserted street and scanning the rooftops.

Five minutes later the bearded Jew came out of the doorway fully dressed in a black jacket, woollen scarf, bright waistcoat and black, peaked cap. He carried a small cardboard suitcase.

The two soldiers emerged followed by the officer who was consulting what looked like a list of names. The bearded Jew was led away by two soldiers while the officer pencilled a tick on the list. Then he pointed up the street. The Germans moved to another door a hundred yards away and the officer began to bang on it with his pistol butt.

The Sicilian turned to Maria and said: "It has begun."

She stared at him for a second. Then said: "My parents."

They dressed rapidly.

"Do you have your forged papers?" he asked.

She nodded. "And you?"

"I don't have to have forged papers." He picked up the Beretta pistol lying beside the knife, then put it down again. "I'd better leave it behind. But you I cannot be without," picking up the knife. "Come," he said to Maria who was dressed in a fawn raincoat with a blue scarf wrapped round her head.

In the street he said: "Walk slowly, look interested. Walk towards them."

The officer with the insignia of the SS barked an order at them in bad Italian.

They stopped. The Sicilian said: "What's happening, Lieutenant?"

The officer ignored him. "Papers."

They handed him their papers.

"A Sicilian, eh?"

"From Messina."

The officer, very young with a razor nick on his chin, said "And on whose side did you fight in Sicily?"

"I was in Rome," the Sicilian said.

"And on whose side will you fight here?"

"I am a good Fascist," the Sicilian told him.

"There is no such thing in Italy. When Mussolini was deposed there wasn't a Fascist to be seen in the streets." The officer stared hard at the Sicilian. "Heil Hitler."

The Sicilian raised his arm. "Heil Hitler."

"And you, senorita. On whose side are you?"

"I am with him," taking the Sicilian's arm.

"Let us hope so."

The Sicilian pointed at the doorway from which two more captives were emerging. "So you are rounding up the subhumans, eh?"

The officer said coldly: "It is none of your business what we are doing." He added: "It is not a job I enjoy. This is a job for other units of the SS." He brandished his pistol. "Be on your way."

As they passed the open doorway Maria and the Sicilian glanced at the two Jews standing in the street. They carried their belongings wrapped in a sheet. They shivered in the cold. A man and his wife, both in their seventies.

Maria and the Sicilian hurried through the narrow streets.

Five trucks stood near the Gate of Octavia. One was already half-filled with Jews huddled together in the rain. Steam rose from their clothes.

Maria gripped the Sicilian's arm. She stared at the soldiers guarding the Jews. "Filthy pigs. If I had a gun . . ."

"Shush," said the Sicilian, his voice surprisingly gentle.

The house where Maria's parents lived still slept behind its shutters. It was part of a terrace of faded orange brick adorned with balconies.

They circled the block and approached from the rear through a small backyard where Maria had once played. She produced a key and they entered the kitchen. Matzos lay on the linoleum-covered table; crockery, washed but obviously not dried, was piled on the draining-board; her father was not the greatest of housekeepers but he did his best.

Maria left the Sicilian in the kitchen and climbed the stairs — she knew every creak — and knocked on her parents' bedroom door.

Her father answered. "Who is it?"

"It's me, Maria."

She heard him mutter, heard her mother's muted voice.

Her father came to the door belting his old dressing gown round his waist. "What is it? What time is it?" peering sleepily at his wrist-watch.

In short, terse sentences she told him what was happening. She went into the room where her mother, as fragile as an autumn leaf, lay on a single bed against the wall.

Her father snapped on the light. "So you were right."

"I was right but that doesn't matter now. We must get you

away before they come."

Her mother who was partially deaf said: "What is it? What does she want, Giuseppe?"

"Nothing, mama. There is nothing to worry about." To Maria: "We cannot move her. She was very bad last night," as his wife began to cough.

"If you don't the Germans will."

"What would they want with us? We are not important."

She gestured wildly with her hands. "You are Jewish. Don't you understand? You are Jewish."

Her father said: "Don't talk like that, Maria. Have respect for your mother."

"Then you won't go?"

He shook his head. "No, we won't go."

"Then we shall take you."

"You would take your own mother and father away from their home on the Sabbath?"

Maria closed her eyes. "Very well, I have warned you."

Her father touched her shoulder. "We shall pray, Maria."

She slammed the door. And on the landing outside, beneath the skylight through which she had first seen the stars she wept. Then she returned to the Sicilian and told him what had happened.

The Sicilian said: "You do not surprise me. My parents would have acted the same. Old people . . ." He shrugged.

"What are we to do?"

He led her out into the rain. "There is nothing to be done." They reached the street. "If you took your mother away she would die. Your father is right."

As they turned into the street a squad of German soldiers appeared round a corner. With them was another SS officer, also consulting a list of names. The soldiers headed towards the Reubeni house.

Fear lurched inside Maria Reubeni.

"Come," said the Sicilian.

They walked towards the Germans. The officer stared appreciatively at Maria but said nothing.

87

Maria looked over her shoulder as the squad approached her parents' house.

"Please God . . . " she whispered.

The soldiers marched briskly past the house and stopped six doors farther on.

*   *   *

In eight hours on that Sabbath morning the Germans collected 1,127 Jews. Old men, young men, pregnant women and children.

They were told to take rations for eight days, blankets and money. They were told to bring their sick: there was a hospital at the camp to which they were being transferred.

Each was given less than half an hour to get ready.

Two days later they were put on a train to the north.

While the remaining Jews of Rome went to ground the Allied forces stormed north. Naples fell but Field Marshall Kesselring (Smiling Albert), master tactician, held them on the Gustav Line which included Monte Cassino.

By this time Italy had formally declared war on Germany and Mussolini had been installed as puppet leader of the Salo Republic to the north; neither event caused much of a stir in Rome.

By this time it was a city of women. Able-bodied men were press-ganged into forced labour camps; anyone with irregular papers or anyone breaking the curfew was taken away. Men took to the cellars as German patrols stalked the streets.

The penalty for harbouring an escaped prisoner-of-war or for owning a radio transmitter was a firing squad. For disseminating news derogatory to the Nazis, or taking outdoor photographs it was life; for failing to notify the authorities of a change of address you got away with twenty years.

Posters on the walls exhorted Italian men to join the German army; allied radio broadcasts exhorted them to sabotage the Germans . . . "strike against them everywhere continuing the fight indefatigably without thoughts of political questions until our troops have arrived."

Food supplies were exhausted and partisani travelled up to fifty miles for a bag of flour. Public transport was thin on the ground; cooking gas was limited to a couple of hours a day.

The Allies bombed the city — and caused more anti-Allied feeling that the bomb-damage caused to the railway marshalling yards. "They want us to continue to fight indefatigably and then they drop bombs on us!" the Romans said.

And there wasn't a Jew — or anyone identifiable as such — to be seen on the streets. The Christian Church had rallied to them: The Vatican had acted.

Jews were given sanctuary in convents and monasteries, churches and chapels and poor houses. The Pope opened his summer residence, Castel Gandolfo on Lake Albano to them, and the Pontificial Gregorian University and the Pontifical Biblican Institute.

He even opened The Vatican to them.

They entered furtively, in disguise, with forged papers. The Vatican's Papal Guard mysteriously increased its strength; it was said that there were more Jews than Christians inside the walls of The Holy See.

The escape plans were organised by DELASEM operating initially from Via Sicilia opposite a prison which the Geheime Staatspolizei, better known as the Gestapo, used as a torture chamber. Refugees to the DELASEM HQ used a side entrance on the Via Buon Compagni, the Street of the Good Companions.

Father Liam Doyle's happiness was boundless. True Christianity flourished around here at the mansion of God, the seat of faith. And he no longer doubted that what he was doing was right. Since the deportation of the Jews in October the Germans were the enemy: he had made his choice. And only in waking moments in the early hours did he wonder why the Vicar of Christ had still not damned the German persecution.

Indeed The Vatican was an exhilarating place to be these days with its population, normally less than a thousand, swelled by Jews, spies, Allied diplomats — and escaped prisoners of war.

It was about this time that Liam came into contact with a wild Irish priest, Monsignor Hugh Joseph O'Flaherty, forty-five years old, nearly fifteen stone, six feet and two inches tall, a one-time boxer from Killarney. He had once been violently anti-British in the days of the Black and Tans. Now, helped by a British Army Major, Sam Derry, he devoted himself to smuggling British, American and other fugitives past the German paratroopers stationed on The Vatican boundaries.

Liam met him one day on the steps of St. Peter's holding a breviary, staring across the piazza through steel-rimmed spectacles resting on his broken nose.

The sky was a bruised grey and a bitter wind nosed its way through the 284 columns that almost surrounded the great square.

O'Flaherty hailed him. "Hallo, me boy, come and have a word. I've heard all about you."

Surprised, Liam mounted the steps. "I've heard about you too," he said.

"Nothing bad I'm hoping."

"All good," Liam said smiling.

"That's not much of a brogue you've got there," the priest with the bruiser's face remarked. "You're from the New World I'm thinking."

"Third generation," Liam told him. "We came from Dublin, on my father's side that is."

"Ah, but you wouldn't be wanting to have a Dublin accent, now would you?"

"They say the best English in the world is spoken there."

"Now don't be talking about English or you'll be getting me roused." O'Flaherty raised a fist like a potato.

"But you're helping the English to escape from the Germans. Or so I've heard." Liam added hastily.

"You've heard that now, have you?" He ran his hand through his thatch of hair. "Now who would have been telling you such a thing?"

"But you are, aren't you?"

"I'll put it to you like this. If you're helping the Jews then I

90

might just possibly be helping the auld enemy. In fact," he said grinning, "I just might be waiting for one of the divils to come by right now."

"If you hate them so much why are you helping them?" Liam asked.

"But you must know the answer to that."

"All —"

"God's children, that's me boy."

Liam hesitated with his next question and O'Flaherty prompted him: "There's something bothering you, I can smell it."

"I was wondering how much support you get."

"In The Vatican?"

Liam nodded; he felt a little intimidated in the presence of this aggressive, stage Irishman who was, in fact, a theologian in The Vatican.

O'Flaherty said: "Why don't you come out with it?"

"I don't know what you mean," said Liam, who did.

"You mean Your Man. You mean the Holy Father."

"I was wondering," Liam said lamely.

"So you were wondering, were you? Well, there's a lot of people wondering what he's up to." O'Flaherty took off his spectacles and polished them with a handkerchief, a little less intimidating without them. He grinned. "He has the divil's own job, you know."

"I suppose so."

"Well I'll tell you." He paused. "Let's say our work has his tacit approval. How does that suit you?"

Liam smiled. "It suits me very well."

O'Flaherty replaced his spectacles. "Now I think I see my man coming. You'd best be off."

"Where will you take him?" Liam asked.

O'Flaherty said: "To the German College. Where else?"

*   *   *

Kappler, now promoted to Colonel, had closed one Jewish

escape route into The Vatican and DELASEM needed another. They approached Liam who immediately thought of O'Flaherty.

"And why should I be giving away my secrets?" he asked in his room at the German College.

"Because they're God's children," Liam said smiling at him.

"Ah well, I suppose you have me there." He finished the daunting task of combing his hair. "And how would you like to be coming on a little mission today?"

"What sort of a mission?"

"Come with me and you'll find out," O'Flaherty told him.

Together they crossed the Ponte Vittorio Emanuele heading towards the city centre.

"Where are we going?" Liam asked, lengthening his stride to keep up with the big Irishman.

"The Via Tasso."

"That's a long way."

"Get some fresh air to your lungs?"

"Isn't that the headquarters of the SS?"

"And the Gestapo," O'Flaherty said cheerfully.

It was a brisk, rain-washed day, the sky a cold blue. A car experimentally fuelled by burning wood inched laboriously past them; an armoured limousine made its predatory way along the Corso Vittorio Emanuele, its loudspeakers blaring exhortations in guttural Italian to Romans to collaborate, and reminding them of the Allied bombs that had killed women and children on the outskirts of Rome the previous night. Fountains splashed as they had splashed for centuries.

O'Flaherty flung money to some boys begging on the sidewalk. "They used to be pick-pockets," he remarked. "But they're out of business — there's nothing to pick."

They passed the five-storey SS headquarters guarded by two SS privates. O'Flaherty pointed at them. "Fine soldiers, me boy, you can't help admiring them."

They entered an old apartment block directly behind the SS building, climbed two floors to a brown-painted door. O'Flaherty gave a mysterious knock. From behind the door came a man's voice. "Who's that?"

"Adolf Hitler," O'Flaherty said.

The door opened and they went into an apartment where five men lounged. "My brood," said the priest. "Two English, a couple of Free French and a Yugoslav."

They greeted O'Flaherty effusively but looked suspiciously at Liam. O'Flaherty introduced him. "A friend. One of us." They relaxed.

"Are you ready?" O'Flaherty addressed a middle-aged Englishman wearing tweeds.

"Quite ready." His voice was clipped, assured — a British General, as Liam later discovered.

Outside they climbed into a tiny Fiat — "I stole the petrol," O'Flaherty explained, "but I've made a full confession" — and headed back towards The Vatican.

They showed their papers to the German paratroopers — the General had become an Irish doctor named Flynn — and headed for the German College where monsignori in black soutanes with red and magenta piping were assembling.

Liam whispered to O'Flaherty: "What's going on?"

"A wee reception," O'Flaherty answered.

"But why is he" — pointing to the General — "coming?"

"A bit of light relief in these dark days."

In a small ante-room Papal dignitaries, diplomats and German officers in civilian clothes chatted and drank wine.

"There's your man," O'Flaherty said to the General. "Time you were introduced."

And that was how a wondering Liam Doyle witnessed the German Ambassador to The Holy See, Ernst von Weizsacker, in animated conversation with a British General on the run. They were discussing acid on the Ambassador's stomach.

*　　*　　*

"But did he show you a new way into The Vatican?" Maria Reubeni asked as Liam told her about the confrontation. They were in a storeroom in the Capuchin convent on the Via Sicilia.

On the table Maria had spread out a green, orange and yellow map of The Vatican City. In one corner of the store-room a young Jew was operating an ancient printing-press turning out forged identity cards, proclaiming that four hundred Jews were French refugees under the protection of the Swiss legation in Rome. They were rubber-stamped with the names of French cities and, as each document slid off the press, the young Jew carefully stuck used French stamps obtained from a Rome philatellist on them.

"Did this priest show you another entry?" Maria asked again as, fascinated, Liam watched the forger at work."

"He did that," Liam said.

"You sound very Irish."

"I've been under a powerful Irish influence."

"He sounds a wild man," Maria remarked.

"That he is."

Liam prodded the map with one finger. "There it is. From St. Peter's steps through the Piazza di Circo Neroniano to the German College."

"And you're sure we can trust him?"

"As sure as the Pope's a Catholic."

"You've changed," Maria said smiling. "For the better."

Liam was pleased. He wondered if she suspected how he felt about her; about the remorse when he prayed in the shabby old church and at his bedside.

He wanted to say: "I've changed because I'm working with you," but instead he said: "I've found a new purpose."

"Not really. You're still working for humanity."

"I was never quite sure that I was before."

He could feel the warmth from her body in the chilly store-room; he edged away.

Father Benedetto came into the room. He looked grave. Pointing at the pile of forged documents beside the young Jew he said: "You might as well burn them."

They looked at him in astonishment. "The Italian Minister of the Interior has been told that there are as many as four hundred French refugees in Rome. He wants a list of their names."

The young Jew stood up. "Well, we'll give them to him."

Benedetto shook his head. "When he's got the names he's going to send them back to France. As soon as they reach France the forgeries will be obvious. And we all know what would happen to four hundred Jews with forged identity papers."

Maria said: "What are we going to do?"

"All is not lost," said Benedetto, Father of the Jews. "We will just have to adapt. The Hungarian counsellor, Viktor Szasz, is under the protection of the Swiss. You," to the young Jew, "will just have to start printing Hungarian papers."

Maria said: "How did the Minister get to know that there were so many *French* refugees?"

"That," Benedetto said, "is what worries me. It seems that we have an informer in our midst."

He looked at Liam Doyle.

IX

By 1944 the German espionage machine was fully installed inside The Vatican.

Among the agencies represented were the Abwehr (Military Intelligence), the Ministry of Foreign Affairs, the Chancellery and the Gestapo. Not even the German Ambassador, Ernst von Weizacker, was immune from surveillance — an associate of Martin Bormann named Ludwig Bremmer was dispatched, under diplomatic cover, to spy on him.

One of the collective achievements of the German agents was to supply the information that enabled Herman Göring's Aviation Ministry to crack the code by which The Vatican communicated with its Nuncio in Berlin, Archbishop Cesare Orsenigo.

The agents consisted of priests infiltrated into papal offices, clerics with Nazi sympathies, diplomats accredited to The Holy See and the *Sotto Vaticano*.

As the war progressed the network expanded methodically within the 42 palaces, 208 staircases and 10,000 rooms that comprise The Vatican. Apart from assessing Vatican policy and trying to peer behind the mask of the enigmatic Eugenio Pacelli, some of the spies were engaged on more defeatist projects: plans to save the skins rather than the souls of members of the Nazi hierarchy.

Among them was a monk named Heinrich Brandt who worked for the SD, the SS security service. He was a plump, jolly man nick-named Friar Tuck who had a good appetite and a hearty laugh. He no longer actively represented his monastic order and, because he had qualified in the subject before taking religious orders, he advised the Pope on archaeology — in particular excavations beneath the altar in St. Peter's to confirm once and for all the burial place of St. Peter.

Brandt was currently engaged in establishing escape routes. But, unlike other colleagues who now accepted the possibility of defeat, he was concerned only with one possible fugitive. One of his two Gods. Adolf Hitler.

*　　*　　*

One wintry day when frost sparkled on the lawns, Friar Tuck walked along a path near the statue Madonna Della Guardia with a young Jesuit priest from Hamburg who worked in The Vatican library.

Brandt liked to stroll round the grounds. He preferred it in the spring and summer when candles were lit on the chestnut trees and there was perfume on the air from the lemon grove; but he walked in all weathers because it was only out-of-doors that he could discuss non-Vatican business out of range of eavesdroppers and microphones.

For a while they walked in silence. Two men of God in meditation. Brandt patted the head of a small boy playing in the long, winter-flattened grass near the statue.

Then they discussed the four bombs that had dropped on The Vatican damaging the mosaic shops. The Germans had blamed the Allies, the Allies had blamed the Germans and the *Osservatore Romano* had complained: "We must deeply deplore this violation of The Vatican City, whose neutrality, recognised by all, safeguards the freedom and religion of the world."

After debating the bombing Brandt turned to the matter in hand. As they neared a statue adorned with spouting angels he turned to the Jesuit named Kruger and said casually: "What do you think of young Father Doyle?"

"Who?"

"Liam Doyle. The language magician."

"I don't think I know him. Why?" making a mental note that he should.

Brandt decided to divert him; perhaps he shouldn't have mentioned Doyle at all; but he wanted to find out if Kruger, who undoubtedly worked for the Gestapo, had any information on Doyle from New York.

Doyle is mine, the chubby monk decided, and said to Kruger: "I merely thought he might be of use to us. You know, fluent in German, Italian, Latin."

Kruger lost interest.

Ostensibly Kruger worked for Chancellery Intelligence. He and Brandt were collaborating in the preparation of sanctuaries for refugee Nazis.

"What we must concentrate upon," he told the pale-faced librarian, "is the methods used by the prisoners-of-war and the Jews. And use them when the time comes."

"If the time comes," Kruger amended. Brandt wondered if he would be the subject of a report. *Defeatist in outlook.*

"We have O'Flaherty under surveillance," Brandt continued. "And Derry. And, of course, Osborne and Tittman."

Kruger said: "Maybe it will all be abortive. Maybe the Führer will decide to seize The Vatican and transport the Holy Father to the north."

But you don't want that my devious scholastic friend, Brandt thought. You're only waiting for the day when you usher your Gestapo friends into the German College.

They walked in silence through The Vatican village, past the pharmacy, the post office and the jailhouse.

In the Street of the Parrots Brandt gently sounded out Kruger. "How many safe houses have you located so far?"

The librarian spread wide his thin hands. "Scores of them. Only yesterday I received a report of one near the Via Nazionale in the Via Firenze right behind the hotel occupied by SS. And another on the SS's back-doorstep in the Via Tasso."

Brandt noted them and excluded them from his own schemes. He needed an exclusive route and haven.

Ten minutes later they parted company.

Miserable little sinner, Brandt thought, watching the Jesuit's departing figure. He glanced at his watch. His fat face broke into a smile. He decided to postpone action on Liam Doyle for a while: it was time for lunch.

*   *   *

Heinrich Brandt was born in Bavaria, stronghold of Nazism and Catholicism, and came to Rome in 1933, the year The Vatican and Germany signed their concordat, when he was thirty-five — and slim.

He was already a disciple of Hitler. He perfectly understood Hitler's hostility to the Catholic Church: he believed there should be a compromise between Catholicism and National Socialism in the interests of Germany. He became a founder member of the SS.

By the time he became aware of Liam Doyle's activities he had been chosen by Sepp Dietrich and his fellow conspirators as Grey Fox's agent inside The Vatican. He was now trying to establish a chain of convents, monasteries and churches from Germany to Rome via the South Tyrol. To observe how other clerics operated in a hostile atmosphere he had visited Father Benedetto.

There was no secret about Benedetto's activities; Kappler knew about them and he was out to get him. But Benedetto was a slippery customer. Brandt rather admired him, even if he was misguided.

He had rung the bell outside the convent and waited while, he presumed, any evidence of unclerical endeavour was brushed under the carpet.

Finally the door opened. Benedetto greeted him cordially but warily.

Inside Benedetto's study Brandt sat down on a leather chair, crossed his chubby legs and asked: "How's the good work going?"

Benedetto sat behind his desk, made a prayer-like motion with his hands and said: "God's work is never done."

"I hear his work is particularly exacting these days," Brandt said. He rather hoped that Benedetto would offer coffee and perhaps a little cake; but the Cupuchin friar seemed anxious to get rid of him; he wondered why.

"It *is* war-time," Benedetto said non-committally.

"We are certainly sorely-pressed inside The Vatican," Brandt said. "The place is teeming with Allied prisoners-of-war. And Jews," he added, forcing himself to remark: "Poor souls." He glanced at Benedetto for his reaction. Nothing.

Brandt went on: "I hear that the Jews have been sent twenty thousand dollars by the Americans." He hoped Benedetto would give himself away by correcting him: the money had been deposited by JOINT in a London bank and the Jews were obtaining lire on credit.

Benedetto remarked: "Really? I hadn't heard that."

Really, Brandt thought, we men of God can be very devious. He noticed what appeared to be an identity card on the desk. It bore a French stamp; he made a mental note of it.

He made a couple more attempts to draw Benedetto but they failed. Brandt didn't blame him.

As he was leaving he met a young priest just about to ring the bell. His face was vaguely familiar; they exchanged hesitant greetings in the way of two people who think they may know each other.

Driving back in a Mercedes with a red-lettered Vatican number plates loaned to him by a Hungarian cardinal, Brandt tried to place the young priest.

It wasn't until later that night when he was tackling a plate of smoked salmon washed down with a bottle of Frascati that he remembered: his name was Doyle and he was The Vatican's American linguistic wizard. Brandt had met him briefly at the German Embassy to The Holy See at the Villa Bonaparte.

Now why, Brandt wondered, as he buttered a slice of brown bread, would an American with access to the German Embassy be visiting the Father of the Jews?

*　　*　　*

100

After lunch on the day that he had walked in The Vatican gardens with the Jesuit librarian, Brandt decided to put Doyle under personal surveillance.

From his apartment he kept watch on Doyle's room with a pair of field-glasses. When he saw Doyle leave he let himself into the block and, with a skeleton key, opened the door to his room.

It was a very humble place, Brandt thought. Darned sheets on the bed, a chest of drawers, gas-ring and chipped teapots, a few dog-eared books, pictures of the Holy Father, the Crucifixion and what he assumed to be Doyle's church in New York.

With the finesse he had learned years ago in Berlin he went through Doyle's personal possessions. Read a couple of badly-spelled letters from his parents, checked the entries in his diary . . . Maria. Who was Maria? A woman's name in this cubicle of devotion and celibacy?

Brandt walked back to the door and surveyed the room. Where to plant the microphone? Inside the base of the bedside lamp, he decided. An electrician on his pay-roll could wire it up the following day.

Brandt closed the door behind him, re-locked it with the skeleton key and walked out into the winter sunlight.

The following day, wearing a collar and tie and heavy, belted overcoat, Brandt followed Doyle when he left The Vatican.

To Brandt's experienced eye Doyle's behaviour was furtive. He kept looking over his shoulder and he back-tracked along a side-street as though to confuse anyone following him. He's learning, Brandt thought. But an amateur. He wished Doyle wouldn't walk so quickly.

Doyle followed the Tiber to the Ponte Cavour, where he crossed the river and headed in the general direction of the gardens of the Villa Borghese. Brandt hoped that one day the young priest would avail himself of a Vatican car so that he could follow in the cardinal's smooth-purring Mercedes.

In the great park spread before the Villa Borghese where Cardinal Scipione Borghese had once collected his art treasure

— Raphael, Titian and Correggio — Doyle paused beneath a leafless plane tree.

An assignation. But the man — or woman — was late. Or, more probably, Doyle was early. He was that sort of man, Brandt decided, shivering as an icy breeze nosed inside his thick coat.

Surveillance now posed problems. Brandt took up a position two hundred yards away and observed Doyle through his field glasses. Luckily there was hardly anyone in the park to notice him: it was too cold.

Doyle kept glancing at his wrist-watch. He was becoming anxious. Then, through the field-glasses, Brandt saw him smile and wave.

Brandt swivelled the field-glasses. A girl was approaching across the frost-rimmed grass. A beautiful girl wearing a fawn raincoat, ankle-strapped shoes — in this weather! — and a blue silk scarf almost covering jet-black hair.

Well, well, Father Liam Doyle!

They chatted for five minutes before making the motions of people about to part.

Brandt didn't hesitate; he followed the girl.

*　　*　　*

That evening beside his bed Liam prayed aloud to God beseeching Him to rid him of his physical desire for Maria.

A hundred yards away Heinrich Brandt listened intently through an amplifier.

Poor tormented soul, thought the monk who had not been entirely dedicated to celibacy in his youth.

Liam finished praying and Brandt switched off the circuit. Soon, perhaps, the young priest might reveal the entire Jewish operation to God — *and to me*.

The monk popped a chocolate with a Brazil nut centre into his mouth and munched contentedly.

102

X

The preparation of Kurt Wolff for his role in Grey Fox proceeded methodically but slowly.

He had to be led gently towards acknowledgement that the war was lost. He had to be *guided* towards the realisation that the only hope of fulfilling the Aryan dream was to save the life of the man who had dreamed it. Not only that but he had to be sheltered from a few brutal facts. You could not totally conceal the existence of concentration camps but you could ensure that he had no contact with the Totenkopfuerbände, the Death's Head organisation of the SS who guarded them.

In this context the conspirators were aided by Wolff's own mental outlook. Hatred of the Jews had been implanted in his mind a decade ago when he was still a schoolboy; he accepted that sub-human races had to be repressed, but his vision was shuttered when he considered the methods of repression. In this he was identical to many thousands of other Germans.

There was one other sublety to be observed. Ultimately, of course, Wolff had to come into close contact with Hitler. But not yet. One glimpse of the Führer in one of his maniacal outbursts and disenchantment might set in.

All Sepp Dietrich's energies were now employed in the great 'tactical withdrawal' across Russia and he appointed a wounded Major-General in the SS personnel department in Berlin to complete the *education* of Kurt Wolff.

The department was one of twelve principal departments in the complicated structure of the SS and it was headed by SS-

Obergruppenführer Maximilian von Herff who was directly answerable to Heinrich Himmler at his offices in Prinz Albrechtstrasse.

The Major-General's name was Werner Harzer. He was an aristocratic zealot who worshipped Hitler but despised Himmler whom he privately described as 'that myopic chicken-farmer.' (Himmler had bred chickens before turning his attention to humans).

He was fifty-two years old, sleek black hair needled with grey, very correct and intelligent. He walked with a stick, his thigh having been shattered by a soft-nosed bullet at Stalingrad, and there was a sliver of shell-casing somewhere in his abdomen which the surgeons had decided to leave there; casual acquaintances left his presence with the firm impression that he wore a monocle: he didn't.

In the spring of '44 Kurt Wolff was posted under protest to Berlin having failed a medical; according to the doctors, acting under orders from Dietrich, his interrogation by the Russians had aggravated his old injuries.

Wolff detested his duties in the personnel archives of the SS; Harzer understood his feelings. "Two war-horses put out to pasture," he sympathised.

"But can't you countermand my posting, Gruppenführer?" he asked Harzer one day, standing to attention in front of the General's desk.

Harzer motioned him to a chair. "You know better than that," he said mildly gazing through the window at the budding linden trees. "Dietrich has refused your request; that's all there is to it."

"I'm perfectly fit," Wolff said. He covered the two nail-less fingers of his right hand with his peaked cap.

"Not according to the doctors."

"They're sending seventeen-year-old boys out to the Russian Front. Surely I would be of more use than them? And what," he demanded, "about my supposed genius with tanks?"

"That is none of my business." A disciplinary touch of frost in his voice. He tossed Wolff a sheaf of papers. "Check out the ethnic origins of these gentlemen. They want to join the SS."

"Are they out of school yet?" Wolff asked.

"That," Harzer said quietly, "will be quite enough of that."

But later he softened. He visited Wolff in his own office, a spartan place furnished with a green, metal desk, two chairs and three filing cabinets.

He offered Wolff a cigarette from a silver case embossed with a family crest. They drank ersatz coffee.

"You've got to learn to relax," he told Wolff.

And he meant it. There was a tautness about Wolff's face that he didn't like: frayed nerves were not acceptable in the man chosen to implement Grey Fox.

Wolff, he thought, had changed a lot since he had first been chosen. Hardly surprising after what he'd been through. But mostly the changes were for the good: there was a leanness of character that had not existed before.

He leaned forward in the stiff-backed chair and lit Wolff's cigarette. Wolff regarded him warily: the general was not one to socialise.

Harzer inhaled deeply, blew out a jet of grey smoke and said: "I'm thinking of taking a couple of days off and going into the country."

Wolff waited.

"I have a place in the Bavarian Alps. You could meet my daughter, I think you may have a lot in common. Would you like to come?"

"I should be delighted," said Wolff because there was nothing else to say. It wasn't an invitation: it was a command.

*　　*　　*

Frieda Harzer served lunch.

Rich meaty soup followed by succulent wurst and sauer-kraut washed down with a Bavarian wine.

Wolff watched her as she moved round the long oak table. Blonde hair coiled in two ropes, alpine complexion, the blue eyes of her father, full-breasted but slender-waisted, head held

105

with the arrogance of her breeding.

Harzer had often talked about her and, from what he had said, Wolff gathered that she could be troublesome. Sometimes the General stopped in mid-sentence when about to embark on one of her indiscretions, but many people did that in Germany these days.

Wolff had gained the impression that the cause of the friction was political. She did not believe in The Struggle. Wolff could imagine the General's pain.

Harzer was a widower. Frieda was his only child. And she despised everything he believed in. *Everything I believe in.*

But, whether or not she believed in National Socialism, Frieda contributed to the war effort. She worked as a nurse in a military hospital in Berlin and now had ten days' leave.

She lifted the bottle of wine from a silver ice-bucket and said: "As you see we do not go short of anything here."

"Why should you," Wolff remarked politely, "if there's plenty of everything."

Harzer said: "It's all home produce. Even the sausage."

The farm-house was wedged into a foot-hill of the Alps south of Augsburg, about fifty miles from Wolff's home. On one side lay a verdant valley, on the other pine-clad mountains.

The window of the stone-flagged dining room was open and spring breathed through it. Wolff smelled blossom and clean air. He bit into the sausage, felt the skin snap in his mouth and the juices flow; he sipped his wine and decided to forget his frustrations, to forget the war for a couple of days.

Frieda Harzer said: "I've heard a lot about you Hauptsturmführer." There was irony in her tone when she gave his rank.

"Kurt, please," he said. "We're not in Prinz Albrechtstrasse now." Although he couldn't imagine himself calling Harzer by his first name.

"Very well, Kurt. But the rank suits you."

"Thank you," he said.

"You are a very military-looking person. But not Wehrmacht material, of course," aware of the SS view of conventional soldiery.

Wolff smiled at her. "I don't think the General would agree at the moment." Wolff wore flannel trousers, an old blue, V-necked sweater and a worn blue sports shirt.

"Nonsense," she said. "You'd look military — sorry, SS — if you came dressed as a harlequin at a fancy-dress ball."

The knowledge pleased Wolff even if it wasn't intended as flattery.

"I should like to see you in nurse's uniform," Wolff said, sensing the girl's hostility which was stimulating because most girls were only too pleased to be seen in the company of an SS officer in his black and silver finery.

"You might one day — if you're wounded."

The General interrupted. "Kurt has already had his share of wounds."

"All for a good cause," said Frieda.

"I'm a desk-bound clerk these days," Wolff told her.

"And you yearn for action?"

Wolff nodded.

"I know, they all do. The SS, that is. First out of their beds, first to be discharged. Heroes every one of them. Except, perhaps those in the camps —"

"Frieda!" The frost was back in the General's voice.

"All right, they don't exist. Do you have any views on racial superiority, Kurt?"

Wolff said: "Yes I do. I believe we're superior."

She was about to reply but Harzer told her to serve the sweet. So at least he still had the authority to discipline a wayward daughter.

The sweet was chocolate cake with three layers of thick cream. And then coffee. Wolff declined the cognac. The General lit a cigar. Wolff relaxed contentedly. One day, he decided, he would retire to Bavaria. After The Struggle was over. He imagined himself in a farmhouse like this, with fumed oak furniture and clean-smelling rooms, dried flowers in the vases and snow falling and melting in the courtyard outside and, to his surprise, he had two flaxen-haired children and Frieda was their mother.

The General rose, reached for his stick and said: "I'm going to take a nap." And to his daughter: "Show Kurt our domain."

"Do you like walking?" Frieda asked. "Or will we have to march."

"I'll stroll," Wolff told her.

* * *

Lying on his bed fully-clothed Harzer pressed his finger into his belly. Sometimes he thought he could feel the sliver of Russian metal embedded there. He wished they'd taken it out. His hand strayed down to his ruined thigh; beneath it, although he tried to exercise, the calf-muscles were withering. After the war, he thought, he would die; not just fade away, as the *Tommis* said.

But first he would make sure that Frieda's future was assured. His beautiful, wilful Frieda, so much like the girl he had courted in those terrible starved days after the First World War; the girl who had died giving birth to Frieda. Why did Frieda have to reject everything that he worshipped?

What if she ever discovered that he planned to rescue the Fuhrer so that his dream could still one day become a reality?

The sliver of metal made its presence felt; Harzer winced.

He wondered if he had made a mistake by introducing Wolff to his daughter. If she could in any way influence him with her rebellious views.

But no, Harzer comforted himself, Wolff was too dedicated a Nazi to accept the arguments of a self-opinionated, twenty-year-old child.

But I would like to have Kurt Wolff as a son-in-law, he thought. He dozed fitfully.

* * *

The distant peaks of the Alps were sprinkled with snow. Wolff believed he could smell the snow; it smelled of iced sugar.

Frieda, wearing a suede jacket, strode manfully beside him.

"You're marching," he told her.

"It runs in the family," she replied.

"Are you ashamed of your heritage?"

"Of course not."

They walked downhill, past cows and goats and chickens, past a water-mill, along a path beside a small, slow river until they came to the village.

A group of old men were putting up a stage in the main street at the point where it was bridged by a closed rooftop passage with a clock set in its walls.

Frieda pointed at them. "There aren't any young men left. Soon there won't be any boys."

"What are they doing?" Wolff asked.

"Preparing for a festival when we drive out the devils from the village."

"And do they go?"

"Not willingly. There are lots of battles."

They left the village and sat in a field. Green pastures tilted away from them down to the foot of the valley; small clouds cast moving shadows on the mountains. A small blue butterfly flitted past.

Wolff lay back with his hands behind his head. He sighed luxuriously. "I'd forgotten all this existed," he said.

"But to you it's just an excursion. You'll be happy to be back in Berlin. You're a town boy."

Wolff shook his head lazily. He told her about his father's vineyards.

"And your father?"

He died when I was in Russia. He had been in the Cavalry and he never wanted me to join the SS. Somehow it put up a barrier between us. I never understood why."

"I do," Frieda Harzer said.

"Please enlighten me," Wolff said, determined not to allow her to spoil the afternoon.

"He was a soldier," Frieda said.

"And what's that supposed to mean?"

"The Army represented our honour. It was the only thing

109

we had left in those days."

Wolff raised himself on one elbow. "The Army was a mess. Its spirit was broken. They were no longer soldiers. The core around which Germany was rebuilt was the SS."

"I've heard all this before," she said, chewing a blade of grass. "From my father." She lay back; the suede jacket fell open and Wolff stared at the swell of her breasts. Why in God's name were they talking politics? She said: "Do you believe in the destruction of a race because they're sub-human?"

Wolff remembered all the anti-Semite teaching at school lodged in his brain as firmly as grammar. He had never allowed himself to question it; he didn't intend to do so now. He knew certain camps existed; he had no wish to know anything about conditions inside them.

He said: "Look, I know I've been pushed onto you. We have been thrown together. I've only got another thirty-six hours." He gestured towards the valley, towards the white-tipped mountains. "I'd like to enjoy this, to share it with you. Can we forget politics?"

She gazed at him, the blue sky in her eyes. "I'm sorry," she said.

He wanted to place his hand on her breast, but he knew it would be rejected. If any feeling grew between them it would be a gentle process, an old-fashioned courtship. There was no immediate, fierce chemistry. What would I find at the end? Contentment, perhaps?

Gently she placed one finger on the scar on his cheek. "You were lucky," she said. "My father tells me that you won the Knight's Cross."

Wolff stood up. "Let's go back to the village and help chase those devils out."

They went to a small cafe filled with old men wearing hats bladed with feathers, and their plump wives. They drank tea and ate pastries and Wolff learned more about Werner Harzer's daughter.

She had studied languages in Munich. She had spent nine

months in Italy — "to learn the language of our allies." But she had rebelled against a future laid out for her as neatly as a landscaped garden. She had taken up nursing; she had seen young men blinded, mutilated, broken; she had sat at their bedsides holding their hands as they murmured the names of wives, sweethearts, parents. "And you wonder why I feel the way I do?"

"They were soldiers," Wolff said. "They knew it might happen."

"None of it need have happened," she said. "None of it."

They walked back towards the farmhouse in the alpine dusk. The mountains seemed to have moved closer, dark and sharp. The air was chill.

Tentatively Wolff asked if she was engaged.

"When I was eighteen I was fond of a man."

"A soldier?"

She drew away from him. "He was a Jew. He was taken to a camp. He's dead."

*   *   *

The two days passed like hours. Then Harzer and Wolff flew back to Berlin in a Junkers 52 transport plane which had dropped some of the first bombs in the Spanish Civil War.

That night Harzer limped through the rubble from the previous night's air-raid to an apartment block not far from the Brandenburg Gate. Or what was left of an apartment block.

Soft rain was falling and the clouds were low; he doubted if the bombers would return tonight. The smell of destruction was thick in Harzer's nostrils as, leaning on his stick, he laboured up a flight of pitted stairs.

He was let into the apartment by a Brigadier in the SS, Fritz von Geissel, a nondescript man with a tactician's brain, not unlike Adolf Eichmann in appearance.

The apartment, furnished with deep leather chairs, red plush curtains and a chandelier, was covered in dust and smelled of whitewash.

111

"So," Harzer said, sinking into a leather chair and accepting a cognac, "they almost got you last night."

"Let's hope it's true about lightning not striking twice in the same place."

Von Geissel spread out a map of Europe on the mahogany table. He prodded it with one well-manicured finger. "The pincers are closing," he said. "Russia, Italy . . . Soon the hammer blow in France."

"How much longer do you think?" Harzer asked.

"I give us another year. The Fuhrer will fight to the last." He ran his finger across Europe to Italy. "But we have to move quickly."

They had joined the SS together and, although they weren't close friends — von Geissel was too clinical for Harzer's taste — they shared common aspirations.

Harzer reached for his stick and joined von Geissel at the table.

Von Geissel's finger stopped half way down the Italian mainland. "Kesselring's doing a superb job but he can't hold Cassino much longer. When that falls the Allies will link up with their forces at Anzio and the road to Rome will be open. By the way, how is our young hero?" pouring them both more cognac.

They retired to the leather chairs in front of the fireplace where wood, salvaged from the debris outside, burned brightly.

Harzer said: "A fire in April?"

Von Geissel shivered. "I've never been able to get warm since Russia." He lit a cigarette. "You were about to tell me about Wolff."

"He's living up to our expectations."

"I knew he would," von Geissel said drily. "I personally pulled out two of his fingernails." He sipped his cognac reflectively. "But we have to speed things up now. His education must be completed."

"I know what you're thinking," Harzer said. "He's got to get to know Rome. I've been working on it," he added.

"Good. It's quite simple really. He's got to visit Rome before Wayne Mark Clark does."

* * *

Two days later Harzer summoned Wolff to his office. "You and I," he said, "are going for a drive," buttoning his long black greatcoat.

"A drive, Gruppenführer?" the informality of the two days in Bavaria forgotten.

"That is what I said, Hauptsturmführer."

Harzer took the wheel of the big Mercedes tourer; Wolff sat beside him.

As he drove along a street of shops, bomb-blasted windows boarded up with wood, Harzer said: "What I am going to say to you now is very important. Listen very carefully and don't interrupt."

"Very well, Gruppenführer."

"You have been chosen for a very important mission. So important that only a few people know about it. It is therefore vital that you tell no one about your movements. Not even Reichsführer Himmler knows about it," he added, glancing at Wolff's face.

The big open car turned a corner where workmen were filling a bomb crater. Harzer skirted the crater and headed west along Charlottenburger Chaussee.

"Rome will fall soon," the General said abruptly.

"But Kesselring is fighting magnificently. They say that more than twenty thousand troops have been killed at Anzio."

"Rome will fall." The frost in his voice again. "But you will have left before it does fall."

"Left?" Wolff stared at the General in astonishment. "Left where, Gruppenführer?"

"You are being posted to Rome for special duties."

Wolff gazed blankly at the General's profile. "I don't understand."

"I don't intend that you do. Just believe me that you have a

vital role to play in The Struggle. A role perhaps in history."
Harzer braked and winced as pain shot up his leg; he shouldn't
have been driving but an open car was the best place for a brief-
ing like this. "I want you to stay incognito in Rome for as long
as you can. I want you to familiarise yourself with the centre of
the city. In particular with The Vatican. We have a man
there," he said. "A monk. He will show you what you will
need to know."

"Can you give me any idea what this is all about?"

"Not yet," the General said, adding: "I'm sorry but that is
the way it has to be. There are too many subversive elements in
Berlin just now. It is in your own interests that you don't know
too much at this time."

"But, Himmler —"

The General cut in tersely: "This order comes from Sepp
Dietrich. As you know he answers only to the Führer. By the
way," in a more conversational tone, "how's your Italian?"

"Non-existent."

"As I thought. You are about to have a crash-course. Five
days. You should be able to pick up enough to order yourself a
bottle of Chianti."

When they reached Spandau, Harzer stopped the Mercedes
outside a suburban house with a green, chalet-type roof. "This
is where your tutor lives," he said.

They walked up the garden-path lined with rose-bushes and
Harzer rang the bell.

The door was opened by Frieda Harzer.

XI

On March 20th, the same day that Kurt Wolff received his new orders, Maria Reubeni had a violent argument with the Sicilian in a deserted chapel near Rome's railway marshalling yards.

Gradually the partisani and the Jewish underground movement had been drawing apart. They no longer had any use for each other; and the Jews feared that any violence instigated by the partisani would bring reprisals on their own heads.

They were to be proved right.

There was also hostility between Jews and partisans, engendered by the suspicion that one was informing on the other.

Liam Doyle was under suspicion, but not by Maria who believed implicitly in the priest. She alone knew the agonies of remorse he had suffered before the round-up of the Jews in October. She alone knew that betrayal was totally repugnant to such a man.

Nevertheless someone was betraying them. Six Jews had been taken by Kappler from an address known only to the nucleus of DELASEM; the cellar in the Borgo had been raided and Carlo — poor winter-crazed Carlo — had died in agony with two bullets fired deliberately into his belly.

It was getting dark as Maria made her way to the chapel which the partisani had taken over since the raid on the cellar in the Borgo.

On the way she paused outside the store where, as a young girl, she had come shopping with her parents although it was non-Kosher. Even now, with its shelves almost bare, she could recall its spiced flavours. Pyramids of lemons and oranges, zucchini laid out as neatly as crayons in a box, piles of artichokes and trusses of pasta, a great barrel of anchovies in brine, forbidden hams hanging from the ceiling, a counter spread with pizza. And always an orange or a piece of nougart slipped to Maria by the owner when his wife wasn't looking. And the noise, ah the noise — bartering, squabbling, boasting, laughing, sometimes weeping. Maria heard it all again as she stood outside the almost empty shop as the dusk turned to blacked-out night.

What was to become of her people? Not just the Jews, the Romans. Embroiled in a war they had never wanted, even though some of them might have thought they did because it was all such a show in those early days and all Italians were actors. They even made a show of their poverty: the young man with the silk suit and camel coat draped carelessly over his shoulders was probably a pauper. Their litigation was a show — the cases were rarely settled; their commerce was a show — impossible promises made to please the customer; their love affairs were a show — litanies of flattery expended on a girl tourist before leaping on the bicycle hidden round the corner and pedalling furiously back to a stout wife and three children. Life itself was a gaudy, glorious show.

If I ever wanted to illustrate the Italian character to a foreigner, Maria thought, I would bring him to this store. As it was in the old days. As perhaps it will be again some day.

Now she took to the back streets. A curfew was in force and German patrols would be out in strength.

When she reached the chapel, a man stepped from behind the portal and clamped a hand round her mouth; she felt the barrel of a pistol in her back.

"When I take my hand away I want you to identify yourself," the man said. "Very softly. No tricks."

She gave the password. Garibaldi.

"Very well. Now walk in front of me." he took her round to a side-entrance and tapped on the door. It sounded like morse, but Maria didn't know what it meant. The Sicilian opened the door. "Is she all right?" the guard asked.

"She's all right," the Sicilian replied.

Three of them were seated by the dusty altar, the light from three prayer candles gleamed on the crucifix. One of the men was Angelo Peruzzi; she could hardly distinguish the features of the other two squatting on the perimiter of the candle-light.

A coffin was open beside them; it was full of grenades.

She sat on the end of a pew.

The Sicilian said: "To what do we owe the honour?"

"I have a request to make."

"Let's hear it then."

The Sicilian hadn't been near her apartment for two days. She knew this was because he was planning an act of violence which he wanted to keep secret from her.

He passed her a bottle but she pushed it away. "Altar wine," he said. "I take your point."

They waited for her to speak.

She spoke hesitantly at first. Then, gaining confidence: "I want you to call off whatever you're planning."

"And what might that be?" asked one of the two unidentified partisani.

"I don't know exactly but," gesturing towards the coffin, "those grenades aren't for playing beach bowls."

The Sicilian stood up. "How do you know that we are planning anything at all?" He held up his hand. They listened. The approaching drone of aircraft.

The Sicilian glanced at his watch. "They're early tonight. Ironic if they should drop a bomb on us just when we're planning to help them out. Now" — he turned again to Maria — "just how do you know that there is any plan at all?"

"I guessed it," Maria said.

"Come now." The Sicilian drew his knife from his belt.

"Can I speak to you privately?"

He shrugged. "If you wish."

They walked down the aisle. "Well?"

"You talk in your sleep," Maria lied because it was Angelo

117

Peruzzi who had told her. "Do you want me to tell the others that?"

His reply was drowned by a bomb exploding near the marshalling yards.

The Sicilian swore. "Do the fools realise what harm they're doing? They pound Monte Cassino to rubble, they shower bombs on the Eternal City . . . If they carry on like this the Italians will hate them more than the Krauts."

Another bomb exploded. Nearer this time. The whole chapel seemed to move and the crucifix toppled from the altar.

They walked back to the altar.

The Sicilian said: "So, what is it that you want of us?" He had dropped the question of Maria's source of information.

"I don't know *what* you're planning," she said. "But I guess that it's something big."

Angelo Peruzzi said: "Very big."

The Sicilian turned on him. "Shut your mouth you."

This time the bomb blew in a stained glass window. They ducked as slivers of coloured glass knifed across the chapel. One piece cut the Sicilian's hand. He wrapped a handkerchief round it.

They stared at Maria as though she had guided the bombers to the chapel. One of the unidentified men spoke. "Well, what is it you want?"

Maria searched for the right words. It was no time to get carried away by uninhibited passion. "As you know," she said carefully, "there are many thousands of people in hiding in Rome. Not merely Jews, gentiles as well. Men like yourself."

"We can take care of ourselves," Angelo Peruzzi said.

She ignored him. "So far the Germans have, by their standards, been restrained. Except, of course, on October 16th. If you pull something big then there will be reprisals. Innocent men and women will be tortured, deported, killed."

Angelo Peruzzi said: "By which you mean Jews."

"By which I mean everyone. The Allies will soon be here. It isn't worth it," she appealed to the Sicilian.

The Sicilian said: "What do you want us to do — collabor-

118

ate with the Krauts?"

"There will be plenty of time to fight them," Maria said, "when they have left Rome. The Allies will need you up north."

The Sicilian shook his head, massaging his bald patch with his wounded hand. "Our place for the time being is Rome. It is our duty to harrass the enemy. You have heard the BBC broadcasts. The Germans are edgy; they know that Rome will fall. We must hit them. After all," he said, "what is a resistance movement for?"

"And he likes killing Krauts," Angelo Peruzzi remarked.

The Sicilian didn't contradict him.

"And you're willing to sacrifice the lives of innocents? Men, women, children . . ."

"War is hell," the Sicilian said sardonically.

It was then that Maria lost control. "You're just a bunch of bastards trying to prove yourselves. Hundreds will die because you want to play at being Errol Flynn. What were you all doing when Mussolini, that blacksmith's son-of-a-bitch, was yelling about power and glory in the Piazza Venezia? Hugging yourselves with delight, strutting around in your black-shirts —"

The Sicilian reached her in one stride and put his hand on her mouth. "Hold your tongue. No one here was ever a black-shirt." He removed his hand. "Now get out, run home." His eyes were dark in the candlelight and she could feel his brutal strength. "If any of this reaches the Germans then we shall know where the information came from. And as for your tame priest . . ." The Sicilian gestured across his throat with his fore-finger.

When Maria stumbled out into the darkness the drone of the Flying Fortresses was receding. She looked around. The bombs seemed to have hit everything except the marshalling yards.

*   *   *

119

Later that night the Sicilian called at Maria's apartment. He had for once made a miscalculation: he had underestimated her, assumed that he had merely witnessed an Italian Jewess cutting loose.

She opened the door of the apartment. "What do you want?"

"I want to talk."

She let him in.

"You have a little brandy?"

She poured him a measure.

He sat down. "Have you ever wondered why the Germans leave the neutral territories of The Vatican alone? Not just The Holy See, all their other little sanctuaries."

Maria shook her head.

"Maybe they want to use them themselves one day."

"Maybe." She wasn't interested, although soon she was to remember his words. "Will you call off what you're going to do?"

"I can't do that. You must understand," his voice softening.

As he reached for her, Maria grabbed a pair of red-handled kitchen scissors. "Keep away from me."

He looked at her reflectively. "And I think you would do it," he said.

She held the scissors tightly.

He stood up. "*Me ne frega.*" And was gone.

XII

The partisani struck on March 23rd.

They had noted that, foolishly, a German military detachment marched down the same small street in the centre of Rome every day. The street was the Via Rasella which lies off the Via delle Quattro Fontane.

At 3.45 pm a bomb exploded killing thirty-two or thirty-three (accounts varied in Rome) members of the 11th company of the 3rd Bozen Battalion.

According to some authorities the bombing was the work of Communists to provoke massive reprisals, instigate insurrection and publicise the Reds as the leading freedom fighters. According to others it was straightforward partisani.

The German Commandant in Rome, General Kurt Maelzer, known as The Drunkard King of Rome, immediately ordered the execution of everyone living on the Via Rasella.

The head of the German Embassy in Rome, Eitel F. Mollhaussen, persuaded him not to make such a savage reprisal. The matter was referred to Berlin.

Hitler and Himmler reacted promptly. Every able-bodied Italian was to be shipped to labour camps in Germany.

At this stage Field Marshal Albert Kesselring intervened. He told Berlin that the deportation of the Italians to Germany would deprive his hard-pressed troops of transport.

Kesselring won the day and signed an order that ten Roman citizens should be killed for every soldier who had died.

But the prisons didn't hold enough Romans to make up the

quota. The Gestapo under the command of Obersturmbann-führer Herbert Kappler took to the deserted streets to round up the balance. Jews in particular.

*　　*　　*

Maria Reubeni heard what was happening at 8 pm. She raced round to her parents' home.

Her father was sitting at her mother's bedside holding her hand. She was unconscious.

Maria told him what was happening. He didn't seem to hear. He said: "Your mother is dying."

Her voice broke hysterically. "Did you hear what I said? The Gestapo are coming."

"So? Let them come. It doesn't matter any more."

"Are you crazy? We can get out through the back-yard. There's a church round the corner where you can hide."

He gazed at her and there were tears in his eyes and he said again: "Your mother is dying, Maria."

"We can get a doctor to the church." She came closer to the bed; her mother's eyes opened and she smiled at Maria; then they closed again.

"You must pray, Maria."

Maria knelt at the bedside as a rifle-butt burst open the door leading to the street. Heavy footsteps pounded up the stairs. The door swung open.

An SS Captain strode in, pistol in hand. Behind him stood two soldiers carrying Schmeissers.

The Captain pointed at Maria's father. "Out into the street." Maria flung herself at the Captain clawing at his face. He threw her against the wall; she hit her head on the corner of the bookcase and fell to the floor semi-conscious.

Her father bent and kissed his wife's forehead. He paused for a moment and then said softly: "It is over."

The Captain dragged him to his feet. "Come with us."

"Willingly," he said.

*　　*　　*

122

Next day 335 prisoners were taken by truck to the Fosse Ardeantine caves — a few more than the ten for one quota.

They were ordered out of the trucks and taken into the caves in groups of five where they were forced to kneel and were then shot in the back of the neck.

Kappler then ordered his men to cover the bodies with lime. The caves were sealed by a blast of dynamite.

Hearing the shooting and the explosion, prisoners-of-war hiding in the nearby San Calisto catacombs assumed that the Allies were on the outskirts of Rome and began to celebrate.

*　　*　　*

On March 25th the German High Command issued a statement which appeared in the newspapers of Rome:

> *On the afternoon of March 23 criminal elements committed acts of violence by means of bombs against a German column passing through Via Rasella. In consequence, thirty-two members of the German police were killed and a number of them wounded.*
>
> *This brutally violent act was committed by Communists of Badoglio's party. Investigations are being made as to the crime being caused by Anglo-American influence.*
>
> *The German High Command is determined to crush the activities of these villanous bandits. No one will be allowed to sabotage the renewed Italo-German cooperation. The Command has ordered that, for every German who was murdered, ten of Badoglio's Communists shall be shot. This order has already been executed.*

Maria glanced at a newspaper containing the order in a car driven by one of her father's friends, a gentile book-seller, who had taken her into his home for a few days. But Maria absorbed none of the German statement.

She hadn't slept and there were stains of grief beneath her eyes. She remembered the gentle authority of her parents and their bewilderment when she left home. When they needed her. She couldn't believe they were dead; she saw them again sitting in the sunlit courtyard in the peace of the Sabbath while she, their only child, played at their feet. *And I deserted them.*

The car approached the small shop where her father had sold his paintings. Her companion, a Neopolitan named Monelli, braked gently and pointed at the shop. "What's going on?"

A truck stood outside. Two men wearing long leather over-coats were loading paintings into it.

Maria said: "Stop the car."

She climbed out. "What are you doing?" she demanded.

One of them said in German-accented Italian: "What does it look as if we're doing?"

Another man emerged into the sunlight from the dusky recesses of the shop. It was the Captain who had taken away her father. He was dressed in a fawn suit and black polo-necked sweater.

Maria said: "I demand to know what's going on?"

The Captain smiled at her. "So you *demand* do you?"

He was slim, athletically-built, with soft brown hair and a cleft in his chin, slightly effeminate and dissipated out of uni-form.

"Those are my —"

Monelli intervened. "The owner of this shop was a friend of hers."

"Ah, now I remember. You were in the room." He stretched out a hand. "Your papers please."

"Come and get them."

Monelli took her handbag from her and handed over the papers.

"These seem to be in order," the officer said. "For one terrible moment I thought perhaps you were Jewish." He smiled, revealing even white teeth. "And why are you interfering with my work?"

"What are you doing with those paintings?"

The Captain shrugged. "The fortunes of war."

"I shall report this."

"Really? To whom?"

The Captain examined an oil-painting one of the men was piling into the truck. "Carefully, please. It might not be a Michelangelo but it will do."

"Where are you taking them?"

"I'm afraid it's none of your business." He took a notebook from his pocket and wrote down Maria's name and address. "But I like a girl with spirit. Perhaps I can call on you. My name is Witt. Otto Witt."

Maria tensed herself, but she felt the restraining hand of Monelli on her arm. "I'm going to the police," she said.

"Please do. Give them my name. They know me well."

Monelli guided Maria towards her car. She felt helpless for the first time in her life.

Witt raised one hand. "To the next time."

But it wasn't until several days later that Maria remembered what the Sicilian had said about the Germans using the Jewish and partisani safe houses for their own purposes one day in the future.

A man like Witt, she thought, would be the first rat to leave a sinking ship financed by loot pillaged all over Europe. And what more obvious escape route than Rome because he knew the city.

She set about learning everything she could about Witt. His standing in the SS, his upbringing, his birthplace. She couldn't act now: the death of an SS officer would merely heap more reprisals on the people of Rome.

But one day, she thought, if God delivers you into my hands, I will kill you.

XIII

Not everyone knows that there is a bar in St. Peter's.

The man in the grey suit hadn't known until he had been told to report there at 11 am. He left his hotel off the Via della Conciliazione, the half-finished avenue to St. Peter's Square, built to replace the old Borgo Vecchio and Borgo Nuovo.

He had all the hallmarks of a raw tourist — head swivelling, attentive to beggars — and The Vatican spivs descended upon him.

"Genuine Vatican coins ... Vatican stamps ... the complete guide to The Holy See ... a lock of the Pope's hair supplied by the Holy Father's personal barber ..."

The latter must be a rare commodity, the man in the grey suit thought, recalling a photograph of Eugenio Pacelli whom God had not blessed with an abundance of hair. He bought a guide-book with a map and snapped at the street hawks who skulked forlornly away; their business, like everyone else's in Rome, was bad.

The April sun was warm and, after he had walked a couple of hundred yards, he took off his belted fawn raincoat and draped it neatly over one arm. He wore black shoes, crisp white shirt and a red tie striped with black.

The street hawks watched him greedily from a distance. They identified him as Swiss, not a difficult assessment; not many countries could afford tourists these days. And he wasn't German because he didn't *march* and he didn't look as if he owned the place. German-Swiss probably. Zurich. Rich.

At the white boundary line of St. Peter's Square the man paused and checked the papers in the inside pocket of his jacket.

Two letters, one in German and one in Italian, certifying that he represented the Red Cross, the Italian document having been obtained that morning from the Comitato Internazionale Della Croce Rossa at their headquarters at 55, Via Campania and signed by Dr. H.W. de Salis. A Swiss passport certifying that he was Hans Doppler born in Zurich on October 10th, 1919. Two Vatican passes, again one in Italian and one, No. 2348, bearing the word *Vatikansstaat*, in German.

Satisfied that he had all the necessary documents, Kurt Wolff walked past the German paratroops posted on the boundary line, crossed the square and mounted the steps of St. Peter's.

*　　*　　*

The bar was in a room next to the Treasury. It was run by a Signora Peroffe, it was open at 6.30 in the morning and was reputed to serve forty-nine different brews.

Heinrich Brandt, wearing black suit and clerical collar, was waiting for Wolff with a glass of brandy in one hand. He stuck out his other hand. "Welcome to the Holy Father's private bar. What will you have?"

"Coffee," said Wolff, looking around in astonishment.

"Anything in it? A little tot, perhaps?"

Wolff shrugged. "It would be a crime not to have a drink in St. Peter's. Do they have schnapps?"

"Of course." The monk gave the order to Signora Peroffe and led Wolff to a table in front of the tiny bar. "I gather you don't fully understand why you're here."

Wolff gazed at the plump cleric through the steam rising from his coffee. "Do you?"

"I'm afraid not. I rather hoped you'd enlighten me."

Wolff had been puzzling over his mission ever since Harzer had briefed him. He had come to the conclusion that he was being prepared for a commando assault on The Vatican. It was common knowledge that the Führer had been contemplating this for some time.

Brandt said: "I have been told to show you round The Vatican City. The full treatment. That's all I know."

"What is the Pope's attitude to the Germans? To us?" Wolff asked, looking curiously at the monk whose loyalties seemed to be temporal as well as spiritual.

"God only knows." He smiled. "And I mean that. Let us say that the Holy Father is a diplomat. He plays one against the other. He knows that if he attacked National Socialism" — Brandt looked round to see if there was anyone listening but the bar was empty — "the Führer would bring Catholicism to its knees. The Vatican would be occupied, the Holy Father would be deported and our, ah, ethnic policies would be implemented on a far greater scale than they are now."

Wolff tossed back his schnapps. "Did he say anything about this business in the Via Rasella?"

"He tried," Brandt said. "He appealed to those responsible — the Communists — to come forward and save the lives of the hostages. But, as you know, they didn't. Quite rightly, the Holy Father believes that the greatest threat to Christianity is Communism." He finished his brandy. "And now, perhaps a tour of the basilica?"

As he had promised Brandt gave Wolff 'the full treatment.' As they paused beside the Papal Altar and the Confession where ninety-nine candles glow daily in honour of St. Peter, Wolff was assailed by an awesome reverence.

Observing him, Brandt said: "No one leaves here unaffected. Not even a Communist."

And when he gazed at Michelangelo's La Pieta it seemed to Wolff that, for a moment, the Madonna holding the body of Christ glowed softly with life.

His feelings disturbed him: it was an experience outside his disciplined beliefs. He said to the monk: "Let's go outside."

They went out into the atrium through the Bronze Door and into the sunlight.

Brandt led the way to the Arch of the Bells guarded by two Swiss Guards in their voluminous blue red and gold uniforms and floppy hats.

"They look like something out of Gilbert and Sullivan," Wolff remarked.

"Don't underestimate them," Brandt told him. "There's a lot of muscle beneath those uniforms. They're trained fighters, they're young — all under twenty-five — and they've all taken an oath to defend the Pope with their lives."

Wolff showed his papers to one of the guards.

"Swiss, eh? Welcome to The Vatican City."

They walked past the guards into the Square of the First Roman Martyrs.

Glancing behind him, Wolff wondered how the two sentries would react to an assault force attacking across St. Peter's Square. A halberd wasn't much of a weapon against a Tiger tank. He grinned and, having shaken off the 'odour of sanctity,' embarked on his tour of the minute Christian kingdom.

*　　*　　*

Brandt showed him the radio station at the end of the Viale Marconi and the pink, green and yellow-marble railway station.

"I thought those would interest you most," Brandt said.

"Why did you think that?"

They stared at each other quizzically.

"They could be useful — whatever Berlin's planning."

"I suppose you're right."

Wolff wondered if the monk was lying. And if, later, he would confess his dishonesty to God.

Outside the radio station Wolff asked: "Where do they broadcast to?"

"The world," Brandt told him. "The broadcasts are relayed to a transmitting station at Santa Maria di Galeria eleven miles to the north."

"Is it used to send messages?"

"Of course. But the codes are pretty basic. Particularly The Holy See's." He rubbed his smooth, pink cheeks. "But perhaps they are meant to be cracked. The Holy Father's a wily old —"

"Devil?"

"You said it," Brandt told him, "I didn't. Of course broadcasts to Spain and Portugal are used a lot as well. Lisbon in particular."

"How else do the diplomats communicate?"

"You mean the enemy diplomats?"

"The British and Americans."

"They use couriers," Brandt said. "Vatican couriers, neutral couriers. And, of course, the telegraph office. But that's all monitored. And any cable we don't like the look of, well, we destroy it."

"You're a ruthless lot," Wolff remarked.

"No man's religion ever survived his morals," Brandt said, adding: "English proverb."

Outside the tiny railway station Wolff asked: "Where does it go to?"

"Onto the main line. There's 160 yards of track. Those iron gates roll back when the Holy Father takes a train ride," he said, pointing with one finger. "Do you think that would be of use to you?"

Again they regarded each other speculatively.

Wolff said: "I'm not lying. Are you?"

"I'm a man of God," the monk said enigmatically.

Later Brandt pointed to the Hospice Santa Marta. "There lies the enemy," he said. "On the second floor Mr. Harold Tittman of the United States of America who is standing in for Washington's personal representative, Myron Taylor, and on the top floor the British in the person of Sir Francis D'Arcy Godolphin Osborne, cousin and heir presumptive to the Duke of Leeds."

"Eton or Harrow?" Wolff asked, amused.

"Haileybury," Brandt told him.

"Of course," Wolff said.

"He was allowed to go to London once. When he returned

every spy in The Vatican pounced on him. And to every question he replied: 'The weather was quite beautiful'."

"Is there anyone in The Vatican you don't know?"

"I don't think so," Brandt replied.

"So Osborne and Tittman, they're prisoners?"

"Virtually," Brandt said. "More so than the Jews and the prisoners-of-war. At least they get out with forged papers."

"I was going to ask you about them," Wolff said.

"I thought you would." Brandt glanced at his wrist-watch. "I'll tell you everything I know — over lunch."

*   *   *

Over breasts of chicken cooked in wine sauce and a bottle of Terlano from the north — "The nearest thing to a Rhine wine" — Brandt told Wolff about the Jews and Allied prisoners being sheltered by the Church.

"But why don't we weed them out?"

"It's not that easy," the monk said, sipping the wine and smacking his lips appreciatively. "Certainly not inside The Vatican. It is neutral after all."

"But The Vatican isn't being neutral if it harbours enemies."

"They're not enemies of The Vatican," Brandt replied.

"Does Berlin know about them?"

"Naturally. I keep them posted. Maybe," he said tentatively, "some of our leaders in Berlin might want to hide out in The Vatican themselves one day."

Wolff didn't react, saying instead: "But what about the hide-outs outside The Vatican?"

"From time to time Kappler picks up a few Jews or escaped prisoners."

"Who's Kappler?"

Brandt told him.

"Ah the Via Rasella affair." Wolff was silent for a while; Brandt guessed he was thinking about the reprisal and, to divert his train of thought, he said: "Kappler's nailed O'Flaherty." He told Wolff about the Irish priest.

"How did he get him?"

"The usual way. Kappler's way. An informer, or someone who was *persuaded* to inform. O'Flaherty has been told that if he sets foot outside Vatican jurisdiction he will be arrested. Not that I think that will stop him," Brandt added.

"Do you approve of Kappler's methods?"

Brandt dodged the question. "I have my own methods of eliciting information."

"You take your suspects to the Confessional?"

"Not exactly. Are you interested?"

Wolff nodded.

The monk opened a cupboard and took out a tape-recorder. He pressed a red button and they listened to the whirr of the big spool rewinding.

"Now listen," Brandt said.

Wolff listened. A low voice that sometimes heightened in intensity. "Please God forgive me ..." And then strange names. "Maria ... Benedetto ..."

"What the hell's that?" Wolff asked. "It sounds like someone praying."

"That's exactly what it is. A priest confessing to God that he's a spy. I had his room wired up."

Wolff jumped to his feet, knocking his plate to the floor and spilling his wine. He took two steps across the room and swept the tape-recorder onto the carpet. The tape stuttered and stopped.

Wolff turned and faced Brandt, the scar on his cheek livid. "You disgust me," he said. He left the room slamming the door behind him.

Brandt stared at the door for a moment, hatred in his small bright eyes. Then he sighed. "Now we have a man with morals. What have I done to deserve this?"

He took an apple from a bowl on the table and bit into it.

*   *   *

Wolff called Harzer in Berlin and told him that he couldn't work with Brandt, but the voice on the other end of the telephone was cold: "You will do as you are told."

Brandt took him to the residence of the German Embassy to The Holy See at the Villa Bonaparte. He said: "I've been told to show you round here, I don't know why."

Brandt was still jovial enough but Wolff didn't respond. After inspecting the low-slung, faded-yellow building that backed onto the Villa Piave, they drove in the cardinal's Mercedes to the German church, S. Maria Dell' Anima.

Wolff thought the Renaissance façade was unimposing. It would have seemed massive by itself but, hemmed in by dusty buildings and mousy alleys, its exterior was ordinary in a city of Baroque splendour.

It looked, Wolff thought, like a warehouse in Kiel.

"And now," Brandt said, "you must meet the Nazi bishop. Known in his earlier days in Austria as the Brown bishop."

As they walked round the Vicolo della Pace, Brandt told him about the Most Reverend Alois Hudal.

Hudal was born in Austria on May 31st, 1885. He was educated at the University of Graz and, at the age of thirty-four, became Professor of Old Testament and Oriental Languages. He also became Procurator of the Order of German Knights.

"Do I have to know all this?" Wolff asked as they waited at the entrance.

"I have been told that you should."

Wolff shrugged.

"He got to know the present Pope when Pacelli was Papal Nuncio in Germany. He was posted here in 1923," Brandt said. "He believes he's the reincarnation of a Dominican saint, Thomas Aquinas, and he sees Hitler as another Charlemagne."

Hudal ushered them into his study and poured coffee. He said: "It's good to see you, Hauptsturmführer."

Wolff started. So the bespectacled little bishop even knew that. For a moment Wolff imagined he was in the presence of an ageing Heinrich Himmler. How much did Hudal know? *More than me?*

"My passport says I'm Hans Doppler from Zurich."

The bishop beamed at him. "I have heard good reports about you, Hauptsturmführer."

"I'm glad to hear it," Wolff said, sipping his coffee.

"We need men like you."

Wolff put down his coffee cup and asked bluntly: "Do you know why I'm here?"

Hudal shook his head. "Only that you are going to play a special part in our crusade. I am honoured that I can be of assistance."

Wolff wondered if he was lying. Perhaps even Frieda had been lying when she had said she didn't know why her father wanted her to give him a crash course in elementary Italian, in Harzer's Berlin residence, spending the last few days of her leave away from the countryside she loved.

While Brandt and Hudal exchanged Vatican gossip, Wolff thought about those few days when, after poring over text books, Frieda and he had walked the streets of Spandau, where daffodils bloomed in the gardens. They had always stopped at a bar down the road for a beer and schnapps before returning to the house when the searchlights began to switch the night sky and the bombers came.

They had grown much closer, although Frieda's political views always loomed between them. He hadn't tried to sleep with her because somehow that wasn't part of this particular picture. And when he had left to fly to Rome he had kissed her gently and felt her respond. As he flew south in another JU 52 he had wondered if he had been naive by not trying to make love to her; this was war-time and these days young men and women didn't bother with the preliminaries of courtship.

"You seem to have left us." Brandt broke into his thoughts.

Wolff apologised — to Hudal not Brandt. "I was back in Berlin."

Hudal nodded understandingly. "A girl?"

"Yes, as it happens."

"Don't let the girls of Rome distract you. Some of them are very beautiful."

Wolff remembered Hudal's words next day in the Golden Gate Cafe at the top of the Via Veneto when a girl with jet black hair contained by a blue silk scarf asked if she could sit at his table.

*   *   *

It was Liam Doyle who had put Maria Reubeni on to Wolff and he was very proud of it.

He had met her as usual in the grounds of the Villa Borghese and told her excitedly: "There's something very strange happening in The Vatican."

After the death of her father it was to the young priest that Maria had come for comfort and guidance. Now he shared her hatred of Otto Witt and didn't seek forgiveness for his feeling.

As they walked in the sunshine he observed other couples strolling hand in hand. He wished he could be like other men and fought the temptation to take Maria's hand.

"What's happening that's so strange?" she asked.

"I don't know exactly. But there seems to be a plot within a plot. Or maybe I'm getting too deeply into espionage."

She smiled at him. "Tell me about it, Liam."

Once it had been *Father*!

Liam told her that it was O'Flaherty whose suspicions had first been aroused. He knew most of the German spies inside The Holy See and now that he was confined inside its walls — although he still slipped out from time to time — he had more time to keep watch on them.

He had also been able to check out their communications: "They're not the only ones who can crack codes, me boy."

O'Flaherty had concentrated on the activities of a monk named Heinrich Brandt because, in the Irish priest's opinion, he was the most sinister of the bunch. "I shouldn't fancy taking that fellow's confession," O'Flaherty had said.

Brandt had made two telephone calls to Berlin. A contact of O'Flaherty's on The Vatican switchboard had listened in — "That'll cost him a few Hail Mary's" — and reported back to O'Flaherty.

The conversations, with a man named Harzer, had seemed innocuous enough; but that wasn't what had intrigued O'Flaherty. "He's not hunting with the pack," O'Flaherty had told Liam. "He usually makes his report to the SS security department. If I'm not mistaken your man is up to something very evil indeed and I doubt if even Himmler knows about it."

Then O'Flaherty had told Liam about the stranger whom Brandt had escorted round The Vatican. "A real Cook's tour — with some differences. They took in the radio station and the railway station, of course. I only saw them from time to time, and then from a distance, but it struck me that Brandt was concentrating on all the buildings where we're hiding our people."

O'Flaherty had then checked with the Swiss Guards at the Arch of the Bells to find out if they knew the identity of the stranger in the grey suit. And they had remembered because he carried a Swiss passport. They couldn't remember his first name but his surname was Doppler.

"And I'll bet you a pound to a pint of stout that he's no more Doppler than I'm George Bernard Shaw," O'Flaherty said.

"It would be interesting to know where he's staying," Liam said.

"Leave that to me, me boy. When he meets Brandt again I'll have one of my lads follow him."

In the Villa Borghese park Maria once again remembered the Sicilian's words — "*Maybe they want to use them themselves one day.*" It seemed to be the only explanation for the intensive interest in the safe houses.

She stooped and began pulling green leaves from the grass.

"What are you doing?"

"Herbs," she said. "You can't get them in the shops any more." He knelt beside her. "You've done well, Liam."

"Do they still think I'm an informer?"

"I don't," she said.

"But they do?"

"They suspect everyone. You see someone *is* informing. Which is why," she said, straightening up, "I think we'll keep

136

this to ourselves."

She told Liam that she suspected that the Germans were planning escape routes to use themselves when they finally admitted defeat. "I don't think we should let them get away with it, Liam, do you?"

"You mean Otto Witt, don't you?"

Her eyes hardened. "He'll come back. And when he does I'll kill him."

Witt hadn't called at her apartment. In fact, she had learned, he had been posted to a unit of Einsatzgruppen responsible for liquidation duties behind the Eastern Front.

Liam was silent.

"You do understand, don't you?"

"I understand," he said. "That doesn't mean to say I can condone it."

He expected her to be angry but she surprised him by saying: "Of course you can't condone it. But as long as you understand . . . Even you can't expect me to forgive him."

"I wouldn't try to persuade you."

"It's something I have to do," she said. "By myself. I pray to God that he delivers Otto Witt into my hands." She looked challengingly at Liam.

When he didn't reply she said: "Will you do one thing for me, Liam?"

"Of course."

"If O'Flaherty finds out where Doppler is staying will you let me know?"

He nodded.

Suddenly she leaned forward and kissed him. On both cheeks like a dutiful daughter, he thought. But still she had kissed him.

And as she walked away swinging her basket he put his hands to his cheeks where her lips had touched him.

*　　*　　*

Later that day, after Liam had found out from O'Flaherty

137

where Doppler was staying, Maria staked out the hotel — and followed him when he left, to the Golden Gate cafe. She hoped she looked like a whore. Bold make-up, top two buttons of her blouse undone, skirt riding high.

The cafe-bar was crowded and, as luck would have it, the only spare seat was at the table occupied by the man who called himself Doppler.

She sat there for a few moments, then asked him for a light.

Without speaking, he pushed a box of matches across the table. She noticed that the nails on two of his fingers were missing.

"Are you German?"

"No, Swiss."

She noticed the scar on his face. A hard man. But a handsome man in a Germanic sort of way.

"A business trip?"

He appraised her through cold blue eyes. Then said: "You're wasting your time." His Italian was terrible.

She smiled uncertainly. "I'm sorry, I don't understand," trying English.

"There are a lot of potential customers here. I'm not one of them." His English was better.

She began to regret her appearance. She pulled her skirt lower. "I am not a whore."

He shrugged.

She snapped her fingers at a waiter and ordered a mineral water. *Whores don't drink mineral water!*

He didn't offer to pay.

She ferreted in her handbag. Finally he handed a note to the waiter.

"You didn't have to," she said.

"I know."

She sipped her mineral water and wondered what to do. In her experience men were only too eager to buy her drinks. But not this one. He wasn't arrogant about it; just indifferent. She was perturbed to discover that she found this attractive. Perhaps he *was* Swiss . . .

"May I ask you a question?"

"It's not a crime."

"That scar. It looks like a bullet wound."

He lit a cigarette. "It is."

"Then —"

"You're very inquisitive," he said. He drew on his cigarette. "I worked for the Red Cross in France during the invasion." He touched the scar. "A German bullet."

"You were very lucky."

"Do you mind if I ask you a question?"

"It's not a crime."

Suddenly he smiled. It was like a flame between them. It shocked her.

He said: "What are you doing out after curfew?"

She improvised wildly. "I went to visit some friends. Their house was hit by an American bomb last night." *Had there been a raid the previous night?* She hurried on. "I managed to find a taxi but the driver wouldn't take me any farther than the Via Veneto. You know, they get a lot of business here."

"And so you're trapped?"

"I'll find a way."

She waited but he didn't respond.

She said: "And you, what brings you here?"

He shrugged. "I felt like a drink. I've had a hard day. Any more questions?"

"No more questions."

He smiled again and the warmth of the smile, so unexpected in his hard, lean features, reached her.

"If you mean what am I doing in Rome then I'll tell you. There are a lot of refugees here. And I do work for the Red Cross."

"I see." She stubbed out her cigarette, closed her handbag and played her last card. "Well, I'll just have to dodge the German patrols."

He reached into his inside pocket, took out a wallet and selected a note saying: "The age of chivalry is not dead." He called the waiter. "Get me a taxi."

"It's impossible," the waiter said.

He took out another note. "Get me a taxi." The waiter still hovered. "I don't want to buy it," he said.

The waiter departed.

"You didn't have to."

"I do work for the Red Cross and you seem to be in need of help. I'll come with you," he added, and she wondered if she had hooked him and in a strange way she hoped she hadn't because it seemed to her that this man wasn't like all the others.

In the taxi he sat apart from her, hardly speaking. She told the driver to stop a hundred yards from her apartment.

She looked at him questioningly. "Would you care —"

He interrupted her. "No, I wouldn't."

She hesitated. "I'm very grateful."

He said: "But I'll buy you a drink tomorrow. At the Golden Gate. But make it midday — before the curfew."

In her apartment she made herself coffee. She remembered wondering when she went to bed with the Sicilian what sort of man she might one day love. Was this the man? Liam Doyle had said that O'Flaherty was convinced that his name wasn't Doppler, that he wasn't Swiss.

If the man called Doppler wasn't Swiss he was undoubtedly German.

Maria hoped desperately that the Irish priest was wrong.

XIV

The meeting had also had its effect on Kurt Wolff. He had never before experienced such an instant feeling for a woman. It had exploded between them.

He wondered why she had engineered the meeting. He didn't think she was a tart, or perhaps he didn't want to think so. Nor did he think she had sat at his table merely because she liked the look of him. Was she a spy of some sort? There were enough of them in Rome. God help her if she hopes to extract information from me: even I don't know why I'm here.

Wolff was still thinking about her as he shaved next morning. When he showered he found himself imagining her naked with water streaming down her body. The image had an immediate physical effect on him.

He towelled himself vigorously and tried to be more practical. He could have her checked out by Brandt; but that might put her in danger whether she was innocent or guilty because Brandt wouldn't be too fussy about proven guilt. And he couldn't approach anyone else in the SS because he was Hans Doppler of the Red Cross.

Wolff dressed in his grey suit, another white shirt and a plain blue tie. His breakfast was waiting for him in the room — orange juice of sorts, rolls, butter and coffee of sorts.

While he breakfasted he listened to Rome Radio. The Allies were still, incredibly, held at Monte Cassino; but that was only a matter of time. Wolff listened anxiously for news of the Eastern Front, wondering at the nerve of the news-reader who only a few months ago must have been hailing every German retreat as a superb tactical withdrawal: now they were just plain defeats. So, the Soviet bastards were pushing into the Crimea.

Could Germany survive? Wolff realised that it was the first time he had honestly faced the possibility of defeat. He wished passionately that he was with the Leibstandarte, fighting instead of wandering round Rome like a tourist.

He yawned and stretched. But I have missed something this morning, he thought. Then he remembered — he hadn't had a work-out; again a first-time sign of weakness. It was the influence of Rome, he decided. Or the girl.

He stripped down to his underclothes and exercised. Fifty press-ups, fifty sit-ups, followed by another cold shower.

When he was dressed again he slid the maps of the Villa Bonaparte, the German College and Hudal's church into his briefcase and deposited it in the hotel safe. He glanced at his watch. Ten o'clock.

He strolled in the sunshine in the general direction of the Via Veneto. He found he was as excited as a teenager on his first date. Shit, Kurt Wolff, he thought, what's happening to you? By the time he reached the Golden Gate he had persuaded himself that her excuse for breaking the curfew had been genuine.

*　　*　　*

She arrived five minutes late. She wore a yellow blouse and skirt and her legs were bare and her black hair was full of sunlight.

He stood up and held out his hand.

"I'm sorry I'm late," she said.

"What's five minutes?"

She said: "I thought perhaps we'd take a walk. I don't feel like a drink at the moment."

They headed for the grounds of the Villa Borghese. After they had walked for a few minutes she said: "There's a friend of mine over there. Will you excuse me for a moment?"

142

Wolff waited while she talked to a priest standing beneath a tree. When she returned she said: "We Italians are never far from the Church. Are you a religious man, Signor Doppler?"

"Hans," he said. And then: "No, I'm not religious. I have my own private code. Nothing more." He paused. "I'm afraid I don't know your name."

She told him it was Maria. Maria Vincelli.

"And are you from Rome, Maria?"

"My family has lived here for five hundred years."

"Then you can be my guide."

Later she took him to a small restaurant on the Via Panisperna where, for a price, you could actually eat meat. They ate a dish which Wolff didn't much like — spinach with a wedge of meat underneath — and drank a carafe of the house white wine.

When they had finished the first course she asked him about his work for the refugees in Rome. Which particular refugees?

He said: "You have refugees from practically every country in the world here. American, British, French, Yugoslav . . ."

"And Jews," she said.

"Ah yes, the Jews."

"The Germans have already taken two thousand of them. The rest are in hiding. Do you have any access to them?"

He shook his head. "That's in the hands of the Italian Red Cross and the Papal assistance board. They have their own organisations here."

"They need your help," she said.

"They're already getting it."

He felt uncomfortable discussing the Jews. He offered her a cigarette but she refused. "If you'll excuse me a minute," standing up and heading for the ladies room carrying a powder compact.

Her open handbag was on the chair beside him. He stretched out one hand and slipped it inside. His fingers encountered some papers. He eased them half way out of the bag and glanced at the first one, black-bordered like a card announcing a death.

Maria Vincelli. Born May, 1924, in Rome.

You slimy bastard, he thought. You've spent too much time with Brandt. As she returned he pressed the papers back into the bag and stood up.

They finished the meal and went sight-seeing.

They visited the Coliseum and the Fountain of Trevi and the Castel Sant' Angelo and then, exhausted, went to a trattoria on the Piazza Navona where they drank too much red wine.

And all the time the feeling between them grew, a fuse spluttering inexorably towards a charge of explosive.

Only once was there an awkward moment — when she asked playfully if she could see his passport, and he thought what a bad actress she was but handed over the passport.

She flipped through the pages, made the obligatory comment about the terrible photograph and handed it back to him.

At dusk he again bribed a waiter to call a taxi. When she climbed out he joined her on the cobblestones.

She said: "Hans, I'm afraid."

And she was in his arms, kissing him wildly.

Then she was gone, high heels clattering on the cobblestones.

He called out after her: "Midday tomorrow." Then told the driver to take him back to his hotel.

When he got back to the hotel the porter handed him a cable with his room key. He guessed what it was before he ripped open the envelope.

CATCH WEDNESDAY'S 0900 ZURICH FLIGHT — HOFER.

which meant Berlin. Tomorrow.

He told the porter to call him a taxi, once again parting with a fat bribe.

For two hours he walked the streets in the area where she had left him asking if anyone knew a girl name Maria Vincelli. No one did.

He left a note with the waiter at the Golden Gate. *I tried to find you. One day I will be back. Please write.* At the bottom of the sheet of hotel notepaper he wrote the address of the German

144

agent in Zurich who would forward mail to Berlin. He gave the waiter a wad of lire and told him to give the note to a raven-haired girl named Maria Vincelli who would be waiting at the cafe at midday the following day.

"Very well, signor. It shall be done. When affairs of the heart are concerned you can always trust an Italian."

When Wolff had gone the waiter, who had been involved in a dispute over his wages, tore the note into small pieces and tossed them into a garbage pail in the kitchen. He felt distinctly better.

XV

Events in the capital cities of Berlin and Rome in the context of Grey Fox now took shape and direction as the Russians pushed forward on the Eastern Front, and the Allied offensive in Italy gathered momentum.

At 11 pm on May 11th, 1944, the Allies mounted a massive bombardment of the 6th century Benedictine abbey at Monte Cassino. In twenty-five hours 174,000 shells were fired. Finally the British XIII Corps and the Poles broke through the northern defences and on May 18th the last thirty Germans defending the abbey were wiped out.

Ahead lay Rome.

Inside The Vatican, and in holy places in Rome where Christianity was partnered by National Socialism, plans were finalised to give sanctuary to Nazi leaders who had written their creed in blood across Europe.

Heinrich Brandt worked closely with Kruger the librarian and Alois Hudal. They compiled maps charting all the routes used by the Jews and the prisoners-of-war and added a few of their own.

But all the time Brandt was working independently. He needed a route and bolt-hole in Rome at the end of his chain of monasteries and churches stretching down the Italian mainland for the exclusive use of one man. And he thought he knew how he could find it.

At the same time Maria Reubeni, with the help of Liam Doyle, was preparing counter-plans. "To forestall all the rats

146

leaving the sinking ship," she told Liam. But they both knew she meant one rat: Otto Witt. And if he didn't come to Rome, then, when the war was over, she would scour Europe for him.

She still helped the Jews in hiding, but she had become a solitary person nursing her dream of vengeance as a recently-widowed woman nurses an only child.

She tried to banish Hans Doppler from her mind but, in the early defenceless hours of the morning, he returned and she stretched out a hand to touch the scar on his cheek.

If only he had left a note. The shock of discovering that he had booked out of his hotel always returned, and she lay awake in her bed seeking the answers to unanswerable questions. She had called at the Red Cross in Rome but they could only confirm that they had written a letter in Italian based on the Swiss documents he presented. She wrote to the Red Cross in Switzerland but received no reply.

Was he a German? She delayed this question until dawn was touching the rooftops of Rome, and then tried to banish it in frantic activity.

Liam Doyle had been unsympathetic. He had asked: "Did you find out anything?"

"Nothing. I saw his passport, that's all."

"That wasn't very much."

"What else could I do?"

"You had great plans for eliciting information."

"He was a clever man."

"And an attractive one?"

She stared at him in surprise. "Liam Doyle, are you jealous?"

The grey eyes had looked sadly into hers; his face was pale and he had cut himself shaving. "I suppose I am," he said.

"Then you must go and confess."

"I already have," Liam Doyle said.

*   *   *

In Rome in the middle of May sunlight lodged in the fountains

147

and gilded domes and spires; in Berlin cold rain spattered the dust and rubble of war.

Harzer and von Geissel paused one day to watch rescue teams pulling bodies from a street of houses devastated the previous night by bombs.

One of the rescue workers had heard the whimpering of a child. The steel-helmeted crew was working calmly and methodically to free the child in the shadow of a wall that creaked and swayed in the wind.

Harzer said: "Brave men."

"Old men too," von Geissel said. "Older even than us. I wonder what they think of those dreams of the thirties."

"We will rise again," Harzer said. "We always do."

Rain drove at them saturating their raincoats, collecting in the brims of their soft felt hats.

Von Geissel shivered and clapped his gloved hands together. "We must speed things along. Is Wolff ready to know yet?"

"I don't know. He's a complex man. And an intelligent one. I don't think even he believes that our secret weapons are going to snatch victory."

One of the rescue workers shouted: "I've found her." Behind him the shattered wall groaned.

"They'd better hurry," von Geissel said.

Three men were clawing at the bricks, masonry and twisted metal.

Harzer said: "Rome will fall any day now. Then they'll invade Europe from the west. God knows how much time we've got left."

"Then you'd better tell him," von Geissel said.

"I suppose so. I wonder how he will take it?"

"How would you take it," von Geissel asked, "if you were his age?"

Harzer, who had been bowed against the rain, straightened himself. "I would consider it the greatest honour that could be bestowed upon a German."

"Then that's the way he'll take it."

"I hope you're right. Some of the young people today have

strange ideas. I suppose you can't blame them," nodding towards the rubble.

One of the rescue workers was holding a small hand and shouting down through the wreckage: "Be patient, little one."

As he shouted a corner of the wall fell away and crashed into the rubble a few feet behind him.

Von Geissel said: "You're thinking of your daughter. Wolff is Leibstandarte."

Harzer didn't reply. He was absorbed with the rescue, hands clenched in the pockets of his raincoat. For a moment it was his daughter of fifteen years ago there under the rubble.

One of the men heaved aside a wooden beam, veins bulging on his forehead. Harzer and von Geissel saw the face of a little girl, smudged, white, terrified.

"There's my pretty one," shouted one of the men as a squall blew down the street and the wall leaned towards them with a last grating roar.

The man snatched the child in his arms and ran towards Harzer and von Geissel as the wall collapsed and thudded into the cradle of rubble where the little girl had been.

The rescue worker smiled at Harzer and von Geissel. "One survivor," he said. "Only a little one but a sweet little one."

He kissed the girl's white wet face and she put her arms round his neck.

* * *

Back in von Geissel's apartment they drank coffee and cognac and stood in front of the debris-fuelled fire, steam rising from their clothes.

Von Geissel opened a wooden box of Dutch cigars and offered them to Harzer saying: "A legacy of the European campaign."

They lit their cigars carefully and stood stiffly staring into the fire, two upright, middle-aged men who looked older.

After a while Harzer said: "And the other man, how is that coming along?"

"I may have found someone," von Geissel told him, drawing on his cigar with satisfaction.

"Really? You didn't tell me."

"I wanted to be sure in every detail before I did."

"There are a lot of details," Harzer agreed. "Weight, age, medical history . . ."

"More than that," von Geissel said. "Much more. Bone structure, skin pigment, scars . . ."

"And you think you've found such a man?"

"I may have. He has to be subjected to several more tests."

"Is he agreeable?"

"He doesn't know yet. But in any case, does it matter?"

"I suppose not." Harzer glanced at his colleague; sometimes there was a chilling quality about him. "Poor devil," he said.

"With respect, this is no time for sentiment."

"Sentiment doesn't matter — as long as it's not put into practice."

"Our mission is beyond the realms of sentimentality."

"I'm well aware of that," said Harzer testily. He studied the glowing tip of his cigar. "When will you know for sure?"

"In about three weeks. Then we can get to work on him." He tossed the remnants of a window-frame onto the fire and watched the sparks spiral up the chimney. "Do you have any trouble with Himmler these days?"

Harzer shook his head. "He knows I'm a friend of Sepp Dietrich. Fall out with Dietrich and you've fallen out with the Führer."

"And he suspects nothing?"

"Nothing. I'm sure of it."

Von Geissel poured them each another cognac. He shivered.

"Still got the Russian snow on your boots?" Harzer asked, thinking that these days the coldness was in von Geissel's soul as well as his body.

Von Geissel said: "If I was roasted on a spit I'd still be cold."

Harzer tossed back his cognac, refused another. "I must get back into uniform and to my office." He picked up his dripping raincoat. "This, ah, subject you have found. Where are you keeping him?"

"In Munich," von Geissel told him. "Steiner and Wenck are looking after him."

"Look after him well," Harzer said. "The poor devil's only got a year to live at the most."

*   *   *

That afternoon Harzer summoned Wolff to his office.

"How was Rome?"

"They don't know the meaning of war."

"They did once," Harzer said.

Wolff stared at him puzzled.

"The Roman Empire," Harzer said. "But they let it go. They needed another Caesar." He stared at the young man standing stiffly to attention in front of him. In some subtle way Rome had changed him; Harzer couldn't put his finger on the change. "Did you do everything you were ordered to do?"

"*Ja*, Gruppenführer."

"I gather you didn't take to Heinrich Brandt."

"*Nein*, Gruppenführer."

"Nevertheless, one of the best men we have."

Wolff stared straight ahead at the linden trees now in full, salad-green leaf.

"Tomorrow, Hauptsturmführer, we return to Bavaria."

Wolff looked at him in surprise. But once again it was an order, not a request.

*   *   *

Twenty-four hours later Kurt Wolff was told what his mission was.

XVI

For three days Wolff lost himself among the mountains and lakes that are the walls and moats between Bavaria and Austria. He climbed mountain roads until his lungs burned with pain; he traversed forests as dark as night; he swam in lakes of melted snow. He observed little, thought little, felt little. He was like a man concussed.

Harzer had said: "Think it over, take your time."

He had packed a small rucksack and left immediately. In the little town of Füssen, nestling at the foot of the Allgau mountains, he bought bread, cheese and fruit and a couple of bottles of Bavarian beer. He contemplated the wicked-witch spires and battlements of Neuschwanstein castle perched among the pine trees and thought vaguely that it was the perfect setting for the mission he had been asked to carry out.

He struck west, hitched a lift, and reached Lindau on the shores of Lake Constance which separates Germany from Switzerland. There he drank a couple of glasses of Riesling without tasting it, and stared across the placid waters and thought how easy it would be to escape.

Escape! The stunning ramifications of Harzer's proposal edged into his consciousness. He pushed them aside, paid his bill and hitched a lift north in an army lorry.

The driver, a corporal with a pock-marked face, glanced curiously at Wolff. "Were you born lucky or did it come later?"

"Lucky?" Wolff looked at him dully.

152

"Not many of us can wander round in sports coat and flannels these days."

"I suppose not."

Wolff's indifference irritated the driver. "I suppose you shot off your big toe or something like that. A fellow I know chewed cordite before his medical so that his heart-beat sounded dodgy. He runs a hotel, lives off the fat of the land."

"No," Wolff said, "nothing like that."

Encouraged, the driver said: "Or maybe you're a Jew?"

"And maybe I'm not."

"Well, what the hell are you?"

"It's none of your business," Wolff said.

"It's my business if I'm giving a draft-dodging bastard a lift." He reached under the dashboard and took out a bottle of schnapps. He took a swig, replaced it and said: "And when the war's over you'll be laughing. It won't have touched you." The driver became philosophical. "But I suppose you were right. None of us should have listened to that little shit Adolf Hitler."

"I see." Wolff spoke calmly. He tapped the driver on the shoulder. "Stop the truck."

The driver glanced sideways at him. "Are you crazy?"

"Possibly." Wolff took his SS identity card from the inside pocket of his jacket and showed it to the driver.

The driver stiffened in his seat, almost drove the truck off the road. "I'm sorry, Hauptsturmführer."

"You will be," Wolff said. "Now stop the truck and get out."

He hit the driver once in the belly and once, as he doubled up, on the chin. He leaned on the side of the truck while the Corporal lay groaning on the road-side. "Now get up."

The driver stood up clutching his stomach.

"You have a dirty mouth, Corporal. It's not fit to utter the Führer's name. Do you agree?"

"*Ja*, Hauptsturmführer."

Wolff reached into the cabin of the truck and smashed the bottle of schnapps on a boulder beside the road. "Now get back

153

in the driving seat."

Neither of them spoke until they reached Nuremberg, walled city of culture, pencils and toys.

For a while Wolff wandered the ancient streets of the city; then he went to a beer-hall and got drunk.

He was served by a girl in Bavarian costume whose breasts nearly popped out of her white blouse every time she leaned over the table. She had pouting lips and beautiful slut's features.

When she had served Wolff his fifth foaming beer and schnapps she smiled at him, breasts suspended over the table, and said: "You shouldn't drink any more."

Wolff stared at her. "Why not?"

"You won't be fit for anything."

"Anything?"

She winked and went back to the bar carrying her tray of empty tankards high above her head.

On his sixth schnapps she lingered, asking: "Are you drinking to forget? The war . . . a girl maybe."

"Both," Wolff said.

"You're a soldier?" And, hopefully: "An officer, perhaps?"

"I'm a rich baron," Wolff said.

"I am only a poor girl. The tourists don't come here any more. Only the soldiers . . ."

"How much?" Wolff asked abruptly.

"If you want to give me a little present we could perhaps discuss it later. In my room," she added.

Despite the liquor Wolff made savage and prolonged love to her in her small room adorned with photographs of war heroes (Dietrich was there) and film stars.

Afterwards she lay back on the pillows panting and said through bruised lips: "What a man. When did you last have a woman? Before the war?"

Wolff lit a cigarette. "I haven't finished yet."

"*Mein Gott!*" she exclaimed. "No more."

Wolff reached for his wallet and extracted a wad of notes. He threw them on her naked belly.

"Those scars," she murmured. "Where did you get them?"

They always asked about the scars.

"Russia," he said tersely.

"*Ach*, I have met other men who have been to Russia. They are all somehow different. Harder, crueller."

It was while he was making love to her for the second time that the bombers came. As the anti-aircraft guns opened up she began to tremble. "We must go to the shelter."

He pressed her shoulders onto the bed as the first bomb fell. She struggled but he held her and pressed his lips against hers in case she began to scream.

More bombs fell closer, flakes of whitewash fell from the ceiling.

Wolff's body moved more urgently and he found that now she was moving with him, not struggling to escape.

"My God," she shouted. "My God we might die together," as her body bucked beneath his. "To die, to love . . ." Her body stiffened and she locked her legs round his body as a bomb exploded close by showering the building with debris and Wolff reached his climax.

Afterwards, as the bombers flew away, she leaned over him. She shivered. "I've never known anything like that." She ran one finger down his face. "*Liebling*, is there any chance that you can stay here?"

"Tonight?"

"Forever," she said.

"No chance," Wolff said.

He turned on his side and slept.

*   *   *

When Wolff awoke next morning sunlight was streaming through the mullioned windows. He stretched out an arm and opened one window; across the street smoke was still rising from the wreckage of one of Nuremberg's beautiful half-timbered houses hit by an incendiary bomb.

Suddenly the mental numbness of the past few days lifted. In its place a fierce pride that, out of the whole German nation, he had been chosen for this glorious mission.

He saw again flags fluttering round a vast arena, heard the thick chant of the crowd, blinked as sunlight flashed on sixty thousand knives.

He stared at the smoking wreckage across the street. Soon all of Europe would be like that. He would take the Führer away from it. Germany would rise from the ashes once again.

The girl reached for him but he swung himself out of the bed and began to dress.

"Can't you stay just one more night, *liebling*?"

"I'm sorry."

"You will come back?"

"Perhaps."

He kissed her on the lips and was gone.

Before returning to Harzer he made one more journey. This time east by train. Sitting opposite him in the train, which was packed with troops, was a girl who reminded him vaguely of Maria Vincelli.

Wolff had never understood happily-married men with beautiful wives and families who were unfaithful. Now he understood. Sometimes you met a woman, just one woman, with whom the attraction was immediate, electric, irresistible. Maria Vincelli was such a woman.

But, just the same, Wolff still envisaged himself married to Frieda Harzer. Saw himself walking in the foothills of the Alps with their two children. My God, he thought, I'm being unfaithful *before* marriage.

The train was nosing through the suburbs of Munich when it occurred to Wolff that he might be able to see Maria again because he now realised why he had been dispatched to Rome.

From Munich, Wolff hitched another lift to the small town of Braunau.

Braunau lies on the River Inn which at that point forms the natural border between Germany and Austria. There at 6.30 pm on April 20th, 1889, a child was born in an inn named the Gasthof zum Pommer to the wife of a thrice-married customs officer. The child's name was Adolf Hitler.

* * *

Harzer was sitting in the garden of the Bavarian farm-house working out a chess problem when Wolff walked up the hill.

He stared expectantly at Wolff. "You'll do it?"

Wolff smiled at him. "Of course."

Harzer leaned back in his chair and closed his eyes. When he opened them he said: "This calls for a drink." He limped into the house and returned with a bottle of Dom Perignon and two glasses.

"Heil Hitler."

"Heil Hitler."

They drank the champagne and sat down. Harzer pointed at the chess pieces. "You play?"

"Set them up," Wolff replied.

Harzer won the white pieces and moved a pawn to king four. Wolff replied with the same move. Harzer brought out a knight and said: "We have a lot to talk about."

"How long do you think we have?" Wolff asked.

"God knows. But I think we both know," glancing at Wolff, "that we cannot win this time. This round," he added moving a bishop.

"I think I finally realise that."

"We could have. The Führer's plans were sound. If Britain had kept out of it, if the invasion of Russia hadn't been delayed in the Balkans . . ." Harzer shrugged.

"But the Germans are never truly beaten," Wolff observed. "They thought we were beaten after the First World War but we showed them how wrong they were."

"And they'll be wrong again," Harzer said, moving a pawn. "Ten years, maybe twenty, and Germany will be great again. Although I doubt if I'll be around to see it."

"Why not?"

Harzer pressed his hand to his belly. "That piece of Russian metal is on the move."

157

"You should see a surgeon."

Harzer shook his head. "I can't afford to lie helpless in hospital at a time like this."

He poured more champagne and gestured at the green valley below them. "It is fitting that we should be discussing your mission here in the mountains. Kings and emperors have made their way through the Alps to Rome." He moved his other bishop pinning Wolff's black knight. "How did your Italian lessons go?"

Wolff sensed that Harzer was sounding him out about his relationship with his daughter. "She's an excellent teacher. Where is she, by the way?"

"Still in Berlin. She's been transferred to a civilian hospital there. The British and American bombers keep her very busy. I think," Harzer said cautiously, "that she is quite fond of you."

Wolff dodged the issue. "But not very fond of the SS. Does she know —"

"Not a thing," Harzer interrupted. "And she must never know. Operation Grey Fox is known only to a few men. Unfortunately Dietrich is too busy fighting to do anything for us. Except, of course, go over Himmler's head when we want anything done." He removed Wolff's knight, forcing Wolff to take the bishop with a pawn and weaken his development. Harzer castled on the king's side and stood up. "I must stretch this damn leg. Take your time."

While Wolff stared at the ivory pieces Harzer limped round the garden with its rockery of alpine flowers and rose-gardens laid out with military precision.

Wolff brought out his queen.

Harzer returned to the board. He nodded approvingly. "You play a good game," moving a rook one square. "I suppose you want to know just how we're going to pull this thing off."

"Through The Vatican presumably."

Harzer winced as pain probed his belly. With an effort he smiled. "Of course. After all, Hitler was born a Catholic. And that reminds me, I want to talk to you about the Führer."

Werner Harzer smoothed his sleek hair and prepared Wolff for his first meeting with Hitler. Hitler was not the man he was in those shining days in the '30's, the SS General said. He had been debilitated by worry and treachery around him. Wolff would have to realise that; would have to remember their leader as he was before the war.

"Do you understand?"

"Perfectly."

"He is given to rages. Small wonder when you think of the sycophants surrounding him. Göring parading around in fancy dress . . ." He paused. Wolff guessed that he had been about to name Himmler.

Wolff said: "And the plan?"

Harzer looked at him thoughtfully. "It isn't complete yet. I would rather that you knew only the basics at this stage." He moved a pawn and said: "How about this? If you win this game I'll tell you everything," a touch of humour in the blue eyes.

Wolff moved his queen again.

Harzer tapped the side of his move. "Daring. You can always tell a man's character by the way he plays chess. And speaking of character, I must warn you about some of the people you will have to meet. You are aware no doubt that there are subversive elements in Berlin?"

"I've heard that some of the Generals are plotting."

Harzer nodded. "They'll get their reward — a firing squad. There are also other elements. Men chosen for their qualities in the glorious days when anything was possible. We didn't realise then that they had character defects. As soon as the game's up these men will scuttle to safety taking as much loot with them as they can."

"But —"

Harzer held up his hand. "Many good men will go too. The cream of the SS. They must get out of the Fatherland until it is rebuilt, otherwise they will be executed. But I am not referring to these men. I am referring to a decadent few . . . You see," Harzer said, "we will have to have what the British and Americans call a dummy run. And the dummy must be someone expendable. In other words you will help someone extremely unpleasant to escape to freedom."

Wolff moved his queen; he felt poised for victory — and Harzer's revelations. "Check."

"So I'm in trouble am I?"

"It rather looks that way," Wolff said.

"Mmmmmm." Harzer winced with pain. "You are an extremely spirited player." He moved out of check and Wolff pressed home with a bishop.

"Spirited but a little reckless." Harzer swept his queen diagonally down the board. "Check-mate, I think."

Ruefully Wolff stared at the board, then stretched out his hand. "Thank you. A good game. Well played, Gruppenführer." He lit a cigarette. "So I can't know the full details yet?"

"First we must rid you of that strain of recklessness."

"I was over-confident."

"Precisely." Harzer poured the last of the Dom Perignon. "But I can tell you this, Kurt. You will have to learn to fly!"

*　　*　　*

That evening after dinner, as they were lighting their cigars, Harzer again raised the question of his daughter. "She's a fine girl," he said. "Just a little misguided."

"She's very young," Wolff said, reflecting that in peacetime he would still have been considered a young man; but not in war; in war you could be old at twenty-five.

"She needs a strong man."

Wolff examined the glowing tip of his cigar. "Are you suggesting me, Gruppenfuhrer?"

"I was merely wondering. I wouldn't presume to pull rank. But I would like to think that when I go she will have someone like you to look after her."

"Do you know how she feels about this?"

"I know my daughter. She leaped at the chance to go to Berlin to help you with your Italian."

"I don't think she would like to be married to a Captain in the SS."

"You won't be a Captain in the SS. There won't be any SS," Harzer said sadly. "But you could be a prosperous Bavarian farmer."

"As you say, she's a fine girl. She would make a wonderful wife. I will see how she feels. After Grey Fox."

"That's good enough for me," Harzer said. He leaned across to light Wolff's cigar which had gone out. "By the way, I've always meant to ask you," pointing at the two fingers without nails. "How did you lose those?"

Wolff stared at him calmly. "I think you know, Gruppenfuhrer."

XVII

Lieutenant Wolfgang Lutz, aged twenty-six, former staffel leader with the Luftwaffe's Kampfgeschwader 51 — the Edelwiss Geschwader — was in a foul mood. Lutz, green-eyed and sardonic, was also a little drunk.

He had flown himself to the point of total exhaustion in the bitter Russian skies in JU 88's; he had dropped thousands of tons of bombs; he had been shot down twice, parachuting to safety on one occasion, crash-landing on the belly of the sinister-looking bomber that he loved on another.

Then the Gruppe had been posted back to Germany. A few days wild leave with plenty of girls and liquor which had left him even more exhausted. And then a conversion course to the new ME 410's which carried four 210 mm rockets, cannon and machine guns.

But men like Lutz were not fighter pilots; they were a different breed. They were the hunted not the hunters. They had been trained to fly with inexorable purpose, dodging flak, evading enemy fighters, anticipating trouble rather than looking for it, concerned only with reaching a target, dropping their bombs and getting safely home again.

Now they were expected to fling themselves around the sky like the glamour boys of the Luftwaffe, the fighter pilots, who had not exactly demonstrated their superiority against the British Spitfires and Hurricanes.

The first sortie with the ME 410's had been a disaster.

They had taken off from Illesheim and attacked two hun-

162

dred American bombers over the Black Forest and engaged them at 16,500 feet. They were enveloped in tracer but they got among the four-engined bombers and took their toll.

But so did the American gunners. It was calculated later that the German squadrons lost as many aircraft as the enemy.

The conversion course continued. The pilots, who knew their JU 88's as a motorist knows a beloved old car, wrestled with the new automatic systems, but repeatedly they put the ME 410's down on their bellies.

Then Reichsmarschall Hermann Göring came personally to find out what the hell was going on. And all might have been well — pilots never forgot that Goring had once been commander of the crack Richthofen Fighter squadron — if rumours hadn't reached the Gruppe that plans were afoot to convert them to the revolutionary ME 262, the wonderbird — the first operational jet fighter in the world.

Fine. A stupendous concept. Hadn't General Adolf Galland, Director of Fighters, commented in May, 1943, after flying the ME 262: "It was just like being pushed by an angel."

But not for the pilots of JU 88's who were currently trying to adapt to ME 410's. "Who the hell wants to fly an oil-stove?" Lutz had remarked to his second-in-command.

By now Lutz had acquired a reputation for cynicism alongside his reputation for being one of the best bomber pilots in the Luftwaffe.

And it was unfortunate that Göring in his silver-grey uniform chose to stop and chat to Lutz when the Gruppen were paraded on the tarmac.

It had been, so it was subsequently rumoured, the Reichsmarschall's intention to present Lutz with the Knight's Cross.

Göring said: "Well, Herr Oberleutnant, and how do you find the ME 410's?"

Lutz stared at the once-handsome face, now pouched with fat, at the corpulant figure. Did he really wear a corset?

"They are a very fine aircraft, Herr Reichsmarshall. But —"

"But, Herr Oberleutnant?" Smile fading a little.

Lutz hesitated: he was not wholly suicidal.

"Come on, man, out with it."

"Well, Herr Reichsmarschall, they have certain disadvantages in close combat."

"Ah, so that is why we have lost so many, is it?"

Lutz gained confidence. "The ME 410 only has single-stage superchargers. They're no match for four-engined bombers with two-stage supercharging."

"Superchargers, eh? So that's the reason why in the past week three pilots crash-landed." Göring's face began to contort with rage. "Could it not be, Herr Oberleutnant, that the pilots of those aircraft had lost the desire to go up there," stabbing one podgy finger towards the sky, "and mix it with these wonderful American bombers?"

Lutz stiffened. "Nothing of the kind," dropping the Reichsmarschall.

A breeze fanned the airfield fluttering the flags on the administrative buildings.

"Are you doubting my opinion?"

"The pilots of those aircraft were not cowards."

A feeling of doom settled on Lutz. His mouth had always been his weakness: it was too big. If it wasn't for his mouth he might have been a Captain or even a Major by now. Instead he would end up in jail or before a firing squad.

"I suggest," Göring said venomously, "that there has been a complete break-down in morale here. I won't use the word cowardice. I was a pilot once, in case you have forgotten." He ran a finger round the collar of his uniform. Suddenly he said: "Do you think we shall win this war, Oberleutnant?"

Self-survival took over. "Of course, Herr Reichsmarschall."

Göring looked at him thoughtfully, then turned to the Gruppe Commander standing beside him. "I think this man has been flying too long." A pause. "I think his wings should be clipped. Ground him," he snapped.

So Lutz was grounded.

For months he skulked around the airfield to which the unit was posted driving nothing more ambitious than his BMW 328 two-seater — and driving it at suicidal speeds. His colleagues commiserated with him but his responses were always bitter; after a while they left him alone.

Then one summer day in 1944 when his colleagues were struggling to adapt to the ME 262 which had an astonishing cruising speed of 525 mph, the final humiliation was administered to Wolfgang Lutz.

He had been watching one of the wonderbirds with its twin jet engines taking off when he was summoned to the Gruppe Commander's office. For God's sake don't fly too fast, he had silently warned the pilot. Although he was no longer operational he hadn't been able to resist studying the jet; he knew that at speeds of more than 585 mph the bastard could go out of control.

Then he made his way to the Commander's office. The Major who wore the Knight's Cross with oak leaves said without preliminaries: "How would you like to fly again?"

A glow of hope expanded inside Lutz. "I think you know the answer to that, Major."

"But you can't expect to graduate straight to ME 262's. You've been a long time on the ground, Lutz."

"It wouldn't take me long to catch up," Lutz told him. "I've been doing my homework."

The Major looked at him almost apprehensively. "I'm afraid that isn't quite what I have in mind."

Lutz stared at him puzzled.

And then the Major told him that he would be flying a Stork. The slowest, lowest aircraft in Germany.

That was when Lutz went to the mess and started to get drunk.

*   *   *

What was worse, Lutz brooded, was the fact that he was to train another man to fly the Stork. In other words he had only been reprieved for someone else's benefit. When he had trained him he would probably be grounded again.

Lutz reached for the bottle of Bols gin. He sat by himself in the crowded mess; that's how it was these days.

He lit a cigarette and when he looked up through the smoke he saw a fair-haired man with a scar on one cheek standing in front of him. He was wearing a grey suit.

"Oberleutnant Lutz?"

"If you say so," Lutz said.

"My name is Wolff."

"My pupil?"

"Correct, Herr Oberleutnant. Do you mind if I sit down?"

Lutz gestured towards a chair and pushed the bottle of gin across the table. "Help yourself."

Wolff poured himself a measure of gin and added tonic water. "When do we start?"

Lutz appraised the man sitting across the table and said: "You believe in getting down to things, don't you."

"I have to learn to fly as soon as possible."

"Perhaps we could finish the job by tomorrow afternoon."

Wolff leaned forward. "I'm serious, Herr Oberleutnant."

"So am I Herr . . . Do you have a rank?"

Wolff showed him his identity card.

Lutz glanced at it casually. "Gestapo?"

Wolff shook his head.

"Then why aren't you in uniform?"

"Because I don't choose to be."

"Perhaps you have heard that pilots have no respect for rank. Or for the SS for that matter." He poured himself a liberal measure of gin.

Wolff smiled at him. "I hadn't heard that. You don't seem to be in a very good mood, Herr Oberleutnant."

"I'm drunk," Lutz said simply.

"I can see that. I suppose I'd better join you. Then we can both start off in the morning with thick heads." He drank some gin. "How long will it take?"

"To teach you to fly?" Lutz shrugged. "Perhaps never.

Some men are born to fly, others to walk. Who knows which breed you are."

"How long?" Wolff asked again.

"Months. It depends on you."

"I want you to teach me in one week."

Lutz burst out laughing and choked on his gin. "Are you out of your mind?"

"One week."

"Totally and utterly out of the question. And please stop issuing orders. You may be a Captain in the exalted SS but I'm your instructor. Your life depends on me. Never forget that."

At the next table a group of pilots were singing a bawdy song. From time to time one of them would glance curiously at Lutz and the civilian in the grey suit.

Lutz said in a slightly slurred voice: "And another thing, Wolff — I see no reason to give you the benefit of rank as you're in civilian clothes — just what the hell is all this about?"

"All you need to know is that I've got to learn to fly."

"A Stork! Why don't you stick to model aeroplanes. Fly them at Prinz Albrechtstrasse."

Wolff said. "This is deadly serious, Lutz."

"For you, yes. For me, no. My friends — my ex-friends," pointing at the other pilots, "are learning to fly the most advanced aircraft in the world, the ME 262, and I'm pissing apround with a Stork! No, my friend, I have to know more about this. Come clean."

Wolff examined the man in front of him. Green cat's eyes, twisted smile. He felt sorry for him. He also liked him. He wanted to tell him the truth, but that was impossible. They had pulled out his fingernails to make sure he could keep a secret.

Wolff said: "I'll explain tomorrow."

"Tomorrow? *Scheisse!* I want to know now."

"Tomorrow," Wolff said, pouring gin into both glasses, "and now let's get drunk."

Lutz thought it over before saying: "I'll drink to that," tossing the gin back in one experienced movement.

*　　*　　*

The Stork stood on the grass at the far end of the airfield, away from the other aircraft with their serpent-noses, their rockets and cannon.

The little plane, Wolff thought, looked lonely, and then thought: "Christ, I'm getting sentimental."

The Stork — official name Fieseler FI 56 — was a spotter plane. It could take off with a fifty yard run and land on a pocket handkerchief.

"Well there she is," Lutz remarked. "A canary among a flock of eagles."

"I think," Wolff said, "that you're a little more fond of her than you make out."

"I don't think anything this morning," Lutz said. His eyes were bloodshot and the ache in his head seemed to furrow his forehead. "I seem to remember you promising to tell me what this is all about. But we'll let that pass for the time being."

Wolff walked round the two-seater monoplane. He looked into the cockpit and imagined himself at the controls. Beside him, as they flew towards freedom, the most important passenger in the world.

"Well," Lutz said, "what do you think? This morning I leave all the thinking to you."

"How fast will she go?"

"Maximum speed 109 miles per hour. A sitting duck for enemy fighters."

"Armaments?"

"A pea-shooter."

"Seriously," Wolff said.

"I am serious. She's got one 7.9 mm machine-gun mounted at the rear. It's fine for spraying crops."

"The Stork has been useful in its time."

"Oh you're so right. It rescued the Macaroni."

Wolff smiled. Lutz was referring to the rescue of Mussolini by Otto Skorzeny. It was a Stork that had taken off from a tiny space behind a hotel on the 9,050 foot Gran Sasso Massif with

168

the Duce inside it.

"And our little Stork has had many distinguished owners," Lutz said. "The Macaroni himself had one. Stalin's got one. Kesselring *had* one."

"What happened?"

"It was shot down," Lutz said.

"When can I start to fly her?"

"Ah, the Hauptsturmführer has learned a little humility."

"I was told you were the best," Wolff said.

"Who told you that, Göring?"

"I know all about that," Wolff said. "They still told me you were the best."

"They?"

"They," Wolff said non-committally.

"You begin to intrigue me," Lutz said, groaning and massaging his forehead.

"Can I handle the controls?"

"Why not? Do some aerobatics while you're at it."

Wolff climbed into the cockpit. Excitement gripped him as he handled the controls, smelled oil and aviation fuel. "Come on," he shouted to Lutz, "let's get started."

"First lesson," Lutz said. "The preliminary check." He walked round the aircraft; then he climbed into the cockpit and checked the controls and gauges. "Do we really have to start now?"

Wolff nodded; Lutz sighed. Then he gave Wolff a brief lecture on aerodynamics finishing with: "I need a beer."

"I'd like to go up."

"You'll go up when I think you're ready for it."

"I meant with you flying her."

"What makes you think I'm ready? I'm a lame duck, remember? I've got to find my wings again."

Two days later they flew. On the third day Lutz let Wolff take over for a while.

"Right wing up," Lutz said as the plane tilted in the summer sky.

Wolff corrected the angle. "Not bad," Lutz admitted.

169

"Now we'll try a turn. Rudder and wheel."

The Stork banked steeply. Wolff straightened her out. He was overcome with exhilaration; he wanted to explore the blue vaults above him, to delve into the banks of cumulus on the horizon, to fly forever. He wished he was alone.

Then the Stork went into a spin.

Lutz took over the controls. They straightened out. "Typical SS," he said. "Arrogant."

They ate a salad lunch in the mess and Lutz asked again why he was teaching an SS officer to fly.

Wolff looked at him steadily. "I wish I could tell you. Will you believe me if I tell you that it's vitally important for Germany? That the whole future depends on it?"

Lutz bit into a tomato. "Future? There isn't any future."

"Do you really believe that?"

"We're finished," Lutz said. "Any fool knows that."

"You disappoint me."

"So you're one of these fanatics, eh? You think our secret weapons will save us?" He forked a piece of chicken. "We're fighting one man's war now. Hitler's war. God knows how many thousands will die before he accepts that he's beaten. He's bleeding us to death," Lutz said pushing his plate aside.

"You're talking treason."

"Maybe. Call Himmler and tell him."

Wolff stared out of the window at the summer day. Whisps of cloud in the sky, a breeze ruffling the butterfly petals of a bed of petunias. Since that first day he had felt a cameraderie growing between Lutz and himself; he had thought that maybe one day when the war was over they might renew their friendship.

"I don't want to hear you talking like that again, Herr Oberleutnant."

"To hell with you," said Lutz.

* * *

Wolff didn't learn to fly in a week. And for the next three

weeks his relationship with his instructor remained distant.

Until one warm, showery day when the sky was patched with cloud and a rainbow rose from the heart of the Black Forest.

Wolff was staring at the rainbow; he was perfectly relaxed, hands and brain attuned to the controls, as though he had been flying for years.

Beside him sat Lutz wearing his leather helmet, goggles pushed up on his forehead. He only spoke if Wolff made a mistake.

Suddenly Lutz grabbed his shoulder and pointed above them. "Did you see that?"

Wolff peered into the leaking clouds. "I can't see a thing."

"*Scheisse!* Here, I'll take over."

Wolff frowned. "What's the matter?"

"A hunter who's found a soft kill if I'm not mistaken."

Wolff saw an aircraft flash between two clouds.

Lutz said: "A Mustang. A long-range bastard with drop-tanks. He must have got lost. Or perhaps," hopefully, "he's wounded."

Lutz spoke tersely into the radio giving their position and the enemy strength — one!

"Maybe he didn't see us," Wolff said.

"And maybe pigs can fly. This, Hauptsturmführer, could be the end of your so-secret assignment." He turned and grinned. "Can you tell me now, just before we die?"

"We aren't going to die," Wolff said as the Mustang appeared behind them and opened up with its machine-guns.

The Stork, zig-zagging above the trees, reached a grey cloud.

"He must be licking his lips," Lutz remarked. "A cat with a very tiny mouse."

Wolff said: "I'm going to try the pea-shooter."

He turned and grabbed the machine-gun as they flew out of the cloud. Ahead the sky was clear.

Then the Mustang was at them again. Bullets plucked holes in one wing and splintered the dials in front of Lutz.

171

"Next time he'll get us," Lutz said. "Do you want to jump?"

"You always were a defeatist bastard," Wolff said. "A sour, defeated, self-pitying bastard."

"Not for much longer," Lutz said. "Anyway he's got to come from above — we're almost taxiing on the treetops."

As the Mustang swooped on them Wolff squeezed the trigger of the bucking machine gun. He was swearing, biting the inside of his mouth so that blood flowed and he was filled with hatred and fear and exultation, as the bullets pumped out of the machine-gun.

This time the Mustang didn't fire. It was banking away, showing its belly. And from its nose black smoke was streaming.

Lutz shook his head in disbelief. "You got the bastard. You actually got him."

"With a pea-shooter."

They watched the Mustang climb. Then suddenly it was a ball of flame plummeting towards the dark-green trees below.

Lutz watched it all the way into the forest; then he made the sign of the cross.

Wolff sat back panting as the adrenalin subsided in his bloodstream. "I didn't know you were a religious man."

"There's a lot about me you don't know."

"I know you're a defeatist bastard."

Lutz grinned at him. "Not any more. Not after I've seen a Mustang shot down with a pea-shooter." He stuck out his hand and Wolff took it.

That night Wolff telephoned Harzer and asked him if he could use his influence at Luftwaffe HQ to get Lutz fully operational again.

One week later, just as Wolff was leaving the airfield for good, Lutz came up to him in the mess. He bought them both beer and schnapps and said: "The lame duck has been reprieved. I'm taking a conversion course to ME 262's."

Wolff held out his hand. "Congratulations."

"Are you going to tell me what this has all been about?"

Wolff shook his head. "I'm sorry."

"Ah well, I have a few hunches. After all, if Skorzeny can do it, why not you?"

Wolff tried to laugh. "But who would I rescue?"

But Lutz just smiled and tapped the side of his nose.

He died six months later when he was attacked by a Tempest fighter plane as he landed an ME 262 wonderbird.

XVIII

Two men of humble origins who knew nothing of each other's existence — in fact, were never to know — now began to play their parts in events leading up to Operation Grey Fox, also known to the conspirators as The Saint Peter's Plot.

One was a Jew in a concentration camp; the other was a thief named Ziemann — the man von Geissel had told Harzer about.

Ziemann had been under sentence of death for looting a bombed store in Munich when he was visited in his cell by von Geissel travelling under the name Sachs. Von Geissel was accompanied by the prison doctor. Von Geissel scrutinised Ziemann who was standing beside his wooden bunk shivering with fear. There was something about von Geissel, even in civilian clothing, that inspired fear.

"Turn around," von Geissel snapped.

Ziemann did what he was told. Von Geissel seemed satisfied, saying to the doctor: "Are you sure of his medical history?"

"Quite sure . . . " The doctor was unsure how to address this nondescript man, but he reacted to his chilling authority. Goebbels was nondescript and Himmler wasn't exactly a pillar of Aryan manhood. The doctor assumed he was Gestapo. "Quite sure, Herr Sachs."

"Mmmmm." Von Geissel ran his finger down a list of Ziemann's known afflictions. "So you were gassed in the trenches, eh?"

"*Ja*, Herr Sachs."

"Take your clothes off."

"But Herr Sachs —"

"Take them off."

Ziemann, medium height, pale-skinned with greying black hair, grey-blue eyes and a straggling moustache, took off his clothes and stood trembling in the cold cell.

Von Geissel inspected the scar on his leg and seemed satisfied. "Did you return to the trenches after you recovered?"

"I was blind for a while, Herr Sachs. You know, the gas —"

"So you didn't return."

"He deserted," the doctor said.

"Do you want to die, Ziemann?"

"No one wants to die, Herr Sachs."

"Put your clothes on again."

Hurriedly the thief put on his shabby suit.

Von Geissel said to the doctor: "He may be what I require." He turned to Ziemann. "I'm going to give you a chance to live. But only if you cooperate with me totally. Do you understand?"

"*Ja*, Herr Sachs." Ziemann hesitated. "But what do I have to do?"

"You will be subjected to some experiments."

Ziemann's trembling became more violent. But the doctor wasn't surprised: it was exactly what he had suspected.

* * *

Ziemann found to his amazement that he wasn't badly treated. He was taken to the basement of a bombed-out house in Munich near the church known as Old Peter.

He was never left alone, two men taking it in turns to guard him. They never called each other by their names but, instinctively, Ziemann knew they were officers. One had a broken nose, the other was tall and handsome with pouches under his eyes.

He was allowed to lie in his bunk until midday, then given a

175

light vegetarian meal. He was also given two pills from a bottle labelled Dr. Koester's Anti-Gas Pills which, although he didn't know it, contained strychnine and belladonna.

When he asked what the pills were for he was told curtly: "For your own good."

After the meal he was allowed into the rubble-strewn courtyard of the house and told to walk round it a dozen times.

On the fifth day he was taken to a dentist's surgery in the centre of Munich next door to a publishing house.

The man with the broken nose handed the dentist a suitcase and said: "Your payment."

When the dentist, sturdy with thick wrists and broken blood vessels on his cheeks, took the suitcase Ziemann noticed that he sagged with its weight.

Ziemann was thrust into the dental chair. He stared at the drill, the spittoon and the probes and fear gripped him.

He turned to the broken-nosed officer and shouted: "I'm not going through with it."

Wenck produced a Luger pistol. "You prefer a bullet in your mouth instead of a drill?"

Ziemann subsided whimpering.

The dentist examined his teeth with a dental mirror, pausing every so often to make notes.

When he had finished Wenck said: "Well?"

The dentist shrugged, appraising Ziemann. "Just about what I would have expected from someone like this. A lot of decay, all the symptoms of undernourishment."

Wenck said: "You know what we want. Can it be done?"

"It will be difficult." He glanced at a sketch of two sets of teeth, upper and lower, which Wenck had provided. "I will have to create some cavities. The bridgework will take time. The materials I need are almost non-existent."

"Make a list," Wenck said. "I'll get them. How long once you have the materials?"

"I don't make the bridges."

"How long?" Wenck snapped impatiently.

"Three weeks."

"I want all the work completed in seven days."

"Impossible."

Wenck picked up the heavy suitcase. "Very well, we'll go elsewhere."

The dentist said: "I'll see what I can do." He picked up his drill. "Now let's make a start."

The drill bit into one of Ziemann's teeth; he tried to scream with pain but the scream emerged as a gurgle at the back of his throat.

Eight days later Ziemann had his bridgework.

That night there was an air-raid. The dentist's body was found beneath a pile of rubble half a mile from his surgery. Bodies were quickly disposed of these days and it never occurred to anyone that there might be evidence of a bullet wound in the shattered remnants of his skull.

Back in the basement Ziemann explored the bridgework with one finger and said to the guard with the pouched eyes: "For God's sake, what is this all about?"

"As Herr Sachs told you — an experiment."

"I think I'm going crazy."

"Aren't we all," remarked Steiner, thinking that this was all to the good because rumour had it that the Fuhrer wasn't quite himself these days and, except for the straggly moustache, Ziemann was now, as near as dammit, Hitler's twin.

*　　*　　*

The Jew who was to play his part in the climactic events of the next few months was named Landau.

He was imprisoned in a pretty little Bavarian town outside Munich where landscape painters once met. It was called Dachau. Landau had been there for three years. He was not all that old — fifty-three, in fact — but his hair sprouting from his shaven scalp was thin and grey; he had once been on the plump side, now he was down to 100 lbs.

He was one of the *lucky* Jews. He was sufficiently strong and healthy to be 'worked to death' instead of being frozen to death or injected with gas-gangrene or just simply being gassed with crystallised prussic acid.

But Landau refused to die. Because he had a mission, an obsession, which had created a resistance to death as bacilli will build up a resistance to a particular drug. Landau wanted to escape and find one man.

Hopes of escape had long since faded from the minds of other Jews, systematically degraded and debilitated so that their only concept of freedom was death. But not with Landau.

He knew he *had* the means of escape. Nothing that could be implemented while the Germans were winning the war. Not even now while some of them still believed that victory was a possibility. But when they were finally on the run, when the Russian tanks were snouting through the outskirts of Berlin then he would make his move.

Already he had selected his man. An Obersturmführer in an SS Death's Head unit. A man so depraved that he must be corruptible, especially if the corruption involved saving his own skin.

So while the other inmates of the billet fell and died, Landau laboured steadily breaking stones and repairing barbed-wire. He patched his striped uniform, ate his potato-peel gruel, slept at the bottom of three tiers of bunks and dreamed fitfully of his mission, his crusade. When that was completed he would die willingly. But not before.

And, like the thief Ziemann, he had no idea that he was destined to play a decisive role in history.

XIX

While Kurt Wolff was shooting down a Mustang, Allied troops were taking Rome. The first American unit, a platoon of the 88th Division, penetrated the city limits at 6 am on June 4th, 1944, but they were repulsed and it wasn't till later that day that The Eternal City was completely cleared of Germans.

However, the Romans had known for some time that the Germans weren't going to make a fight of it. The movement of military traffic south had suddenly turned north. Big guns, searchlights, armoured cars and trucks piled high with food and loot trundled along the Via Flaminia. Installations at Campino and Urbe airfields had been mined; the torture chambers of the Pensione Jaccarino fired, ammunition dumps and railway yards blown.

Already in the outskirts of Rome partisani were shooting collaborators.

By dawn on the 4th, a Sunday, radio and telephones had been cut; there were no trams, buses or newspapers. Gun-fire crackled in the distance. Rome, seized by armies ranging from the Gauls in 390 BC to the Germans in 1943 AD, waited expectantly to greet the new victors unaware that the victors' generals had been in dispute as to who should take Rome: the American 5th or the British 8th Army.

It was the army of the American General, Wayne Mark Clark, which finally entered the city in force.

* * *

Maria Reubeni watched from the back of the crowd as American troops poured through the Porta Pia in the old walls of the city.

The soldiers were caked with dust and mud, draped with garlands of flowers. They grinned hugely as they doled out cigarettes and gum, kissed the girls, drank from bottles and wiped streams of wine from their chins with big, battle-bruised hands.

Since Salerno the 5th Army had lost 20,389 men.

But Maria didn't rejoice. Rome hadn't belonged to the Germans, nor did it now belong to the Americans. She waited only for two men — Hans Doppler and Otto Witt.

An American soldier broke away, pushed through the crowd and put his arm round her. "How about a kiss?" he said. She let him kiss her, feeling the stubble of his beard on her skin, and when he let her go he said: "Jesus, it was like kissing a nun."

And that's what I've become, she thought, as she watched children fighting for gum, priests running with the crowds, black cassocks flying — like crows as the Germans had contemptuously described them.

Maria turned and headed away from the jubilation towards ancient Rome, the tranquil ruins that were all that remained of the violent past. She paused at the moonlit Forum where, spurred by Mark Antony's words, the crowds mourning the death of Julius Caesar had once made a funeral pyre of furniture. What ruins would there be in 2,000 years time to remind people of the Via Rasella, of the Ardeantine Caves?

She thought of Caesar lying in Pompey's Theatre, his body pierced by twenty-three dagger wounds. And she thought of Otto Witt.

She turned and walked back towards her apartment.

*　　*　　*

Slowly Rome began to relax as the British and Americans pushed through the city in pursuit of the Germans. Semprini played at the Brancaccio Theatre; Olivia de Haviland and Charles Boyer starred in *La Porta d'Oro* at the Quirinetta Cinema.

In St. Peter's Square 100,000 people gathered to hear Pope Pius XII offer a prayer, his white-robed arms outstretched:

We must give thanks to God for the favours we have received. Rome has been spared. Today she sees salvation with new hope and confidence. This day will go down in the annals of Rome.

"So will the Ardeantine Caves," said a Jew standing next to Maria Reubeni.

King Victor Emmanuel II abdicated and Prince Humbert took his place. Badoglio quit as Prime Minister and Bonomi — the only man faintly acceptable to the warring political factions of Italy — took his place.

The beleagured Allied diplomats inside The Vatican departed and the Germans moved in; the Black Market flourished; partisani execution squads gunned down Fascist sympathisers; the Jews went back to their homes. One day the Sicilian came to Maria's apartment. He held out his hand. "I come to say good-bye. I would like us to part as friends."

She took his hand. "It is all in the past now."

"Not for me," he said. "Now we fight properly. We go to the north where we are strong."

She made him coffee and, sitting opposite him across the marble table, remembered the first time he had taken her. He had awoken her. *And now I am dead again.*

He put down his cup and said: "Your hate is destroying you, Maria. But revenge . . . It is something a Sicilian understands." He lit a cigarette and they watched the smoke billow along a shaft of sunlight.

She gazed at him; she felt nothing for him; it had all been a long time ago.

"Do you think this man will return?"

She spread her hands. "This is one of the routes the Nazis will take. Otto Witt knows Rome. He will have the money to buy his way out."

"But you must be careful. Maybe he will come looking for

you. He will realise that you know the escape routes, the safe houses —"

"Safe houses? But they were for Jews. The priests wouldn't give sanctuary to Nazi criminals."

"You don't know your priests," the Sicilian said. He took his Beretta pistol from his belt. "Here, take this, just in case." He put the pistol on the table in the ray of sunlight. "So your work is finished?"

"Yes," she said, "it is finished. The doors of the Synagogue are open once more." She finished her coffee. "Is Angelo Peruzzi going with you?"

"Angelo is dead," the Sicilian said. "We found out that he had been paying visits to the Germans in the Via Tasso. He had to die. In Sicily we call it *infamita*."

Maria shivered.

The Sicilian stood up. "And now I must go." He kissed her on both cheeks. "At least you will always remember me as the first."

From the window she watched him as he walked away along the cobbled street below. Then she picked up the gun and began her long wait.

PART II

XX

Sitting in his office, Major-General Werner Harzer reviewed the course of the war. In front of him on his desk lay the *Berliner Morgenpost* dated December 19th, 1944 — hardly worth the ten pfennig they charged for it, in his opinion — with a report and map on the front page of the German offensive in the Ardennes forest.

Von Rundstedt's divisions were pushing into Belgium while the bewildered Americans fell back. Harzer smelled the smoke of battle, heard the grinding roar of Tiger tank tracks. Jochen Peiper was there, Sepp Dietrich was there, the Leibstandarte was there.

What wouldn't he give to be there. Pain stabbed him in the belly. He sighed and lit a cigarette.

Was it just possible that Hitler's instinctive genius had reasserted itself? Harzer doubted it, but for a few moments he allowed himself the luxury of contemplating a German advance. Antwerp was only a hundred miles away. Smiling to himself, Harzer extended the luxury to ultimate victory.

He turned the page of the newspaper and the euphoria drained from him. He was too old a soldier to be fooled by reports of enemy losses on the Eastern Front, of strategic withdrawals and regrouping. The raw facts were that the Russians had taken Rumania, Bulgaria and large tracts of Poland and were about to lay siege to the Hungarian capital of Budapest. In the North of Italy the Allies had foundered to a halt; but Harzer knew that it was only the weather that had temporarily washed away the enemy's initiative. How much longer? Six months at the most. But, since the fall of Rome, preparations for Grey Fox had been proceeding satisfactorily.

On June 6th the expected invasion of Europe had been launched when Allied forces stormed the beaches of Normandy. By August 25th Paris had fallen and the Allies were fanning across Europe while seven divisions, landed in the south of France on August 15th, were nosing northwards.

None of this interfered with Operation Grey Fox. But it seemed likely that one event would: the attempted assassination of Adolf Hitler on July 20th. Shortly after 12.30 pm a Colonel Claus von Stauffenberg attended Hitler's daily conference at Rastenburg in East Prussia and departed — to make an urgent phone call — leaving behind his briefcase containing a time-bomb.

The bomb, under the table close to Hitler, exploded ten minutes later. But miraculously Hitler survived the blast. Harzer was overjoyed, but the Führer's condition presented him with problems. The tympanic membranes of Hitler's ears had been damaged by the explosion: the membranes of his double imprisoned in the Munich cellar would have to be similarly damaged — without killing him.

While the purge following the assassination attempt was in full swing, Harzer instructed von Geissel to fly to Munich to see what was to be done.

He was lucky. The night before von Geissel arrived Liberators and Flying Fortresses bombed Munich. One bomb exploded a few yards from the cellar and blew in the heavy, studded door as though it were paper. Wenck, who was on guard at the time, suffered internal injuries but managed to draw a pistol and keep Ziemann covered until Steiner returned.

Von Geissel called in a local doctor and told him to examine Ziemann thoroughly. "What's wrong with him?" he asked half an hour later.

"Nothing much."

"Nothing at all?"

"He may have damage to the tympanic membranes."

* * *

In his office Harzer drummed his fingers on the newspaper map of the Ardennes offensive with its splendid arrows biting into Belgium. He gave it ten days, no more, before it spent itself.

He tossed the newspaper into the waste-paper basket, reached for his stick and limped to the window where he stood gazing at a bomb-shattered building, its sharp edges softened by mist and frost.

The dummy-rum would have to be made soon. Now! First they needed a suitable subject, an expendable one, to test with Wolff the dangers through which the Führer would have to pass. Harzer picked up a manilla folder. He thought he had found just such a man; he wasn't in personnel for nothing.

He returned to his desk and began to read the life and times of Otto Witt.

* * *

Next morning Steiner, wearing a dark suit, long brown leather coat and slouch hat, called at the Munich apartment of Standartenführer Otto Witt who had been mysteriously granted leave from his duties in Eastern Europe. Steiner rather enjoyed the role; perhaps he would become an actor when it was all over.

Witt, wearing a red silk dressing-gown and smoking a cigarette in a holder, opened the door. His eyes were puffy, soft brown hair tousled. "Who the devil are you?" voice faltering as he took in the *uniform*.

Steiner flashed his identity card at Witt and pushed past him into the apartment. It must have been some party! Ash-trays overflowing with butts, cut-glass tumblers still half full of liquor, gramophone turn-table still revolving, perfume and cigar smoke on the air, pornographic photographs spread over

187

the table.

Steiner appraised the apartment. Richly — no lavishly — appointed. Steiner thought of the cellar where he had spent the past few weeks with Ziemann and determined to enjoy himself.

Witt poured himself a brandy with a shaking hand and made an effort to assert himself. Steiner sensed that it would be his last effort.

"Do you know who I am?" Witt asked.

Steiner smiled at him. "I not only know who you are, I know everything there is to know about you. Your birthplace, education, career and your, ah, inclinations."

"I am a Colonel in the SS and I demand to know on whose authority you are here."

"Himmler's," Steiner said simply. "And when you say SS you should be more specific. You are not a fighting man." Steiner took a notebook from the pocket of his leather coat and consulted it. "You were in command of Einsatzgruppen, liquidating the sub-humans in Eastern Europe. There is a difference you know."

"I was merely —"

"Shut up." Steiner ran his finger down a page of the notebook. "Not only that but you are a thief," pointing at the silver candelabra, cut-glass decanters and oil-paintings on the walls.

He crossed the room and kicked open the bedroom door. The bed was big and circular with a blue silk canopy over one end.

On it lay a man and a woman, both obviously naked beneath a silk sheet. "*A menage à trois?* Very pretty. Still, everyone to his own taste." To the man and the girl he said: "*Raus!*"

"Hey," said the man, "what the hell . . ."

Steiner pulled back the sheet and gazed appreciatively at the girl trying to cover her breasts. "So," he said, "what was it like being in the centre of a sandwich? Or perhaps," glancing at Witt, "you weren't the centre." He flung a handful of flimsy underclothes at her. "You both have three minutes to get out if you don't want to suffer the same fate as your host."

Steiner walked back into the lounge, sat down, selected a cigarette from a silver case and told Witt to sit down.

Consulting the notebook again, he said: "You have an impressive record in Eastern Europe. How many thousand Jews and gypsies did you polish off?"

"I did my duty," Witt said.

"And you did it very well." A pause. "But that is not why I'm here."

Witt began to shiver. "Why *are* you here?"

"As you know there was a plot in the summer to assassinate our beloved Führer."

Witt stared at him uncomprehendingly.

"Most of the conspirators have been executed. Some were hung from meat-hooks with piano wire," glancing at Witt. "Estimates of the number executed vary but I have heard it put as high as five thousand. The sort of figure you would appreciate, Colonel."

Pouring himself more brandy, Witt said: "I don't see what any of this has got to do with me."

Steiner waited while the man and the girl slunk, half-dressed, across the room and out of the door to the apartment. Then he said softly: "Don't you, Standartenführer?"

"I have always been loyal to the Führer."

"Very praiseworthy," said Steiner consulting his notebook. "I believe that about three years ago you were friendly with Count Helmut von Moltke."

Witt bunched his fists in an effort to control his trembling. He gulped more brandy.

"I knew him, yes."

"He was the head of what was known as the Kreisau Circle. Did you know that, Colonel?"

"I have never heard of the Kreisau Circle."

"Come, come," Steiner said mildly. "It was the political opposition to the Nazi Party. Traitors, in other words. Even you must have known that."

"I didn't know anything about it."

"Ah well, have it your own way. The fact remains that, as a

189

result of our interrogation of the criminal elements who tried to kill the Führer, a lot of information has come to light about von Moltke, the Kreisau Circle — and its members." He paused. "Do you have a glass of mineral water, Colonel?"

Witt blinked. "Mineral water. No —"

"Then champagne will do," Steiner said, settling back in an easy chair and crossing his legs.

When Witt had poured the champagne, spilling a lot on the polished surface of the table, he went on: "Your name has cropped up, Colonel."

"Mine? That's nonsense."

"That's what they all said." Steiner sipped his champagne. "It must be a terrible death with a piano-wire cutting into your throat. I'm told it nearly decapitates the victims. Slowly," Steiner added.

"For God's sake I had nothing to do with it."

"The July Plot? No, I don't suppose you did. You were too busy carrying out your own executions in Eastern Europe."

"Then what do you want with me?"

"There have been other plots, other conspiracies. In his statement on July 21st, the Führer himself spoke of two other attempts to kill him. He also said that the conspirators were 'a group of criminal elements who will now be ruthlessly exterminated.' That is what I am helping to do."

"I didn't know anything about any of it." Witt's dressing gown had slipped open at the chest revealing what looked like cigarette burns. He brushed the soft hair from his forehead. "You must believe that."

"I might," Steiner said abruptly.

"What do you mean, *you might*?"

"You will have to convince me." Steiner sipped his champagne appreciatively. "Good stuff this. Moet Chandon. But, of course, you were in the French campaign."

"How can I convince you?" Witt lit a cigarette from a stub. "I can't disprove something that hasn't any basis of fact."

"Difficult, I agree. But I have an open-mind in the matter." Steiner stood up and grasped a silver candle-stick. "Russian?"

"Polish," Witt muttered.

Steiner pointed at an old painting of a church with a river flowing in front of it. "Italian?"

"It was given to me in Rome."

"*Given*, Colonel?"

"Does it matter?"

"Not really. But these, ah, gifts, might be important if you really want to convince me of your innocence."

Suddenly Witt caught on: they were two of a kind. "How much?" some of his self-assurance returning.

"A lot," Steiner told him. And then: "But it's not as easy as that." And, when Witt tried to interrupt: "You see I have to take you away."

Witt slumped back in his chair. "I don't understand."

"It's very simple. I have to arrest you. But perhaps you weren't at home this morning ..." Steiner sat down again.

"What do you want?" Witt asked. "You talk in riddles."

"I'll explain," Steiner said, crossing his legs. "I think you're innocent. You know, I really do. But as you and I are both aware, man to man, that doesn't count for very much when a purge like this is taking place. However, I personally don't like to see an innocent man *interrogated*." Steiner managed a silky emphasis. "Or executed for that matter. Especially on the end of a piano-wire. Now if I were to delay your arrest by, say, two days you would be able to ... let us say gather enough evidence to prove your innocence."

"Escape you mean?"

"I didn't say that."

"But you meant —"

Steiner broke in: "You must make your own interpretation of what I meant. You know," he said casually, "I think the best place for you to gather this evidence of your innocence would be Rome."

Witt stared at him. "Are you crazy?"

"You were in Rome, weren't you?"

Witt nodded.

"And what was the safest place in The Eternal City?"

191

"The Vatican I suppose."

"A man could stay there for years undetected." Steiner leaned forward, his voice cold. "Now listen, Witt, and listen carefully. I am your only chance, your one and only chance."

Witt sloshed more brandy into his glass. "I'm listening."

"In the next few months lots of high-ranking officers will be leaving Germany. The end, as you well know, is near." Steiner held up his hand. "Treasonable talk? Perhaps. But self-survival is the most primitive instinct. Even if you escaped the Gestapo — an unlikely event — you would be executed by the British and Americans for what you've done in Eastern Europe." He smiled at Witt. "Am I right in assuming that you have already considered these possibilities?"

"I may have," Witt admitted.

"And you know Rome. Did you perhaps have The Eternal City in mind?"

"It has always been a possibility."

"There is a way," Steiner said and sat back to observe Witt's reactions.

The trembling had stopped; Witt was consumed with self-survival. "How?"

"As I said it will cost you."

"I don't have much money."

"Come now. You may not have much money but you have considerable resources."

Witt adjusted his dressing-gown. "How much do you want?"

"Everything," Steiner said simply.

"But —"

"You aren't in a position to bargain. Everything you possess — or your life."

Witt bowed his head, pressed his fingers to his bloodshot eyes. "Very well."

"What, for instance, is in that packing case over there?"

"A few treasures I collected."

"Let me see them. I'm quite a connoisseur, you know."

"Take my word for it, it's good stuff."

Steiner stood up. "Let me see."

"It's sealed. The lid is nailed down."

"Hand me one of those beautiful Sheffield-steel knives with the silver handles."

Steiner stuck the blade under the lid. It took him five minutes to prise it open. Underneath was a tray of rings, earrings, necklaces; diamonds, sapphires and emeralds glittered in the light from the chandelier.

Steiner started to lift the tray but Witt held his arm. "They're all yours," he said.

"I'm sure they are. But what's underneath?"

"Just packing materials. Paper and cotton-wool."

Steiner pulled his arm away and lifted the tray.

Underneath was a ply-wood box, about three feet by two feet.

"The key," Steiner snapped.

"I haven't got it."

"The key," Steiner said wearily.

Witt went into the bedroom and returned with a key.

Steiner slid it into the lock and opened the box and looked down upon a great mound of gold teeth. He stood very still for a moment, trying to contain his revulsion. Then he said quietly: "You have been a busy boy, Colonel, haven't you?"

"Well, is it on?"

"Oh yes," Steiner said softly. "It's on all right." He poured himself some brandy to drown the sickness that was rising inside him. "Now this," he said, "is what you have to do."

* * *

At the same time that Steiner was talking with Witt in Munich, Harzer, von Geissel and Kurt Wolff were studying a large-scale map of Europe in Harzer's farmhouse in Bavaria.

Harzer had drawn a line in red ink from Berlin to Rome. The line came almost straight down Germany — Leipzig, Nuremberg, Munich — bisected Austria through Innsbruck, and entered Italy through the Brenner Pass.

Harzer pointed at the northern reaches of Italy. "That," he said, "is the crucial area of operation." He turned to Wolff. "I assume you know about the South Tyrol?"

"I know it's sometimes said to be more German than Germany, more Austrian than Austria."

Harzer nodded. "We call it the South Tyrol, the Italians call it the Alto-Adige. It was given to the Italians at the end of the First World War because they supported the winning side. In 1939 the people of the South Tyrol were given two options — to take out Italian citizenship or be repatriated to Germany. Two-thirds of them voted to come to Germany. But so far only about half that number have been moved. About 80,000, I believe."

"In any case," von Geissel remarked, "we are in occupation now."

"Agreed. But the point is that, irrespective of whether or not we're in occupation when Grey Fox goes into operation, the South Tyrol will still be a stronghold. In fact," Harzer said, "I think the South Tyroleans will always have the good sense to be more German than Italian."

"Not only that," von Geissel said, "but we have the Bozen SS there. Mostly South Tyroleans giving a good account of themselves against the Italian partisans."

Wolff, dressed in a red turtle-neck sweater and black ski-trousers, glanced at von Geissel. Instinctively he didn't like him: he had ice in his veins instead of blood, more like a mortuary attendant than an SS officer.

Wolff warmed his hands in front of the log-fire. Outside snowflakes flakes fluttered against the window and the mountain peaks were hidden by grey sky.

The map was spread on a table which had been drawn up to the fire. The two older men wore sports jackets and sweaters.

Harzer said to Wolff: "On the dummy run you will fly half the way. But not, of course, over Italian territory occupied by the Americans and British. We shall have to adapt the final flight according to the prevailing military situation."

Von Geissel said: "Luckily the Red Cross has two Storks.

Yours will have red crosses painted on its wings and fusilage."

"Not *luckily*," Harzer corrected him. "I arranged the gift of the Storks to the Red Cross." He straightened up from the map. "But even so we can't run the risk of you being accidentally shot down flying over a battle area."

"So what do I do when I reach the fighting?"

"You take a train," von Geissel told him.

"Through the enemy lines?"

Harzer said: "An exchange of wounded prisoners has been arranged. You, of course, will be Hans Doppler of the Swiss Red Cross."

"And my . . . dummy?"

"He will be a priest. Someone has to administer last rites."

"Have we found this dummy?"

Harzer glanced at his watch. "He is being interviewed at this minute. I expect a phone call in about an hour's time."

"Do I know him?"

"I doubt it very much. I don't think he is the sort of person with whom you would associate. His name," Harzer said, "is Otto Witt."

Wolff shook his head. "I don't know anyone of that name."

Von Geissel said: "Consider yourself lucky. He's a degenerate. Someone slipped up at the selection board."

"With respect, I don't see how an exchange of wounded prisoners is going to get a German-Swiss Red Cross official and a German-Swiss priest into enemy territory. They'll have their own officials and priests."

"It won't," von Geissel told him. "We're hedging our bets, as the British say. You have a dual purpose. You are acting as an intermediary between Berlin and The Vatican. You have vital dispatches — and written authority from both. When you've dealt with the wounded you will cross the Gothic Line to the north-west of Italy."

Harzer limped over to the window and stared through the falling snow at the white valley beneath. He wondered if he would ever see it green again. He said to Wolff: "First you make for Meran — or Merano as the Italians call it — in the

195

South Tyrolean region of northern Italy. You should feel at home there — they grow grapes. We had thought of Bozen — or Bolzano as the Italians call it — but it's a little too obvious."

Von Geissel picked up a fountain pen lying on the table and made a cross on the map. "We have a man there and he will be waiting for you. But," von Geissel warned, "he only knows that Meran is a link in the chain for Germans leaving the Fatherland. He doesn't know the identity of the person you will ultimately be bringing through."

Von Geissel made three other red crosses down the great Jack-boot of mainland Italy. "These are the three other *sanctuaries* arranged by Heinrich Brandt. An abbey, a monastery and a church."

"Stations of the Cross,' Harzer observed drily.

"And finally The Vatican." Von Geissel slashed a big cross over Rome.

"When do I go?" Wolff asked.

"The day after tomorrow," Harzer told him. "Provided Herr Witt collaborates. He will meet you in Berlin. You will take off from Templehof. Although I doubt very much if you'll be able to do that when the day comes."

Wolff threw a log onto the fire. "And what happens to Herr Witt when he gets to Rome?"

Von Geissel's voice was clinically cold and Wolff imagined him dispassionately examining a corpse on a slab. "You kill him, of course," he said.

* * *

Forty-five minutes later the old-fashioned telephone on the desk beside the book-shelves rang. Harzer took the ear-piece from the hook and spoke into the mouth-piece. "*Ja?*"

The conversation lasted thirty seconds.

Harzer turned to the other two men. "He's hooked," he said.

As he spoke they heard a grinding metallic sound outside. It sounded, Wolff thought, like the treads of a half-track on the

Russian snows.

He peered through the window and saw a van with snow-chains on its tyres coming slowly up the hill. "Visitors," he said.

Von Geissel folded up the map and slipped it into his brief-case.

Wolff watched the van stop at the gates. Frieda Harzer stepped out.

She flung herself into her father's arms; kissed Wolff on both cheeks, lingering fractionally against him; shook hands with von Geissel.

Her father smiled at her. "What are you doing here?"

"Five days' leave," she said. "Isn't it wonderful? And finding you here, too." She frowned. "By the way, what are you doing here?"

"A reunion," her father said. "Three old soldiers — one not so old — re-fighting their battles."

"Ah, the SS." She pulled off her fur-trimmed hat and said: "I promise I won't say anything."

After lunch Wolff drove Frieda in the van to the house in the vineyards where he had been brought up. The snow had stopped falling and there was a bluish glow in the grey sky.

"I love the snow," she said. "It never seems cold to me."

"I dream about the snow in the summer," Wolff told her. "When it snows I dream of the summer."

"You're very awkward," she said, glancing at him. "A tough customer, too. Who is that man?" she asked.

Von Geissel? An old SS friend of your father's."

"I don't like him," she said. "I don't trust him. I can't make out why he should be a friend of my father's."

"I don't know either," Wolff said. "Perhaps he was different when he was younger. Perhaps the war has changed him. It's changed everyone — you and me."

"Not you," she said. "You wanted the war in the first place."

He stopped the van. "You promised."

"All right, I'm sorry."

He started the engine again. Ninety minutes later the pulled up outside the big gabled house cossetted in snow.

A grey-haired woman with untroubled features came to the door. Wolff introduced himself — the son of the previous owner.

The woman's face lit up. "Ah, young Kurt. Everyone in the village has followed your career with great interest. Where are you stationed these days?"

"Berlin," Wolff told her as they went into the oak-beamed lounge where he and his father had once argued about his military career. *Wehrmacht* versus SS, the familiar friction.

"And this is your wife?"

"This is Frieda Harzer. She's a nurse."

"You're doing a wonderful job, my dear," said the woman. "Do you work near Kurt?"

"In Berlin," Frieda said. "I've just been moved to a civilian hospital, the Charite."

Wolff gazed through the window at the rows of vines like gravestones under the snow. He didn't like this woman; she was an intruder; what's more she asked too many questions.

They excused themselves and Wolff drove to the village where they drank hot chocolate in a cafe. She asked him about his Italian.

"I need some more instruction."

"Then you shall have it. Perhaps tonight?"

He glanced at her to see if there was another implication there. He thought he saw a softness in her eyes that he hadn't detected before.

Forgetting that he had to return to Berlin, he said: "Perhaps."

She placed her hand on the top of his. "What's going on Kurt?"

"With us?"

"No, with you." Softly: "I know what's happening with us."

"Nothing is happening with me. I'm getting older, I know now that we'll lose the war . . ."

198

"To hell with the bloody war." She lit a cigarette and blew an angry jet of smoke towards the ceiling. "What are you and my father plotting?"

Wolff sipped his hot chocolate. For the first time since he had undertaken the mission, he was tempted to share it with someone else. He compromised. "You must never tell your father that I've told you anything. Do you promise?"

"I promise."

"I can't tell you exactly what's happening. But, well, your father and I are engaged on something that is vitally important to Germany."

"The war?"

Wolff thought about it, then compromised again. "No, the peace that will follow. I can't tell you any more. I don't want to begin by telling you lies."

"Was that the truth?"

He nodded because he didn't want to hear deceit in his own voice.

"You talk about peace. But you people, my father and you, have never even thought about peace. Only war, victory, battle."

"Battle is a prelude to peace," Wolff said.

"Or defeat. I don't believe people like you can accept defeat. You'll want to start all over again. Build Germany up from the rubble. Twice this has happened, you'll be looking for the third chance. More uniforms, more guns, more blood. You'll find another Hitler."

The cigarette in Wolff's hand snapped.

"Have I said something a little too near the truth?" Frieda asked.

"On the contrary," Wolff said, "you couldn't have been further from it."

She frowned. "I don't understand."

"You're not supposed to."

"Is it something . . . bad?"

Wolff shook his head. He gripped her hand. "Just trust me," smiling. "And stop trying to trap me."

"Is von Geissel involved?"

"I said stop asking questions."

"Because if he is, then there can't be anything good about it."

"Come on," he said, "it's getting late."

He paid the bill and they walked out into the snow-quiet village. The air smelled of burning pine-wood. A small boy and a girl careered past them on a home-made sled into a snow-drift. They stood up laughing and for a moment they were *their* children in the years ahead. In the years of peace.

It had begun to snow again. A few soft flakes from a pewter sky. They climbed into the van.

As they neared the farmhouse Wolff stopped the van beside the dusk-dark pine forest. And then they were kissing, and her cheeks were cold and her lips warm and open, and there was joy and anguish in the soul of Kurt Wolff.

When they got back to the farmhouse Harzer and von Geissel were ready to leave.

Frieda said: "But I thought —"

Harzer looked at them, understood and said: "Berlin have just been on the phone. We have to leave tonight."

"And Kurt?"

"All three of us."

Wolff kissed her once more before they left and whispered: "I'm sorry."

"The damn war," she said hopelessly. "The damn, damn war."

"Don't forget the peace," he said.

She looked up at him. "You haven't lied to me?"

"I haven't lied."

She kissed his eyes, his cheeks, his mouth and said: "Do you love me, Kurt?"

"I love you," he said.

But seated in the JU 52 behind Harzer and von Geissel as it droned through the snow-flying night, Wolff found that his thoughts preceded him to Rome. To a girl named Maria Vincelli.

XXI

The bomb-scarred suburbs of Berlin lay beneath them.

Wolff relaxed after the tension of taking-off and glanced at his companion. A cruel, spoilt face, features blurred by indulgence; at the moment they were still tight with the fear of the past two days. Was this man really SS? They had told him how Witt had been *persuaded* to make a run for it; they had told him about the gold teeth. Witt, he thought, would have even more reason to be scared if he knew how many flying hours his pilot had recorded, thirty at the most.

He eased the Stork — white, with red-crosses on fusilage and wings — towards the grey clouds crumpled like brains above them; but the clouds were too high to penetrate to the blue sky and sunshine beyond. Below, the suburbs were thinning out into white quilts of snow as they flew south towards Leipzig where, after refuelling, they would cross the Thurringian Forest and head for Munich. Then Austria, finding the valleys of the Alps, and finally a field cleared of snow near Merano in the South Tyrol.

Wolff jerked his thumb at the machine-gun mounted behind them. "Do you know how to use that thing?"

Otto Witt glanced over his shoulder. "Of course." He was gaining a little confidence now. "I am told that you are an officer in the SS. May I enquire what rank?"

Wolff told him.

"Then you will agree that I am in command?"

"Don't make me laugh," Wolff said. "I might choke and

we'd spin out of control."

"On the ground I'm in command."

"On the ground I can always pick up a telephone and call the nearest Gestapo Headquarters. In fact," Wolff told him, "I could call them on the radio right now."

A JU 88 passed above them. Sadly Wolff remembered how Lutz had loved the aircraft. Otto Witt wasn't fit to sit in the same seat that Lutz had once occupied. Wolff contemplated a few aerobatics to put the fear of God up his passenger; but no, you didn't jeopardise the mission just to scare one degenerate.

He peered ahead and tried to enjoy the flying; but he was too tense. He was competent enough to fly under normal conditions but there were unpredictable factors ahead — winds sneaking through the valleys of the Alps for one — and he wasn't sure of himself.

Witt lit a cigarette.

"Put that bloody thing out."

"Who the hell —"

"I said put it out. I don't like smoking in the cockpit."

Witt squashed the cigarette under his foot. "All right," he said, "you're the pilot. But when we get to Rome . . ."

Yes, Wolff thought, when we get to Rome.

Would he be able to find Maria Vincelli? Perhaps I shouldn't try, he thought tasting Frieda Harzer's lips against his. But he knew he would: it was written.

*　　*　　*

They spent that evening in a small hotel in Munich off the Ludwigstrasse. The Föhn — the unpredictable wind that blows from the mountains — was bowling small whirlwinds of snow along the streets. Pedestrians in snow-pasted coats leaned into the wind and headed for home; at least the Föhn was preferable to bombs.

They ate a frugal meal without speaking; Wolff drank a beer, Otto Witt put away two bottles of Rhine wine.

Wolff took the bed nearest the door in their room. While

Witt was in the bathroom he slipped a Walther pistol beneath his pillow. When Witt re-emerged Wolff said: "Don't come blundering this way during the night."

"Don't worry," Witt said, "I find you equally unattractive." He was dressed in silk pyjamas and was smoking a cigarette; Wolff rather hoped he would set himself alight in bed.

Witt said with elaborate politeness: "Do you mind if I ask a question?"

"If you must."

"Why did I have to go to Berlin? I'm back in Munich where I started out from."

"Because," Wolff said.

"I'm entitled to know. After all, I've paid."

"Oh yes," Wolff said, "you've paid all right."

"There's something about the whole thing I don't like."

"There's something I don't like," Wolff said. "And it's lying in the bed next to me." He reached out for the switch on the wall and turned out the light.

For an hour Wolff lay awake. And all the time Frieda Harzer's words came back to him. "I don't think people like you can accept defeat . . . You'll want to start it all over again . . . more uniforms, more guns, more blood . . ."

Wolff thought of the carnage and misery he had witnessed since the war began. Did he really want to start it all over again? Angrily he tried to push aside the questions; finally he slept and, by the morning, sleep had steeled his resolve once more.

He woke Witt roughly and threw him a black suit, dog-collar, black hat and overcoat that he had brought with him in a suitcase. "Get dressed, Father," he said. And, as Witt dressed: "Do you know your stuff?"

"My name is Hahn," Witt mumbled. "I was born in Innsbruck. I'm thirty years old — although I look younger," peering at himself in the wall-mirror.

"Why are you flying to Italy?"

"To administer last rites to dying prisoners."

"And to Rome?"

"To deliver vital dispatches to the Pope."

"And my name?"

Witt frowned. "I've forgotten."

Wolff swore at him. "You don't forget. It's your skin that's at stake. Doppler. Hans Doppler. I'm from the Red Cross in Switzerland."

The sky was diamond bright when they reached the airport and the runways had been cleared of snow. With the thoroughness that Lutz had instilled into him Wolff checked out the Stork and, when it had been refuelled, taxied to the end of a runway to await radio clearance.

Then they were soaring into the bright sky; ahead lay the white fortresses of the Alps.

Wolff navigated the first valley marked on his map in red ink. A white peak loomed in front of him. He pulled on the stick and they climbed, but it seemed that the razored peak must rip through the belly of the little aircraft. Then they were over it.

Witt was shivering. With fear, Wolff presumed. "Don't worry, Father," he said, "God is on your side."

It was then that the Föhn hit them. Stole slyly between two white fangs of rock and pushed them sideways. Wolff struggled with the controls; then they flipped. The Stork was upside down and beside him Witt was screaming.

"*Klappe halten!*" Wolff shouted.

He tried to remember everything Lutz had taught him. He wrestled with the stick as blood rushed to his head. He righted the plane and saw ahead a wall of white spiked with pine trees.

Otto Witt was still screaming.

Wolff fought the little plane shouting: "Come on, you bitch," as they banked, one wing-tip grazing the branch of a pine tree, and straightened up.

Wolff hit Otto Witt across the face with the back of his hand. "Did *they* scream when you gunned them down in Poland, Father?"

Blood oozed from the corner of Witt's mouth. "You bastard," he said.

204

Far below them was a village asleep in the snow. Above them, the peaks. They burrowed on through the white corridors until, far below, Wolff saw smoke rising from a fire, a cross picked out in the snow with logs and an area of green where the snow had been cleared.

Merano. They were ten miles inside Italy. Well, Wolff thought, if Skorzeny can do it I can. He landed with twenty yards of grass to spare.

Wolff turned to Witt. "Now all you've got to do is say as little as possible."

A big man with aggressive features and bushy eyebrows came running through the snow. He wore a sheepskin jacket and ski-boots and there was a sheen of good-living to his complexion not common in Europe these days.

As they climbed down he shot out a large hand. "Welcome to Italy. Or," appraising them, "Austria as we still like to think of it."

Wolff shook his head. "This is Father Hahn. You are Herr Gert Deussen?"

He nodded and shook Witt's hand. "*Gutten tag*, Father," winking broadly to show that he *knew*.

"You will be staying the night I trust?" Deussen asked as they walked towards the little town.

"I think so," Wolff said. "I don't think Father Hahn can take any more flying today."

"Good, good." Deussen rubbed his hands. "I've prepared a room for you and we're not short of food and drink here."

As they walked down the main street, Corso della Liberta, Wolff again felt himself cut off from war. The Germans were in occupation but there weren't many uniforms to be seen. Most of the inhabitants seemed to be old; he felt as though he were in Austria in 1935. The architecture, the chalets in their envelopes of snow, the old cathedral.

What of Deussen? Wolf distrusted his bonhommie; it didn't partner the harsh features. These days there weren't many people he did trust.

They went into a half-timbered house with huge wooden

205

doors. It was cool but not cold, similar to Harzer's Bavarian farmhouse. A log fire was blazing, and a heavy wooden table was set for three.

"A drink, gentlemen?"

"A Scotch if you have one," Witt said quickly.

"Not altar wine, Father?"

"The joke is beginning to wear a bit thin," Witt said.

Deussen chuckled and produced a bottle of Dimple Haig from a cupboard. "And you?" to Wolff.

"A beer would be fine," Wolff said. He sat at the table and removed his flying jacket; underneath he wore a brown sport coat and flannels. "What do the good people of Merano think about our arrival?"

"Just what they're supposed to think," Deussen said pouring Wolff a beer. "Schnapps?" Wolff shook his head. "They know that prisoners are to be exchanged. They know that a member of the Red Cross and a priest are passing through. Whatever happens in the future," he said confidentially, "you will be sure of a welcome here." He put one finger to his mouth as a red-faced girl came in carrying a tray of food. "We will have ample time to talk later."

They ate smoked pork with sauerkraut washed down with the aromatic local wine; Witt hardly touched his food but helped himself to the Scotch.

When the girl had gone Wolff said: "Where are the British and Americans?"

"Bogged down," Deussen told him lighting a cigar. "The British 8th Army has come to a standstill with the capture of Ravenna and Forli to the east. The Americans stopped just south of Bologna last month. And they'll stay there until the weather changes. Even then I doubt if they'll make much progress through the mountains. We're truly in the Fuhrer's Alpine Fortress, the National Redoubt," referring to the area including the northernmost tip of Italy, Austria and Southern Bavaria which was said to be impregnable.

"The French thought the Maginot Line was impregnable," Wolff said.

Deussen laughed it away, but his eyes were cold.

"Do you still think we'll win the war?" Wolff asked.

"We have our secret weapons."

"The rockets didn't make much difference to the Londoners. Merely hardened their resolve."

"Just as the bombing of our cities is hardening our resolve."

Wolff told himself: "You've got to stop needling him. Don't alienate your one contact here. What's got into you, Kurt Wolff?" But he wished Deussen had been in just one air-raid in Berlin.

"I hope you're right," Wolff said.

"I'm sure I'm right." Having won his point, Deussen relaxed again and told them that Heinrich Brandt had been in touch with him the previous day by radio. The exchange of prisoners was to be made at the front line just south of Bologna. Wolff and Otto Witt would then come north by rail with the prisoners as far as Parma. From there they would take the rail-link to La Spezia and then south to Rome.

"I don't see why we have to bother with the prisoners," Witt remarked. "Why don't we just head straight for Rome?"

The reason was simple. But you couldn't explain it to a dummy, Wolff thought. When the time came for the real run south the top Nazis would be fleeing in their thousands. Through Switzerland, Spain and Portugal en route to South America. And the British and Americans would be hunting them. A Red Cross official and a priest making their way to Rome on Vatican business would immediately be suspect. But not if they were once again accompanying the wounded from the battlefields of Northern Italy. But the next time the wounded would be Italians — the puppet dictator Mussolini's Fascist troops. They would be going south and with them would be an Italian priest, a German-speaking South Tyrolean priest.

"I'm not sure I know the answer to that," Deussen said when Wolff didn't reply.

Otto Witt looked at Wolff. "Well, why don't we?"

"Because I say so!" Wolff snapped.

"*Scheisse!*"

"That," Wolff said, "used to be a favourite expression of a friend of mine. I'd rather you didn't use it." He stood up. "I'm going for a walk."

At the door Wolff said to Deussen: "Don't let the bastard out of your sight."

The sky was studded with hard bright stars and the snow underfoot had been crisped by frost. The air was cold and sweet.

For an hour Wolff tramped the streets memorising them. One day in the near future, if there were any hitches, he might have to spend a long time here.

* * *

They flew to a landing strip north of the American 5th Army's line and left the Stork in a small corrugated-iron hangar.

They drove to the railway line where, in some sidings, two hospital trains were drawn up, one filled with seriously-wounded Germans, the other with Americans and British. When they arrived a head count was being carried out. A serious matter. You mustn't allow the enemy to have back one more legless man than yourselves.

German officers chatted and smoked cigarettes with Allied officers. They laughed and swopped names and addresses and, just for a moment, Wolff wondered why the hell they were fighting each other.

Wearing a Red Cross armband he joined the other officials supervising the exchange while Witt wandered up and down the train talking to bandaged, bleeding men. At least, Wolff thought, he was a good actor: a dying soldier wouldn't doubt that he was in the presence of a priest.

At midday the two trains moved off in opposite directions. By the time they reached Parma two men had died and Witt, who had studied his part, had administered last rites.

Twenty-four hours later they were on their way south in a snowstorm.

XXII

It was also snowing at Dachau when the prisoner named Landau made his first move.

The snow softened the hopeless scene, even blessed it with a certain desolate beauty; it also doubled the death-rate. Smoke rose steadily from the crematorium; in the watch-towers the guards tried to stamp the cold from their feet.

At 8.30 am a Lieutenant and a Sergeant carried out the weekly inspection of the billets. It was a duty that Untersturmführer Bruckner heartily detested; the smell for one thing, and the expressions of men who had given up all hope. Bruckner, once a clerk in a shipping office, got it over as quickly as possible, imposing a few statutory punishments, kicking over a couple of buckets.

On this bitter morning Bruckner moved through the billets quicker than ever. He was therefore considerably irritated when one of the prisoners spoke to him. "Untersturmführer."

Bruckner stopped. Prisoners did not address officers. He stared at the man standing in front of the three tiers of bunks; he was vaguely familiar; he must have been around a long time because that was the only reason that his features could have registered.

The prisoner handed him a piece of paper. Bruckner took it in astonishment. He read it, hesitated, and stuffed it into the pocket of his coat.

He turned to the Sergeant. "He wants to see the Commandant!"

The Sergeant laughed cautiously.

"No food for this man today."

Bruckner carried on briskly with his inspection but there was a thoughtful expression on his face.

Two days later he summoned Landau to his office. It was a Sunday and the office-block was almost empty. Landau stood in front of his desk.

Bruckner picked up the scrap of paper. "What is the meaning of this?" On the piece of paper Landau had written in German: I HAVE GOLD.

"What it says, Untersturmführer."

"And why should that interest me?"

"Everyone is interested in gold."

"And how the devil can you have gold here?"

"Not here, Untersturmführer. In a village in Bavaria. A lot of gold," he added, eyes fixed on the fleshy features of the young Lieutenant who was plagued with boils.

"But why are you telling me?"

Landau plunged in. He had rehearsed this moment for years: he mustn't fail.

"Soon," he said carefully, "Europe will be in total chaos. The Russians will be on the outskirts of Berlin; the British and Americans will be sweeping across Germany from the west."

"This is treasonable talk," Bruckner said, but he didn't stop Landau.

"With respect, Untersturmführer, it is the truth and we both know it. What," he asked softly, "do you think the *Amis* will do when they find camps like this?"

Bruckner shrugged. "Perhaps they won't find them. Perhaps we will burn them down — and all the people in them."

"Oh no, Untersturmführer, they will find out. You cannot destroy a decade of horror just like that. And, when they find out, they will execute those responsible. And not even a Lieutenant will escape their vengeance. But, if he had the resources . . ."

"Gold?"

"If he had the resources then he could escape. I don't

210

doubt," Landau said, "that hundreds, maybe thousands, are planning to escape at this moment."

"Where is this gold?"

"I can take you to it."

"You mean you want me to help you to escape?"

"It is the only way, Untersturmführer."

"You must be out of your mind!"

"Is that surprising?"

"You will pay for this," Bruckner said. He stood up and went to the door and shouted to an orderly who had been discreetly stationed at the end of the corridor. "Take this man back to his billet."

But Landau didn't pay for it. He was assigned to the kitchens where favoured prisoners could steal a little extra sustenance. He knew he had won the first round and he began to build up his body for what lay ahead.

* * *

In the cellar in Munich, Wenck, who had recovered from his injuries, consulted the latest report on Hitler's health.

He said to his prisoner: "Stand up."

Ziemann stood up. According to the report, the Führer suffered from attacks of palsy. There was nothing palsied about Ziemann. However, Wenck reflected, it wasn't important: you didn't look for palsy in a corpse.

"You'll do," he said to Ziemann.

"For God's sake, what is this all about?"

"You'll find out," Wenck said. "Quite soon now."

XXIII

Father Liam Doyle finished praying in the chapel that reminded him of his church in the Bronx and walked out into the bleak day.

It was ironic, he thought, but he missed the excitement of the German occupation. Here I am, a priest beseeching God to grant us everlasting peace, and yet I yearn for that time of adventure. Always the contradictions!

Liam still worked clandestinely but it was purely for the sake of Maria Reubeni. And that, surely, was wrong. Maria claimed she wanted to map out the Nazi escape routes before they arrived, but Liam knew that she meant one Nazi — and he knew what she planned to do to him.

He headed for The Vatican through streets which seemed to be dominated by G.I.'s on furlough. There weren't that many of them but, chomping cigars, chewing gum, clicking cameras, they seemed to be an occupying army even in civilian clothes. Rome didn't yet belong to the Romans. But, very soon, it would all be over and life would revert to normal. Liam Doyle wasn't sure that he looked forward to that day.

Once again he would be remote from the people, serving God amid the glittering, yet curiously remote, pageantry of The Vatican. A prisoner rather than a servant of religion.

He skirted a group of G.I.'s buying hot chestnuts. For a moment he wished he was one of them, as other men.

If only the Pope had utterly condemned the Nazi atrocities then I might accept my role in The Holy See. Liam recalled the

212

Pope's Christmas message:

There is a duty binding on everyone, a duty which can tolerate no post-ponement, delay, hesitation or reversal: namely to do everything possible to prohibit and outlaw definitely, aggressive war as a lawful solution of international disagreements and as an instrument of national aspira-tion . . .

Liam Doyle sighed. Postponement, delay, hesitation. Were these not the very qualities Eugenio Pacelli had displayed? Would the persecution of the Jews have been accelerated if he had spoken out? Could it have been any worse? Liam didn't doubt the sincerity of the Pope but if only he had shown . . . A phrase used by the partisani surfaced unsolicited and, shocked, Liam Doyle thrust it aside.

Now it was dusk, smelling of frost and knifed with cruelty, or so it seemed to Liam Doyle, as he mounted the stairs to Maria Reubeni's apartment.

*   *   *

Maria was sitting talking to an American wearing civilian clothes. An intelligence agent working for the Office of Strategic Services, according to Maria.

His name was Anderson. He was a Captain in the Army, in his early thirties, crew-cut with a lean, Red Indian face; he wore a blue mohair suit, slightly draped. Liam suspected that he was fond of Maria but it didn't worry him. Jealousy, dark and primeval, had only taken hold of him once — when he saw her with the man named Doppler. Frightening, sickening, as though forces beyond any known discipline were at work.

Maria had told him that Anderson was concerned with apprehending war criminals — before they escaped into neu-tral and sanctified havens where they couldn't be touched. That was how she had met the American.

Liam noticed a carton of Lucky Strikes on the coffee table. And two pairs of nylon stockings. The usual American service-man's payment for whatever favours that might be bestowed. In this case nothing more than information — and perhaps friendship — because these days Maria lived like a recluse.

"Sit down, Liam," Maria said.

Anderson, who had met Liam before, nodded at him politely. Not devastatingly pleased to see me, Liam thought, and smiled; a man like Anderson could never really accept the role of a priest in matters like this.

Maria said: "Liam has been a tower of strength during the German occupation. He knows as much about Vatican intrigue as anyone."

Anderson regarded him doubtfully. "Miss Reubeni has already told me what good work you did. May I ask why?"

"I should have thought that was obvious." Liam took the coffee that Maria had offered him and sipped it; better than any coffee he had tasted outside The Vatican for years. He assumed the source was Anderson.

"The Vatican and the Jews haven't always seen eye to eye," Anderson remarked.

"I think," Liam said, "that you are a little out of date. Where are you from?"

"Washington D.C.," Anderson told him.

"If you'd lived in the Bronx you might understand a little better."

"I didn't mean to offend, Father. I'm just finding my way around."

Maria said: "Captain Anderson wants us to give him a complete break-down of the bolt-holes the Germans will make for. Inside The Holy See, Vatican premises outside the boundaries and any other safe houses."

"I'll do my best to help," Liam said. "But I don't think Nazis will be very welcome in any places where Jews were harboured."

Maria had already briefed Liam: to give just so much away, no more.

"You may be right. But, after all, a House of God is open to everyone."

Maria said passionately: "But not to murderers."

"But the Church preaches forgiveness. Would a priest

really hand over a German to the authorities knowing that he would probably face execution?"

Maria turned to Liam. "Would you?"

"I suppose theoretically the priest would then be guilty of murder."

Maria looked at him in horror. "You mean to say —"

Liam held up his hand and said softly: "No, I would hand him over. You see, Captain Anderson, you haven't seen what we've seen."

"Supposing," Anderson said, "that he was not a criminal in the strict sense of the word. Just a man who considered that he had been carrying out his duty. Would you turn him in?"

Liam sighed. "I think I would," and wondered if even now he was telling the truth.

"You surprise me," Anderson said. Turning to Maria he said: "Please understand me, I know what you've been through. If I personally come across Otto Witt I will strangle him with my own hands. I merely wanted to sound out Father Doyle here on the attitude of the Roman Catholic Church to these men when they arrive. And, believe me, they will arrive." He stood up, lean and straight, and said: "Would it trouble you too much to prepare me a dossier on what you know? I believe a certain Father O'Flaherty will be able to help. Now he was quite extraordinary. You know, he hated the British and yet he helped them."

"Father O'Flaherty is an extraordinary man," Liam said.

*   *   *

Heinrich Brandt cut into his fillet steak with displeasure. It was tough and overdone. If his new man didn't improve he would have to get rid of him. And what a wailing and gnashing of teeth there would be then because the fear of all domestic staff was to be ejected from The Vatican to the hard realities of life outside its walls.

He pushed the steak aside and tackled the sauté potatoes and sprouts. Eatable but without style. Brandt sighed and poured himself a glass of Chianti; he preferred German or French vintages because there wasn't much to be said for Italian wine except its high alcoholic content. But stocks were running low, the war affected everyone.

Brandt glanced at the clock on the wall. If all had gone well Wolff and his companion should be somewhere between No Man's Land in the north and Rome. The dummy run ... such Germanic preparation and precision. Perhaps that had been their undoing in the war. But no, even Brandt had to reluctantly admit that the Führer, like Napoleon before him, had underestimated the Russians.

Brandt's worship of Hitler was founded in the little town of Landsberg fifty miles west of Munich where Hitler had been imprisoned after the abortive putsch in November 1923. Brandt, then a young archaeologist had also been flirting with National Socialism. It was his good fortune to have been arrested and sent to Landsberg at the same time as Hitler.

He had become hypnotised by him; those mesmeric eyes, the rhetoric, the idealism, the ruthless undercurrents. And he had been privileged to attend Hitler's 35th birthday celebrations in Room No. 7 — conditions were far from stringent — where Hitler was to write *Mein Kampf.*

Once he had been closeted alone with Hitler and Rudolf Hess, and Hitler had said: "I hear that you once had ideas about entering the Church."

Brandt had looked at him in surprise. He seemed to know everything about the private lives of the other forty political prisoners. Brandt admitted it was true. Like so many other young people he had been wandering among the ruins of World War I looking for a faith. The Church had attracted him, so had National Socialism.

Hitler had said: "I admire the Catholic Church. Its power, its organisation. It has no place in my scheme of things but nevertheless there is a lot to be learned from it, from the Jesuits in particular. Don't lose sight of the Church, Herr Brandt."

Twelve years later, after his recruitment into the SS, a Major had produced his file and said: "I see you were once interested in Catholicism. It has been suggested by a higher authority than me that you take Holy Orders." And the officer explained why.

In 1939, when Pius XII was elected Pope, Brandt was posted to The Vatican as an adviser in archaeology. Brandt often wondered if the Führer himself had played any part in his appointment. Fervently he hoped so when he remembered the young man with the hypnotic eyes who had emerged from imprisonment to make the Fatherland great again.

When Brandt remembered the early days he recalled how slim and supple he had once been. His appetite, he believed, was a substitute for sex — not that he had observed total celibacy — aggravated by his enforced absence from Germany. But he wasn't alone in his hedonism: Hermann Göring had been among those who had marched on November 9th, 1923, and look at him!

Brandt finished his supper and opened the wall-safe behind a painting of the Crucifixion. He removed a black file and studied the documents inside it. Details of all the routes and hiding places that would be used by the escaping Nazis. All very efficiently executed by Kruger the librarian. But not sufficient for Brandt's own purposes: he needed an exclusive bolt-hole. And he thought he knew how he could find it.

As an archaeologist he had handed over all his information about The Vatican grottos and catacombs to Kruger; if he hadn't the Jesuit's suspicions would have been aroused. But, in the latter days of the German occupation, Father O'Flaherty had been smuggling refugees into The Vatican through a route which Brandt had been unable to find. The Jews had known about it. Therefore the Jewess, Maria Reubeni, had known about it. Therefore Father Liam Doyle had known about it.

Brandt took a small envelope from the black file, put the file back in the wall-safe, replaced the painting of the Crucifixion and, carrying his tape-recorder, went out into the night to find Liam Doyle.

*   *   *

217

Liam had just returned from his visit to Maria Reubeni when Brandt knocked on the door of his room. He was kneeling on the threadbare carpet warming his hands in front of the gas-fire.

"Who is it?"

"Heinrich Brandt."

Liam stood up puzzled. He glanced around the room but there was nothing incriminating on view. He opened the door and Brandt came in rubbing his hands. "It's as cold as charity out there," he remarked. "Ah, but charity is your business. No offence, Father."

"What can I do for you?" Liam asked.

"How about a cup of tea to warm the cockles of my heart?" Brandt shivered. "It's almost as cold in here as it is outside."

"You can't expect central heating when all over Europe people are dying of the cold."

"I suppose you're right," Brandt said sitting down on a rickety, stiff-backed chair. "But how about some tea?"

"I was just going to turn in," Liam said.

"This early?" Brandt consulted his wrist-watch. "It's only nine o'clock. And in any case," he said, "I have something very important to discuss with you."

Liam shrugged. "Very well." He lit the gas-ring and put on the kettle.

Brandt said: "You really should look after yourself better than this. After all, you can't be expected to carry out God's work in these conditions."

"I'm quite comfortable," Liam said, regarding the plump monk with distaste.

"Ah, perhaps you have other creature comforts to compensate?"

"I've no idea what you're getting at," pouring scalding water into the teapot, "and if you have something to say I wish you'd get to the point."

"All in good time. All in good time."

Brandt laid the tape-recorder on the bed and checked the spool.

"What in heaven's name have you brought that for?"

"I have a proposition to put to you," sipping his tea. "I want you to listen to me very carefully and not to make any rash decisions." He smacked his lips. "Do you have a little more sugar?"

Liam poured more sugar into his cup from a twist of paper. "Now please get to the point. I'm feeling very tired."

"Very well. But you would never have made a diplomat."

"That doesn't disturb me," Liam said.

"The Holy Father is a consummate diplomat."

"I happen to think there are more important functions in the Church than diplomacy."

Brandt said: "You haven't by any chance any biscuits?"

Liam shook his head.

Brandt put his cup down beside him. "Listen carefully," he said.

He told Liam that he was aware of his activities with the Jews. Of his liaison with Father O'Flaherty and Father Benedetto — "If you remember we met outside his front door."

None of this surprised Liam. "So? It's all over now. The Jews were saved with the blessing of the Holy Father."

"It's not quite over," Brandt said. "You see there are others who will want to find sanctuary here."

"You mean Nazis?"

"I mean Germans who fought a war in which they believed. Germans who, now that they have lost, will have to escape the wrath of their enemies. Self-survival is no crime."

"But *they* have committed crimes."

"According to which side you were on. A victor must have his scapegoats and many who merely did what they believed to be their duty will be executed or, at the best, incarcerated for years to come."

"I don't see how any of this concerns me."

"Would you condemn a man, any man, to a firing squad, to the noose, to the executioner's axe, Father?"

Twice in the same evening, Liam reflected, recalling Anderson's questions. "It depends on the circumstances," frowning

219

as Brandt chuckled and said: "So you *are* something of a diplomat, Father."

"You said you had something important to say."

"I have. I suggest that if a German should come to you seeking refuge then you should treat him in the same way that you treated the Jews."

Liam paced the room, cup of tea in his hands, before replying: "I couldn't do that."

"Why not? We're all God's children."

"Some of God's children have committed crimes outside the comprehension of religion."

"So did the Jews. But Christ forgave them." He handed his empty cup to Liam. "Is there a little more in the pot?" And as Liam refilled his cup: "Well, let me put it to you this way. I know perfectly well that you and Father O'Flaherty have a secret entry into The Vatican. Would it offend your ethics too much if you shared your secret with me? Then, you see, you wouldn't be directly involved."

"Why don't you ask Father O'Flaherty?"

"Because he would probably knock my head off."

"What makes you think I won't?"

Brandt sighed. "You make it very difficult. You see I shall have to resort to other devices. I'm not a hypocritical man and, quite simply, the device is blackmail."

Liam stared at him in astonishment. "Blackmail?"

"You have been rather indiscreet, Father."

A terrible sickness suddenly descended on Liam Doyle. "How do you mean, indiscreet?" as Brandt said: "I think you know, Father," handing Liam the envelope.

Liam's hand shook as he opened the envelope because Brandt was right: he did know.

The first photograph was innocuous enough. He and Maria Reubeni walking down a street somewhere in Rome.

But Liam guessed it was merely to whet the appetite. The second photograph showed them in earnest conversation outside a newspaper kiosk. The photograph must have been taken with a long-distance lens because there were other people in the picture and none seemed aware of a photographer.

The third jolted Liam with an almost physical force. He felt the blood drain from his face; he sat down on the edge of the bed and put his head between his knees.

The photograph was innocent enough — if you weren't a priest. It showed Maria kissing him. Liam remembered the kiss, two in fact, one on each cheek, in the grounds of the Villa Borghese. But the camera angle was such that she seemed to be kissing him on the lips.

He raised his head as the blood flowed back. "And you a man of God . . ."

Brandt's voice was impersonal, professional. "There are more, Father."

Liam wiped the sweat from his forehead with the back of his hand and looked at the next photograph. There he was entering Maria's apartment block, Maria just in front of him. And then there he was leaving the apartment. The implications were obvious. The sequence had been put together with professional expertise.

"You filthy scum."

"I'm sorry," Brandt said, "but you have forced my hand. And," he said, "I'm afraid there's more."

"More? What more can there be?"

The answer came from the tape-recorder. Brandt plugged it into a wall-socket. The spool with the carefully-edited tape began to revolve.

"Maria, my love . . . What have I done . . . ? Please, Lord, forgive me . . ."

It went on repetitively, sickeningly. Until Liam leaped to his feet and snatched the spool from the tape-recorder. The tape unwound around his feet like a treacherous serpent; the spool continued to rotate with a faint whirring noise.

Brandt said: "You needn't bother to destroy it. I have another recording."

Liam stared at him, shuddering uncontrollably. "How long has this been going on?"

"Some months I'm afraid."

221

"How could anyone do this? Eavesdropping on a man's prayers to God. How?" Liam's voice rose to a scream. "You don't work for God, you work for the Devil."

Brandt began to rewind the spool. "Come now, don't be hysterical. Every priest in the land listens to confessions. In this case I didn't consult you."

"I was talking to God."

"And to me, I'm afraid."

"But I've done nothing wrong. I have nothing to confess."

"Then why did you?"

"We all suffer temptations. I overcame them."

"Not according to the evidence," Brandt said. "But come now, don't get so agitated. No one need know. Just you and me. Provided . . ."

"I give you the information you want? Never!"

Brandt shrugged and picked up the photographs. "Do you want these? I have plenty more."

"Get out," Liam shouted. "Get out or, as God is my witness, I'll kill you."

"I doubt it," Brandt said. "I may be a little on the, ah, plump side but I have been trained in unarmed combat."

"Get out!"

"Then I have no alternative. I shall have to hand over the evidence to the appropriate authorities."

"Do what you like with them."

Brandt picked up the tape-recorder and walked to the door. "And not only the authorities."

Liam stared at him uncomprehendingly.

"I think your parents and some of your little flock in New York would be most interested to see the photographs and hear the tapes."

He closed the door behind him.

* * *

For nearly an hour Liam paced around the small room, sometimes with his hands clenched, sometimes with head buried in

222

his hands. What had he done? He knelt to pray. Then realised that he might still be sharing his prayers with Brandt.

He tore the mattress and pillows from the bed, looked behind pictures, under the carpet, behind books. It took him ten minutes to locate the microphone in the bedside-lamp. He ripped it out and smashed it to pieces on the floor.

At 10.30 pm he put on his coat and left the room. For an hour he walked the streets without seeing or hearing. He strode without direction, and yet some instinct must have been guiding him because just after 11.30 pm he found himself outside Maria Reubeni's apartment. He went up the stairs and knocked on the door. It didn't matter who heard. Nothing mattered any more.

He heard her voice from the other side of the door. "Who is it?"

"It's me, Liam. Please let me in."

She unlocked the door. "Liam, what on earth . . ."

He shut the door behind him. "Have you got a drink?"

"Yes, of course. But you look terrible. What's happened?" She handed him a glass of cognac.

Liam gulped it, coughed, retched.

"Here, take it easy. Sit down. What's happened?"

"Do you have any more?"

"Of course. But do you think you should?"

Liam nodded, his eyes wild. She poured him another cognac, smaller this time. "Drink it more slowly. Then tell me what's happened. But take your time."

In between sips of brandy, Liam told her about the meeting with Brandt.

"The bastard," she said when he had finished. "Oh the bastard." She had never before sworn in Liam's presence; she didn't apologise. She took Liam's hand. "And it's all my fault. I didn't realise . . ."

"It's not your fault, it's mine. All mine."

"I didn't know that you prayed about me."

"I thought only God knew that."

"I'm so terribly sorry." She smoothed his tousled hair. "I

223

suppose I did know how you felt. But a priest . . ."

"It doesn't matter," Liam said. "Nothing matters."

When she came back with the coffee he had recovered a little as the brandy went to work. She poured them both black coffee. She was very thoughtful. "And what are you going to do?" she said after a while.

"Do? Nothing. I may have sinned —" pausing as she interrupted: "But you haven't, Liam," and then continuing: "But it would only make the sins worse if I gave into a man like that. It would be a confession of guilt."

"Guilt? But you aren't guilty of anything, Liam. Your feelings for me . . ." she groped for words, " . . . nothing has ever happened. We're all tempted, but you overcame temptation."

"Can you imagine that tape being played in the Bronx?"

"That worries you more than The Vatican?"

"Of course. That's the closest I've ever been to the true meaning of religion."

Maria, wearing a pink dressing-gown over her nightdress, stood up and faced Liam. "You've got to tell him about the very last route we used. Not O'Flaherty's — our own."

"Tell him? Just to save my own face?" Liam shook his head.

"Not to save your face, Liam. Now listen to me — don't you realise that Brandt has played right into our hands?"

The brandy glowed inside Liam; he felt more confused than ever, but the confusion had a mellow quality that he hadn't experienced before.

Maria explained. If Liam revealed the one bolt-hole unknown to the Germans inside The Vatican then that was the one they would use. "We will know exactly which way they will come and we will catch them." *We will have Otto Witt.*

"I suppose you're right," words sliding into each other. "I didn't think of it that way." His eyelids felt heavy.

"So you must go to Brandt and tell him. Tell him the truth. Then, just think of it, Liam, no one will hear the tapes, no one will see the photographs. Everything is going to be all right." And, softly: "Trust me."

He smiled at her. "When you talk like that I know everything will be all right."

"And now go to sleep." She brought a blanket from her bedroom, hitched his legs onto the sofa and covered him with the blanket.

"I must get back ..."

"You'd fall into the Tiber."

Just before he fell asleep he opened his eyes and asked: "Would things have been different if I hadn't been a priest?"

"You know they would," she said.

The smile was still on his face as he slept.

*　　*　　*

Next morning Liam visited Brandt in his apartment.

Brandt looked at him speculatively. You could never tell what the Irish might do. "Well, Father?"

Liam spread his hands hopelessly. "I can't face the disgrace."

Brandt's eyes twinkled. "I knew you would see commonsense, my son. Coffee?"

"I don't want your coffee. It disgusts me even to be in your presence."

"Very well. No one's perfect. Now tell me everything you know."

So Liam told him.

XXIV

They could hear the occasional crack of a sniper's rifle, sporadic bursts of machine-gun fire and, from time to time, the roar of a mortar.

When it seemed to be getting closer Witt shrank back in the passenger seat of the old, 1938-vintage Volkswagen with the red crosses on doors and roof.

"For God's sake," Wolff said, "you must have been under fire before."

Witt didn't reply.

They had left the train near La Spezia on the north-west coast of Italy and were heading towards the Gothic Line where the Allied advance had been halted by winter. It was snowing lightly, just enough to blurr a gunner's vision.

"I doubt if anyone will be able to see the red crosses when we go across," Wolff remarked cheerfully.

"We'll have to wait till it stops snowing."

"No such luck. We cross at a fixed time agreed by the Germans and Americans."

"We can change the time."

"And run the risk of the Americans changing their minds? No, my friend."

"We should have flown straight in," Witt said sullenly.

"And been shot down?"

"I think this job has been botched."

Wolff stopped the car. "*Raus!* I'm sure we can find at least a few Gestapo here."

226

"For Christ's sake, drive on," Witt said as a mortar exploded a hundred yards away tossing snow and earth into the air.

Wolff put the Volkswagen into gear and they moved off. Three minutes later they stopped at a small hotel bordered on one side by barbed wire, slit trenches, concrete anti-tank blocks and a pill-box. Hidden in the trees to one side of the hotel were the tanks: Wolff could feel their presence.

Wolff went into the hotel, showing his papers and pass to the shivering sentry outside.

A young Captain looked up from a table in what had been the lounge of the hotel. The windows were boarded up and the floor was littered with broken glass and debris. He looked very tired.

"Herr Doppler?"

Wolff nodded and began the normal courtesies but the young Captain brushed them aside. "Don't waste your breath. You have ten minutes to get across, then we start firing again. It must be very important to halt a war for as long as that. However, I have my orders from Berlin . . ."

"It is very important," Wolff said, nodding towards Witt hunched in the Volkswagen. "It's a message from the Führer to the Pope."

The Captain didn't appear to be impressed. "The Americans won't give you safe conduct if you're carrying a dispatch from Hitler."

"They will," Wolff told him, "if the message is the Fuhrer's reply to peace proposals from The Vatican." He paused. "They've agreed to a cease-fire, haven't they?"

The Captain nodded. "They have." They both listened. The only sound was the creak of a broken shutter. "You'd better be on your way, Herr Doppler. Give my regards to the Pope. And the crow out there," pointing at Witt.

Snow was still falling as Wolff drove the Volkswagen, a white flag fluttering from its bonnet, across No Man's Land.

"How long have we got?" Witt asked.

"Ten minutes."

227

"Put your foot down."

"And drive into that!" Wolff said as he braked on the lip of a shell-hole. He backed up and gingerly skirted the crater.

They were half way between the two lines when a machine-gun opened up.

"Get out," Wolff snapped.

They threw themselves face down beside the road as bullets whipped up a line of white feathers in front of them.

"You'd better pray, Father," Wolff said.

But Witt's face was pressed into the snow.

The firing was coming from behind them. German gunners. Communications were even worse than they had been in Russia. "You stay there," Wolff said. "Don't move," as though there was the slightest likelihood of Otto Witt moving an inch.

Wolff crawled back to the Volkswagen and wiped away the snow covering the red crosses. Then he began to back up the car in the direction of the shooting.

The shooting stopped. Wolff turned the car so that they could see the crosses and shouted in German: "Red Cross. Get on your field telephone. You stupid bastards," he added in a whisper.

He waited a couple of minutes. Then cautiously turned the car and inched forward. The machine-gun was silent. He accelerated, picked up Witt and headed for the American lines.

The American field HQ was a village school. An American Captain wearing a steel helmet and battle-dress sat in front of a blackboard on which the presumed German positions had been drawn in red and blue chalk.

The Captain, thirty-ish with a freckled face, was reading a document on which Wolff could see the word VATICANO in black letters. At the bottom was the signature; it looked like Brandt's.

"Could you please identify yourselves. You'd better bring Father Hahn in here as well." Wolff decided that his accent was mid-western; he looked like a farmer.

Wolff brought Witt in. Somehow he had managed to convert the evidence of debauchery into the stamp of suffering.

They handed the Captain their documents. He read them carefully and then said to Wolff: "I visited Zurich before the war. Quite a city."

Wolff nodded; he had been there once.

"There used to be a great little bar near the railroad station . . ."

"The Limmat," Wolff said wondering if there was such a bar; there was certainly a river of that name.

The Captain frowned. "That sure rings a bell . . ."

"There are more banks than bars," Wolff said quickly.

"You can say that again." The Captain picked up Witt's papers. "Innsbruck, huh?"

Wolff prayed that the Captain hadn't visited Innsbruck.

"I guess I never got there," he said. And to Witt: "You're doing a great job, Father. As a matter of fact I'm a Catholic."

"Practising?" Witt asked in German.

"What did he say?" the Captain asked Wolff.

"He asked if you were a practising Catholic."

"I used to be. Not much time these days for church-going." He grinned and looked very young. "Well, I wish you both luck in your mission. If you can help to bring about peace the world will be eternally grateful."

He stared through the window at the falling snow and Wolff guessed that he was seeing a cornfield in the mid-west rippling in the breeze. He would have like to stay and talk to him: but there wasn't time and, in any case, he was afraid that Witt would make a mistake.

"Coffee, gentlemen?"

"It would only delay the possibility of peace." Wolff held out his hand. "It's been pleasant meeting you, Captain."

The Captain stood up. "May God be with you," he said awkwardly and sat down again.

Three minutes later Wolff was driving through enemy-occupied Italy.

*   *   *

On the way Wolff checked out two of the staging posts for the final journey. A monastery south of Pisa and a church between Montalto and Viterbo.

Everything seemed to be in order; the good priests had been briefed — and paid — by Brandt. Both places contained deep cellars sealed by heavy doors with keys as big as rolling pins.

At 4.39 pm, five days after leaving Berlin, Wolff and Otto Witt entered the city of Rome.

But, instead of making for The Vatican, they headed straight for the church of S. Maria dell' Anima where the Nazi bishop, Hudal, held court.

*　　*　　*

The Most Reverend Alois Hudal was in buoyant mood.

For months he had been brooding about the failure of his scheme to unite America, Britain and Germany against the Russians. The scheme was simple: Hitler would halt the persecution of the Jews and the Church if the Allies joined his crusade against the Bolsheviks.

The scheme had certainly got as far as Dr. Josef Goebbels, Hitler's propaganda minister, through an intermediary, Dr. Waldemar Meyer, an SS intelligence agent who made frequent visits to Rome. And, according to Meyer, Goebbels had been receptive. For his own purposes, Hudal now realised — Goebbels was conducting an anti-Bolshevik campaign and could do with some anti-Communist comments from Pius XII.

Meyer claimed that Hitler had been handed an emasculated version of the plan. Anyway he had turned it down. The Pope had never known anything about it. Which was all to the good now, Hudal realised, because it would only have served to further fray his own relationship with Pacelli.

Hudal now knew about Brandt's secret plan. He was overwhelmed, overjoyed. Not only would he be helping run-of-the-mill Nazis to escape: he would be helping Hitler himself. To have the Fuhrer in his own church!

Before the arrival of Wolff and Otto Witt the bishop had

been told by Brandt that the plan was known only to the two of them — and Wolff. No one else — certainly not Witt — must ever know.

Brandt had also given Hudal a list of names of leading Nazis who would be sought by the victors. "The list comes from a good source," Brandt had told them. "It's the Allies' own wanted list."

Beside some of the names were black crosses. These were the men who would travel via Rome. Among them, Hudal noticed Martin Bormann, Adolf Eichmann, head of the Jewish Office of the Gestapo, Gruppenfuhrer Heinrich Muller, head of the Gestapo, and Otto von Waechter, the SS Vice-Governor of Poland, who in July, 1934, led the Nazis who broke into the Viennese Chancellery and murdered the Austrian Chancellor, Englebert Dolfuss.

Some of the refugees — if you could call the Führer a refugee — would be housed in the German College where, ironically, British and American POW's had been harboured. They would stay there, on neutral territory, until the first fury of the witch-hunt died down.

Others, less notorious in the Allies' eyes, would hide in the students' pensione at S. Maria dell' Anima and the Collegio Croatia on the Piazza Colunna. Some would find safety at the headquarters of the PCA, the Pontificia Commissione Assistenza (for which Father Liam Doyle worked), which was to be located at the Villa Bonaparte where the German Embassy to The Holy See had once been housed.

Hudal already had his man established at the Papal Assistance Commission. He was a former priest who had become a Sergeant in the paratroopers; now he was a priest again and it was he who would liaise with the department of The Holy See responsible for issuing refugee documents and identity certificates. Luckily the Nazis were also in possession of 10,000 blank Argentine passports provided by Juan Peron.

There was no difficulty about money. Funds for the great escape had already been lodged in numbered accounts in Switzerland. When the Allied purge had lost momentum the Nazis, mostly disguised as priests, some as Red Cross officials, would be shipped from Naples or Genoa to Barcelona and thence to South America. There they would build the foundations of the Fourth Reich. And among them would be the Führer.

Apparently the dummy run had been successful. There in front of him sat the first SS officer to escape, Otto Witt, a somewhat depraved looking young man wearing a clerical collar. But, Alois Hudal comforted himself, depravity was contagious and somewhere during the brutalising experience of war Otto Witt had been exposed to it. Life in Rome would soon cleanse his soul.

One climactic step remained: the transfer of Witt to his hiding place. As yet Brandt hadn't elaborated. Hudal looked at him expectantly, but Brandt said nothing. Nor did Wolff, a fine-looking young man, the personification of Aryan manhood, who had first been introduced to him as a German-Swiss named Doppler.

Hudal asked: "When do we make the next move?"

"Tomorrow night," Brandt told him. "Can Witt spend tonight in the pensione?"

"Of course. And Herr Wolff?"

"He can stay where he likes. At his old hotel. After all it makes no difference to a Swiss whether the Germans or Americans are in occupation."

They were seated in Hudal's study. And, as it was apparent that he wasn't as yet going to share the secret, Hudal suggested coffee.

Brandt shook his head. "We must be off. There is a lot to be done."

Hudal was disappointed. He would have liked to chat with Wolff and Otto Witt. To hear about their experiences fighting the Russian barbarians who threatened to overwhelm Christianity.

Brandt said to Wolff: "I suggest we leave separately. There is no need to arouse unnecessary suspicion. We've been seen together inside The Vatican in the past. If we were seen emerging together from here . . ."

232

They arranged to meet at the church next morning at 11 am.

Wolff made for the hotel near The Vatican where he had previously stayed. First he bathed to rid himself of the dust of travel — and the smell of Witt. He put on his grey suit, white shirt and blue tie. Then he headed for the Golden Gate café.

XXV

It was O'Flaherty who first reported that Hans Doppler was back in town. He knew ten minutes after Wolff booked into the hotel. The receptionist, who had been on O'Flaherty's payroll, called him at The Vatican.

O'Flaherty strolled round to Liam Doyle's room. "Your man's back," he said.

"Which man?"

"The German who said he was Swiss. Hans Doppler, remarkably friendly with Brandt as I recall it."

Depression pricked with jealously immediately settled on Liam. "How do you know?"

"One of my boys telephoned."

When O'Flaherty had gone, Liam sat brooding. He was sorely tempted not to tell Maria. But temptation was created to be overcome. After a while he put on his overcoat and went to Maria Reubeni's apartment. But he took his time.

When he told her that Doppler was back he was pained by the sudden animation on her face. It was as though she had emerged from hibernation. "I thought you would want to know," he said.

But she barely heard him. She was looking in a mirror, pushing at her hair with long fingers, considering the clothes she was wearing. "Yes, Liam, thank you." She went into the bedroom where she pulled clothes from a chest of drawers, holding a grey woollen dress to her body.

Liam let himself out of the apartment and, outside on the

landing, faintly heard her call "Goodbye, Liam," as though he were some casual acquaintance who had called with a message.

An hour later, bathed and perfumed, wearing the grey dress beneath the old Persian lamb fur coat which had once been her mother's and still retained a little faded glory, Maria left the apartment, leaving a note on the door for Anderson who was to have taken her to dinner.

She caught a taxi to the Golden Gate café. Wolff, who had given up hope of seeing her that night, was standing on the other side of the Via Veneto looking for a cab. He ran across the road and climbed into the taxi which Maria had just vacated, and told the driver to take him to Hudal's church.

* * *

At 11.30 pm Maria Reubeni gave up. She hailed a taxi, more plentiful these days, and told the driver to take her to the hotel where Doppler had stayed on his previous visit.

Without consulting the register the receptionist confirmed that Herr Doppler was staying there. He had gone out several hours ago and hadn't returned.

Maria considered leaving a note. But no, it would spoil the electric moment of their meeting.

She thanked the receptionist who was just going off duty and returned home in the waiting taxi. She would, she decided, come to the hotel at 9 o'clock the next morning.

* * *

Wolff had just finished shaving when he heard the knock. He dried his face with a towel and opened the door. Outside stood Otto Witt.

"What in God's name are you doing here?"

Witt, still dressed as a priest, pushed his way into the room and shut the door behind him. "I'm not going through with it," he said.

"What do you mean, you're not going through with it?"

235

Witt sat on the chair in front of the dressing-table, his old arrogance rekindled. "Just that, I quit."

Cold anger gripped Wolff. "I told you to stay in the pensione."

"The days when you give me orders are over. You seem to forget that I out-rank you, Hauptsturmführer."

Wolff reached under his pillow and produced the Walther. "I'm taking you back."

"Put that thing away. You can't afford to go shooting people in quiet little hotels near The Vatican."

Wolff sat down on the bed facing Witt. "Why the change of heart, Obersturmbannführer?"

"Because I have no intention of being confined in The Vatican murmuring Hail Mary's. You forget that I was in Rome. I have friends among the Italian Fascists. They will put me up. You see," Witt said, patting the pocket of his black top-coat, "Hudal has given me all the papers I need. I have a complete new identity. I'm free to walk the streets of Rome without being shut up like a monk."

"Why did you bother to come and tell me?"

"Because I wanted to see the expression on your face. I wanted to tell you what a sanctimonious shit I think you are."

"Very well," Wolff said, "now you've said it," reaching for the telephone beside the bed.

"What are you doing?"

"Making a few calls. I should think you will be picked up within the hour."

The arrogance began to deflate. "Who are you calling?"

"The Americans. The first SS escapee to be picked up. Quite a catch." His hand rested on the receiver. "Every Fascist sympathiser is known to them, thanks to the partisans, so I wouldn't go to them if I were you. I'll furnish the Americans with a full description — you're quite outstanding in a repugnant sort of way — and I'll tell them about those scars on your body. That must have been quite an orgy. What's more," Wolff said, picking up the receiver, "I'll tell the Jews; A few of them have arrived from Palestine and they'll be hunting people like you for decades to come. I wouldn't care to be in your shoes if they pick you up, especially if they've visited the Ardeantine Caves." He said to the switchboard operator: "Get me Allied military headquarters."

But Witt had launched himself across the room. He grabbed the receiver. "Cancel that call," he told the operator, and to Wolff: "You win, I'll do it your way."

"Very well," Wolff said. "When I've finished dressing I'm taking you back to the church."

He dressed quickly, slipped the Walther into the pocket of his tan rain-coat and pushed Witt out of the door.

They were stepping out of the elevator in the hotel foyer when Maria Reubeni walked through the swing doors.

She stared first at Wolff and her face began to light up. Wolff would always remember that first fleeting expression on her face.

Then she took in Otto Witt.

Her face looked puzzled as she grappled with the double impact. One hand darted to her mouth.

She said: "You!" but Wolff never knew which of them she meant.

She took a step forward and said again: "You."

Wolff said: "Maria," and Otto Witt said: "I think I know —" but Wolff rounded on him: "Shut your mouth."

"The two of you," she said as realisation hit her. "Oh my God!"

For a fraction of a second the three of them stood frozen in the foyer of the hotel.

Then she turned. Moaned. Stumbled. And was gone through the swing doors.

*　　*　　*

Liam Doyle, motivated by a brooding jealousy which he didn't try to conceal, called at Maria's apartment at 10.30 am.

She opened the door, said: "Hallo, Liam," and sat down on the sofa. She sat there without speaking, hands tightly clenched, staring in front of her.

Liam said: "What's the matter, Maria?"

She hardly seemed to hear him.

"Shall I make some coffee?"

"If you wish."

Liam made coffee in the tiny kitchen, occasionally glancing into the lounge. But Maria hadn't moved. She seemed to be in a state of shock, face ashen, eyes staring.

He handed her a cup of black coffee. She took it and put it on the table.

"Maria?"

She looked at him. "Yes, Liam?"

"Please tell me what's the matter. Perhaps I can help you."

"No one can help me."

He sat in front of her. "You must never say that," pushing the coffee towards her.

She sipped the hot black coffee. Then she put the cup down and wept uncontrollably.

Liam watched her in anguish but he knew better than to comfort her. So he waited until she had spent herself.

When it was over she went into the bathroom. When she returned she had bathed her face and her features were composed. "I'm sorry," she said.

"Don't be. I only want to help."

"He's back," she said.

"Who's back?"

"Otto Witt, the man who killed my father and looted his shop."

"And Doppler?"

"He was with him."

"So he's —"

"SS."

Liam was silent. He understood.

She glanced at her wrist-watch. "We know which way they'll go — we gave Brandt the route."

Liam said: "Listen to me, Maria. You must not take this into your own hands." He wanted to say: "Thou shalt not kill," but

238

it would have sounded incongruous. "We must tell the authorities."

She looked at him steadily. "No, Liam. This is something I have to do. I don't ask you to understand. But please, don't tell the authorities. If you do, whatever it is we have between us will cease to exist."

He bowed his head.

Then she said: "Please go now, Liam." She touched his cheek with a cold hand. "Don't worry, everything will be all right."

When he had gone she put on the Persian-lamb coat, took the Beretta the Sicilian had given her from a drawer, checked to see if it was loaded, slipped it into her handbag and left the apartment.

*   *   *

The secret route revealed by Liam Doyle to Heinrich Brandt was really no secret at all. In fact Brandt admitted to himself that he had been blinded by the obvious. It was the *passetto*, the historic escape route through which, among others, Clement VII fled from The Vatican during the sack of Rome in 1527.

It was a narrow, brick-paved corridor a quarter of a mile long surmounted by an open-air, fortified passage. It led from the gardens of The Vatican to the Castel Sant' Angelo, the great rotunda of a fortress on the banks of the Tiber whose dungeons had once rung to the cries of incarcerated prisoners.

If you had the contacts in the castle, latterly a tourist attraction, it wasn't difficult to enter the *passetto*. Nor, in the days of the German occupation, was it difficult to get out through the gardens of The Holy See: the ranks of the Papal guards had been swelled by refugee Jews and it was a simple matter to post a Jewish guard, armed with the keys, at the exit to the *passetto*.

Brandt had no German sympathisers within the Guard. Instead he bribed two of them with Allied lire, pointing out that helping a refugee in no way contradicted their oath to defend the Pope with their lives. With the help of more Allied lire he also obtained duplicates of the keys to the castle which were copied by a locksmith in one of the little streets between the Tiber and the Piazza Navona.

He planned to smuggle Otto Witt through the *passetto* at midnight.

*　　*　　*

It was 11.55 pm. Moonlight silvered the waters of the Tiber and polished the bronze angel on top of the Castel Sant' Angelo.

Maria waited in a Fiat 500 that she had borrowed from Anderson. There was an American pennant on the bonnet and no one bothered her. She had waited a long time. But she hadn't given up hope. She knew he would come.

At the stroke of midnight a black Mercedes drew up by the Piazza Pia which flanks the castle on one side. Three men got out, one in a tan raincoat, the other two in black coats, clerical collars gleaming in the moonlight.

Maria stepped out of the car. She held her handbag in her left hand; her right hand was inside it gripping the butt of the Beretta.

She was twenty-five yards away from them when she called out: "Herr Witt" because she wanted to see his face as he died.

Witt spun round. The Beretta was now out of her bag pointing at his startled white face.

Her finger was squeezing the trigger when Liam Doyle hurled himself from behind an empty parked car shouting: "No, Maria, no!"

Shocked, she hesitated for a moment. The hesitation gave him enough time to reach her. He slashed down with one arm knocking the Beretta onto the ground.

And yet there was an explosion.

Maria and Liam stared as Witt doubled up, hands clawing at his stomach. And then another explosion from the Walther in Wolff's hand. The second bullet took Witt between the eyes.

*　　*　　*

Two days later the scarred body of a naked man was fished from the Tiber. The man had died from two bullet wounds, one in the belly and one in the head. It excited little comment because the Tiber was a common dumping ground for the victims of partisani vengeance.

XXVI

On February 13th, 1945, Kurt Wolff became one of Adolf Hitler's special bodyguards: an appointment which raised no eyebrows because he was a member of the Leibstandarte, Hitler's original bodyguard, he had an excellent war record and his loyalty to the Führer was unswerving.

The appointment was arranged by Sepp Dietrich and Harzer and it excited no comment from Heinrich Himmler who was now occupied with military as well as police duties, having been put in command of the Army Group Vistula.

Wolff was also promoted to Major.

When he reported to the Reich Chancellery in Berlin — Hitler had moved there from his Adlehorst HQ in the Taunus Mountains on January 15th — the end was in sight.

On the Eastern Front the Russians were on the banks of the Oder, 40 miles from Berlin; on the Western Front, the Allies — Americans, British, Canadians, Free French — were on the banks of the Rhine poised to cut off the Ruhr and strike across Germany to meet the Russians. Berliners no longer prayed for victory: they prayed that the *Amis* would reach Berlin before the pillaging Bolsheviks.

Before Wolff presented himself at the bomb-shattered Chancellery, Harzer and von Geissel took him aside to warn him once again about the condition of the Führer. They sat on a park bench in the Tiergarten near what remained of the zoo in the early morning lull between the departure of the RAF Mosquitos and the arrival of the USAF B-17's.

They wore civilian clothes to avoid attracting attention; they also kept identity cards to hand in case they aroused the suspicions of the German execution squads who were rounding up deserters and hanging them from street-lamps.

It was a sweet, fresh morning, morsels of white cloud in the blue sky and the scents of spring struggling through the stench of destruction and carnage.

Harzer leaned forward, both hands clasped on the handle of his stick. His face had a yellow tinge about it and he spoke with an effort.

"We ask you to see the Führer as he was. As we knew him ten years ago. As perhaps you remember him." Harzer leaned back, one hand to his stomach.

Von Geissel said: "The Führer is a sick man. But he will recover — when he is away from all this," gesturing at the tooth-stump horizons of the captial. "At the moment he is surrounded with sycophants, traitors, cowards."

Wolff wondered if, behind the cold exterior, von Geissel wasn't also a little mad. It didn't bother him one way or the other: since that night in Rome two months ago his senses had been dulled. *The gun in his hand, the hatred in her eyes . . .* But he still retained a core of resolve to carry out this mission.

Wolff said: "I understand."

"Ironically," von Geissel said, "it is the Führer's great strength of will that may be our greatest obstacle."

Harzer leaned forward again. "You see he may refuse to go. If he does then we have a plan . . . But it would be better if he could be persuaded to leave," wincing with pain.

Two members of the Volkssturm, now preparing to defend Berlin, walked past and looked contemptuously at the three men in civilian clothes. One of the Volkssturm looked about sixteen, the other was in his seventies.

Harzer sighed. "Ah, so it has come to this." He leaned back again and breathed the air of premature spring.

Wolff said: "You mean you want *me* to persuade the Führer?'

Von Geissel said: "Who knows? He may not need persuading. He may realise that Germany still needs him — but safely away from the enemy. On the other hand he may decide to die in his capital — even if he always preferred Munich. You see," von Geissel said urgently, "he may listen to you. You are young, you are strong, you are the sort of man to whom he once entrusted our future. You will be able to convince him that the historians must not be able to close this chapter in the glorious history of the Fatherland with —" von Geissel seemed hardly able to say the word — "suicide."

"You really think he would contemplate that?"

"Who knows the mind of the Fuhrer?"

An air-raid siren sounded close by. Pedestrians headed back to the shelters and subways which they had only just vacated. Wearily the gunners on the 100-foot high Flak tower in the Tiergarten returned to their posts.

Wolff said: "I think, gentlemen, it is now time that you gave me exact details of your plan." In the past two months his relationship with his two superior officers had changed: despite their rank he no longer felt subordinate. Without him they were nothing.

Von Geissel and Harzer exchanged looks. Harzer nodded weakly. "It is time that he knew."

So they told Wolff about Ziemann and they told him exactly what was to happen when the time came. There were variables according to the conditions at the time but, Wolff had to admit, it was as foolproof as anything could be. Or, to be more cautious, it could just work.

"What do you think?" von Geissel asked.

"I have to admit that it has touches of Teutonic genius."

"You must keep in close touch with us. Let us know when the time is ripe."

The fervour left his voice as though he had flicked a switch. He was a mortician again.

In the distance they heard the drone of approaching bombers and the thump of anti-aircraft fire.

Wolff said: "I think we ought to take cover. It would be a pity if an American bomb killed off Grey Fox at this stage."

244

*   *   *

Later that day Wolff called at Harzer's house in Spandau, comparatively undamaged despite its armament factories.

It was 8 pm and Frieda had just got back from the Charite Hospital. She looked exhausted, the Bavarian sheen wiped from her cheeks.

He had called several times since his uneventful return journey from Rome. At first their relationship had been almost formal, and she hadn't questioned it; like a wife, he thought, who senses fleeting infidelity, but doesn't want confirmation.

Now some of the old warmth had returned. His feeling for Maria Reubeni had been a tongue of flame: his feeling for Frieda Harzer was a glow that expanded with time.

One day soon he would be returning to Rome. He knew that he would be tempted to seek out Maria; he also knew that, if he did, it would be futile because the hatred in her eyes had been implacable.

Frieda lit a small fire with chopped wood, stripped from bombed houses and sold in bundles, and made a potato stew in which pieces of tough meat bought on the Black Market bobbed like corks.

They ate the meal in the dining room which, like the rest of the house, was as neat and impersonal as any serviceman's married quarters. (These days Harzer slept in a bunker near the Prinz Albrechtstrasse.)

"So," she said as they ate, "you are to guard Adolf Hitler."

"A great honour," Wolff said, spearing a piece of bobbing meat.

"Very great. By keeping him alive you are prolonging the war. He is the only man in the whole of Europe who wants to go on fighting."

"It's incredible when you think about it," Wolff said. "The whole nation still bending to the will of one man.

"One madman," Frieda said.

Wolff selected a piece of black bread and mopped up the last of his stew. "Now let's not start that again."

245

"You needn't worry," she said. "I hope he continues to hold out. That way there's still a chance that the Americans will get here before the Russians. The patients I've seen today . . ." she put down her knife and fork as though she had lost her appetite. "Women raped until they nearly bled to death, until their minds cracked . . . Did you know that women in Berlin carry poison and razor blades with them so that they can kill themselves before the Russians get them?"

Wolff pushed his plate aside. "I didn't know." He lit a cigarette. "But for God's sake let's talk about something else."

He sat on the sofa and patted the space beside him. "Come and sit down." And when she did he put his arm round her and they stayed like that in the blacked-out room lit by two candles and the light from the fire, and it seemed then to Wolff that this was how life should have been, sharing the candlelight, and then a bed, and then the peaceful dawn, if . . . In the distance they heard the first air-raid siren.

He glanced at his watch. "I must be going. I report for duty tomorrow at eight."

"Kurt?"

"Yes?" He kissed her gently and stood up.

"These new duties. Are they anything to do with what you and my father were discussing at the farmhouse?"

He sighed. "There is a connection."

"At least you're not lying. I only pray . . ."

"What do you pray?"

"It doesn't matter," standing up and putting her arms round him and clinging to him. "Perhaps one day . . ."

"Yes," he said, "perhaps one day . . ."

Wolff caught a subway train back to the small hotel off the Bismarck Strasse where he was staying. In his room he laid out his uniform. But, as he thought about the old men, women and children he had seen camped on the platforms of the subway, it seemed to Wolff that the silver threaded into the black uniform had become a little tarnished.

*　　*　　*

246

The Führerbunker where Hitler lived and worked was part of a vast subterranean complex beneath the old and new Reich Chancelleries.

The biggest part of the complex, its concrete walls not yet dried out, was located under the new building. It could accommodate seven hundred men and women, and that was where Wolff would be quartered alongside the other bodyguards.

From this area a tunnel led to the Vorbunker beneath the old building. This contained the kitchens and servants' quarters; it also housed Professor Theodor Morell, Hitler's personal physician, condemned by the rest of the medical profession as a quack. Among the drugs prescribed by Morell for his patient were Dr. Koester's Anti-Gas Pills, containing strychnine and belladonna.

A flight of steps led from the Vorbunker to the Führerbunker consisting of eighteen rooms, mostly about ten feet by eight in size. Two rooms were larger — a waiting room and the room which Hitler was to use for his daily conferences when he finally vacated his study in the Chancellery.

Adjoining the conference room were Hitler's personal quarters, a telephone switchboard, accommodation for his military aides and valet, and a couple of offices for the head of the Party Chancery, Martin Bormann, and the head of Propaganda, Josef Goebbels.

There were two exits from the Führerbunker and it was these that were to attract the attention of Kurt Wolff. One emerged through a half-finished observation tower; the other through a block-house into the garden.

By the time Wolff arrived at the underground complex it had become a warren of intrigue and suspicion dominated by one prematurely-old man.

Wolff was quartered with another SS officer in one of the tiny rooms under the new Reich Chancellery. His name was Lubrich, a saturnine captain who chain-smoked and barely spoke.

The walls of the room were still damp from the fresh concrete, there was no furniture and, during the daily and nightly raids, a film of dust settled over everything.

When he first arrived in the cramped quarters at 8.30 am Wolff attempted conversation with Lubrich who was lying fully dressed on his bunk smoking.

He asked: "Do you often see the Führer?"

"Occasionally."

"How is he looking?"

"You'll see," Lubrich said, turning on his side.

Wolff shrugged and waited for the summons to Hitler's study which, he had been assured, would occur some time today. But not until after midday: Hitler worked at night and slept till noon.

The summons came at 2.35 pm.

Even Lubrich was impressed. "You must have connections," he said.

An aide led Wolff along the tunnel. Wolff felt excited and scared; there was a tightness in his chest and he could feel the beat of his heart. At last the boy whose dagger had once been one of 60,000 forming a dazzling metallic flash of light was about to meet the man in whose honour the dagger had been raised, the man who had resurrected the Fatherland.

At the entrance to the Führerbunker Wolff deposited his pistol. He was also subjected to a body-search: no one was above suspicion since the July Plot.

But his first impression of Hitler was anti-climactic. Hitler sat behind a desk in his sparsely-furnished study. The familiar lock of greying hair and the moustache were all that remained of the man the schoolboy Wolff had once seen from a distance.

Hitler's left arm lay on the desk, apparently with little use left in it. His right hand, with which he was turning the pages of a dossier, trembled. His features had slackened into old age; his skin was grey.

He wore a grey, double-breasted uniform jacket and black trousers, and for a while he didn't look up. In the background a woman stenographer hovered anxiously.

Finally he looked up and it was then, as the hypnotic eyes stared at him, that Wolff felt Hitler's strength and his disappointment lifted, and he thought only of the sacrifices and Wehrmacht treachery that had brought about the physical degeneration.

"So," Hitler said, "you're Sturmbannführer Wolff." He flicked through the dossier. "Dietrich speaks very highly of you."

Wolff stood rigidly to attention. He hesitated. "It is an honour to be chosen for these duties."

Hitler turned and dismissed the stenographer, then said abruptly: "How do you think the struggle is going, Sturmbannführer?"

We're at the edge of defeat, on the brink of an abyss. "Your troops are fighting heroically, *mein Führer.*"

Hitler didn't appear to hear him. He stood up and walked to a wall-map of the Eastern Front clawed with arrows. He prodded it with one trembling finger. "We have taken the bridgehead from which the Russians planned to attack Vienna. See that triangle?" turning to Wolff. "It's formed by Lake Balaton and the Danube and Drava rivers. That is the crucial area of the campaign today. We have an opportunity to mount a Blitzkrieg there. To hurl the Russians back across the Danube and retake Budapest. Just like the old days, eh, Sturmbannführer?"

"*Ja, mein Führer.*"

Hitler sat down again. "And I'll let you into a secret as Dietrich seems to think so highly of you. Dietrich himself is there!"

Wolff was surprised. He had heard that the Leibstandarte had been withdrawn after the failure of the Ardennes offensive but he had no idea Dietrich was in Hungary.

"Dietrich is the man for the job," Hitler said. "He is one of the few men I can still rely on."

"He is magnificent," Wolff said with total sincerity.

Hitler pointed to a seat. "Sit down. Tell me about your experiences with Sepp. He has been with me from the beginning. Tell me about Russia," Hitler said and Wolff realised that he had withdrawn to 1941 when 3,580 tanks stood poised to decimate the Soviet Union. Hitler glanced at the dossier on Wolff and then at his war wound medal. "I see you were one of the unlucky ones."

Wolff sat down and told Hitler about Dietrich and Meyer and Peiper. And he told him about courage and sacrifice in the bitterness of winter. But he spoke only of heroics, never of defeat.

Hitler sat enraptured as the dreams of the early days took substance once again. And when Wolff was finished he said: "And we will rise again, Sturmbannführer," unconsciously admitting the inevitability of defeat.

Hitler leaned back in his chair. "Already the Russians, Americans and British are falling out among themselves. Who knows, it isn't beyond the bounds of possibility that they will fight each other. Fight to a standstill and leave the Fatherland in control of Europe once more."

Wolff said nothing.

Hitler gazed at him speculatively for a few moments. Then said: "I need men around me like you. Men who still believe. Men with whom I can talk . . ."

Wolff felt his face flushing.

"Young men," Hitler said. "Not infirm Generals incapable of making any decision except the wrong one."

He pressed a button on his desk. Albrecht Bormann, Martin Bormann's brother and Hitler's personal adjutant, came in.

Hitler spoke briskly. "I want you to arrange accommodation for Sturmbannführer Wolff next door to my valet."

Bormann showed no surprise. "It shall be done, *mein Führer*."

Hitler indicated that the interview was over. Bormann and Wolff saluted and left the study, Wolff stunned by Hitler's words.

Within seven hours of his arrival Grey Fox had infiltrated into the innermost sanctum of power.

XXVII

Landau was worried. It was March, the end was near, and still the SS Lieutenant Bruckner hadn't made a move.

Landau looked fitter these days than he had since he came to Dachau. His skin still had a corpse-like pallor about it and his cheeks sank like pockets into his face but, as he fed himself on gruel, frost-bitten potatoes and crusts of bread, the sharp outlines of his bones had become rounded with flesh. His stomach was still a mess but he managed to keep his food down as he prepared his body for the ordeal ahead.

But where was Bruckner? Instinctively he knew he had picked his man well. The trouble was that, apart from air-raids, Bavaria had hardly been touched by the last throes of the war. Bruckner had probably been lulled into a false sense of security.

But Landau hadn't much longer to wait. On March 30th, 1945, Good Friday — still observed in the Catholic strongholds of Bavaria — Bruckner summoned him to his office.

His tone was more reasonable than it had been before as he told Landau that, according to the latest military information, the American 7th Army planned to sweep south into Bavaria.

Landau waited expectantly.

Bruckner fingered the boils on the back of his neck. Then he said: "Tell me about the gold."

"What more is there to tell, Untersturmführer?"

"I want to know where it is."

"You would never find it without me."

"How do I know this gold exists?"

"You have only my word."

"The word of a . . ." Bruckner cut himself short.

"The word of a Jew. Yes, that is all you have. Did you know it was Passover yesterday?"

Bruckner ignored him, still feeling the angry red pustules on his neck.

Landau said: "I don't have to remind you what action the Americans will take against SS officers in camps like this."

Bruckner snapped: "You don't have to remind me of anything."

"And you could be a rich man."

Bruckner made his decision. "Very well. And if the gold doesn't exist then I will kill you."

"The gold exists," Landau said simply. "A trough of gold, Untersturmführer, where the rainbow ends."

"Very well," Bruckner said. "We leave tonight."

And soon, Landau thought, the crusade to save one soul will be over.

*   *   *

Now Landau had the upper hand. Bruckner was terrified of what the Allies would do to him — and he would do almost anything Landau commanded.

Before they left the camp Landau told him to steal certain documents and photographs from the Dachau files.

They left at 10.35 pm in a field-grey, Jeep-type Volkswagen with Bruckner in full SS uniform at the wheel and Landau hidden beneath a pile of prisoners' striped clothing in the back.

Seeing Bruckner at the wheel, the guards saluted smartly and opened the gates. The gates of hell, Landau thought, as he heard them clang behind them.

Dachau lies to the north of Munich. Half way between the camp and the city, Bruckner swung the Volkswagen off the main road and up a dirt-track. At the end of the track stood a rusty, corrugated-iron building.

Bruckner stopped the Volkswagen, doused its lights and opened a padlock on the doors of the building. Inside stood a civilian ambulance, a darker grey than the Volkswagen, the metal above the red crosses ripped by shrapnel.

Bruckner drove the ambulance out of the building and drove the Volkswagen in. From the back of the ambulance he produced two suits of civilian clothing, shirts, underclothes, socks and black shoes. And two sets of identity papers. He threw one set of clothes to Landau. "Put those on." The jacket was crusted with blood.

When they had changed Bruckner threw his uniform and Landau's wretched clothing into a pit already excavated beside the building. He covered them with soil.

He locked the padlock on the doors and pointed to the back of the ambulance. "Get in." He jumped in beside Landau and produced a sling and a blood-stained bandage from a metal first-aid box underneath one of the stretchers. He wound the bandage round Landau's head and slipped his arm into the sling. "Now get under a blanket and look as if you're dying."

Landau lay on one of the floor-level stretchers and pulled a soiled brown blanket up to his chin.

"Right," Bruckner said. "Now you say this village is near Tolz?"

Landau nodded. "It shouldn't take long."

"Let's hope there's an air-raid. No one will bother with us then."

Tolz lay to the south, a little over half way between Munich and the alpine border separating Bavaria from Austria. Landau had pointed out to Bruckner he would be able to enter Austria through the Aachen Pass and cut straight across to the mountains of northern Italy. With, of course, gold to pave his way. And he would still be inside the National Redoubt where fugitive Nazis would already be going to ground because it was the logical place.

Ten minutes later the Allies obliged Bruckner and Landau as they drove south through the outskirts of Munich. The sirens wailed, searchlights switched the sky; the sky exploded with flak and Munich exploded with bombs.

They drove steadily through the night and, when Bruckner slowed down at an intersection, Landau opened the rear doors of the ambulance and jumped onto the road.

As the ambulance drove away he headed in the opposite direction towards a village where, as a boy, he had often spent happy days with another Jewish family.

In the village he found a telephone kiosk. He dialled the operator; after a minute or so a sleepy girl's voice answered. Landau told her to give him the number of the police station at Tolz where, he knew, a Gestapo agent would be in residence.

He dialled the number and told the police officer who answered: "There is an ambulance two miles out of Tolz heading south. It is being driven by an Army deserter carrying forged papers."

Then he hung up and walked in the direction of the village where he was born.

XXVIII

In the weeks that followed Kurt Wolff's admission into the Führerbunker his faith frequently wavered.

He witnessed Hitler's attacks of illogical rage; he saw him dimiss and humiliate the wisest and most clear-headed of his advisers.

And for the first time he came into close contact with the clique who had ruled Germany, the men who seemed to have had a God-like quality when viewed from the stalls of a cinema. How different they were now in the face of defeat, a collection of mediocrities upon whom greatness had been thrust by one man. Now they were as scared as an ordinary soldier facing a bayonet charge.

He saw Hermann Göring twice. A buffoon from a comic opera in his blue, bemedalled uniform planning his escape to the south with his loot.

He saw Heinrich Himmler, grey-faced and myopic behind his wire-rimmed spectacles, who had feigned illness on the Russian front and gratefully handed over the command of Army Group Vistula to Colonel-General Gotthard Heinrici, a soldier of the old school.

He saw Martin Bormann, the 'brown eminence' who had schemed his way to virtual omnipotence in the Nazi hierarchy beneath Hitler, and was still scheming in these last weeks. Probably, Wolff decided, to save his own skin.

He saw Josef Goebbels, the demoniac, club-footed genius who moulded the minds of the German people like putty. Now he was recommending the slaughter of 40,000 prisoners-of-war in retaliation for the bombing of Dresden. But at least Goebbels retained his loyalty to Hitler which was in itself outstanding in these mad subterranean halls of injustice in March 1945.

Wolff also found to his chagrin that the men he most admired were the military leaders, not the SS. Men like Field-Marshal Wilhelm Keitel, Army Chief of Staff; Colonel-General Alfred Jodl, Chief of Operations and, in particular, General Heinz Guderian, Chief of the General Staff of the Army High Command, the last of the legendary generals since the death of Rommel who was forced, so Wolff now learned, to commit suicide for supposed complicity in the July Plot.

On March 19th Hitler began to issue a series of crazed directives aimed at the scorched-earth destruction of what was left of Germany. Horrified, Wolff envisaged the villages and pastures of Bavaria being razed; heard the crackle of flames engulfing the Harzer farmhouse, saw Frieda running from the fire, clothes ablaze.

But this last act of wilful destruction was forestalled by Reichminister Albert Speer, head of Armaments and War Production and, paradoxically, a man of culture. He contacted gauleiters and military commanders and countermanded Hitler's orders, persuading bewildered officials and officers that, if they obeyed the Führer, Germany was doomed for ever.

Wolff's faith came close to cracking wide when he attended one of Hitler's midday conferences. The subject: the failure of a German counter-attack at Kustrin, a town on the Oder where the Russians were poised for the final offensive against Berlin.

Guderian was present; so was General Theodor Busse, commander of the 9th Army, which had made the attack. Busse was under fire from Hitler, whose eyes were staring wildly as he shouted: "Incompetence, negligence ..." And to Guderian: "Why didn't you supply Busse with enough ammunition?"

It was then that the grey-haired, moustached Guderian, one of the best of the Generals, lost control. He shouted and prodded his finger at Hitler while the other leaders listened in horror. "You say the troops are to blame. Look at the casualties. Look at the losses. The troops did their duty. Their self-sacrifice proves it."

Hitler screamed at him: "They failed."

Hands clenched, cheeks flushed, Guderian shouted: "I must ask you not to level any further accusations at Busse or his troops."

The row heightened in intensity with Hitler screaming invective and Guderian yelling back. Finally the General was led away while Hitler fell back in his chair wiping his lips with a handkerchief.

Wolff knew Guderian was right. He stared at Hitler with disgust. Was this the man he had to rescue?

Later that day Guderian, the brilliant strategist who had invented the panzer techniques of attack, was relieved of his command and dispatched for six weeks convalescence leave. He departed for South Bavaria.

Wolff's disgust lasted until he was summoned to Hitler's study. Hitler sat at his desk holding in one trembling hand a pair of green-tinted spectacles; his blue-grey eyes were bloodshot but, when they looked at Wolff, the old mesmeric effect was immediate.

He gestured to a chair. "Sit down, talk to me." He sipped a cup of peppermint tea. "I suppose you were disenchanted by this afternoon's performance."

"*Nein, mein Führer*," the tone of his voice belying the words.

"You must understand," Hitler said, "that I am the only man keeping Germany together. I cannot afford insubordination. I have to attack, attack. If I didn't they would lose respect. They expect it of me," he said sipping the aromatic tea. "And as for Guderian, he is well out of it. He has served the Fatherland well."

Wolff didn't reply; he understood now that his role was that of a captive audience; that Hitler used him as the catalyst to purge his tortured mind.

"I suppose you've heard," Hitler said, "that I have spoken

257

about committing suicide."

Wolff took his chance. "That, *mein Führer*, would be a negation of everything you have achieved. In the future millions of schoolchildren will read about those achievements," playing on Hitler's vanity. "I implore you not to take this step. It would play into the hands of your enemies. That is just how they would like to portray you — killing yourself by your own hand. The dishonourable way out," Wolff said tentatively.

Hitler stared at him. "Do you really care, Sturmbannführer Wolff?"

"I and millions of other Germans care," Wolff said. And then, cautiously: "But if we are defeated, it might be expedient if the world *thought* you had committed suicide. At least for a while."

Hitler put down the tea-cup. "What exactly do you mean, Sturmbannführer?"

"It is my belief," Wolff said, "and the belief of many men whose loyalty is beyond question that you should take" — he deliberately avoided the word evacuate — "your headquarters to Bavaria. To the Eagles' Nest on the Obersalzberg."

Wolff was referring to Hitler's mountain fortress near Berchtesgaden, surrounded by peaks rearing up to 9,000 feet, each spiked with anti-aircraft guns. It was in the heart of the National Redoubt that covered nearly 20,000 miles of mountainous territory.

Lately the National Redoubt had become an obsession with the Americans to the extent that they were more concerned with reaching it than taking Berlin. It was reputed to be virtually impregnable. According to Allied intelligence, German fanatics assisted by crack mountain commandoes could hold out there for two years or more.

Hitler said: "Please continue, Sturmbannführer, you interest me."

Wolff mustered his thoughts: the opportunity was too good to be missed. "If we left clear evidence here that you had committed suicide then you would be able to withdraw to Berchtesgaden without harrassment. I have no doubt that when it was announced that you were dead an armistice would immediately be negotiated. But the National Redoubt could still be defended. You would regain your health and emerge once more while the Allies and the Russians are at each other's throats."

Hitler nodded: "You have a lively mind. Your plan is worth considering." He leaned back in his chair, face drained of all colour, hands brushing weakly at his forlock of hair. "I am grateful to you, Sturmbannführer. I shall apply my mind to what you have proposed."

And it was then that Wolff realised that, after the spleen of the working day had spent itself, Adolf Hitler was an exhausted old man malleable in his hands. The proposal that he could hold out in the Eagle's Nest for two years was nonsense, but Hitler no longer seemed to have the acumen to realise this.

However Berchtesgaden was half way to Rome.

*   *   *

A cold wind loaded with rain was blowing through the ruins of Berlin when Wolff left the presence of Hitler; in Rome it was a warm spring night.

Without hope Father Liam Doyle made his way to Maria Reubeni's apartment. Since that terrible night when he had stopped her from shooting Otto Witt she had refused to see him. She had spoken to him once — as the finishing touches were put to the macabre scene in the Piazzi Pia, as Witt's body was bundled into the black Mercedes and driven away with Brandt at the wheel.

He had tried to put his arm round her to comfort her but, fiercely, she had thrust it away and said: "That was all I had left. Now you have taken that away from me."

She had driven back to her apartment leaving him standing alone in the square where he had been waiting all day knowing that she intended to kill Witt.

He had called at the apartment three times. He had written twice but both letters had been returned unopened. But still he knew he had been right; he had prevented her from becoming a murderess. He had to find a way to talk to her.

He walked up the stairs leading to her apartment block and knocked on the door. No reply. He assumed that she recognised his footstep on the stairs.

He knocked once more, knelt and slipped a note under the door and sadly made his way down the stairs.

As he walked into the street Anderson was alighting from a taxi. He crossed the road with quick athletic strides, acknowledging Liam as he entered the door of the block.

Liam waited for five minutes but he didn't reappear. He went to a café at the end of the street and waited.

* * *

As he entered the apartment Anderson picked up the note lying on the floor and handed it to Maria.

She tore it up without looking at it.

"Hey, why did you do that?" Anderson said in Italian.

"Because I know who it's from."

"The priest?"

She nodded.

"You should take pity on him."

"Why? He shouldn't have done what he did."

Anderson put a carrier bag down on the table — cigarettes, chocolate, stockings, canned food and coffee.

Maria, wearing a blue blouse and black costume with a nipped-in waist, sat down and watched him. The lean, alert face, thick, crew-cut hair. An attractive man. But she had met *the one man*. Perhaps in the world there was just one man for every woman; very occasionally they met. Maria had met the one man born for her and he had betrayed her. She would never forget him, but she might adapt and find a sort of happiness.

"Give the guy a break," Anderson said, sitting opposite her. "He was pretty fond of you. It must have been hell for him."

"He shouldn't have done it," she said tonelessly.

260

"Of course he should. I know it, you know it. He did what was right, Maria. He stopped you killing a man."

"It's no crime to kill in war-time. He was the enemy. He killed my father. Took him away from my mother as she lay dying. Looted his shop when he was dead, shot him in the back of the head and buried him in lime." Hatred rasped her voice. "Do you really think I should have forgiven him?"

"No, I don't think that. But I think you should see Father Doyle. He did a hell of a lot for you when the Germans were here."

She didn't reply. She stood up, face pale, eyes tired. "Well, are you taking me to dinner?"

He shook his head. "I'm afraid not. I have to meet a General. Tomorrow?"

She shrugged. "Tomorrow."

He kissed her on the cheeks and left the apartment. As he walked down the street Liam came up to him. "Can you spare me a few moments, Captain Anderson?"

Anderson glanced at his watch. "I guess so. But I don't have much time."

When they had sat down in the café Anderson said: "If it's about Maria —"

"It isn't. I understand how she feels."

Anderson looked at him curiously. "What can I do for you, Father?"

"Your assignment is to apprehend Nazi war criminals on the run?"

"Something like that," Anderson said warily.

"But you let Doppler get away after Maria had told you he was in Rome."

"We were just behind him,' Anderson said. "But he changed identities."

"Maybe it's a good thing."

"How's that, Father?"

Liam told him that Brandt and Doppler had been working outside the established organisation for spiriting away Nazis. The only conclusion was that they were planning the escape of one particular person.

"Not Otto Witt surely," said Anderson who had heard about the shooting from Maria Reubeni long after it had happened.

"No, not Otto Witt. Someone much more important to them than that."

Realisation dawned on Anderson. A shiver of excitement, the hunter's first intimation of a kill. "You think they'd bring Hitler out this way?"

"Why not? It's the safest."

Anderson forgot the general he was supposed to see. He leaned forward, Red Indian features alive. "You could be right. And Otto Witt was a dummy run, I guess."

"That would seem to be the explanation," Liam said. "I can't see any other reason why they should bother with a man like that. And Doppler shot him. He can't have been that important."

"If you're right," Anderson said, "they were probably going to kill him anyway. But," he said thoughtfully, "they won't use the *passetto* again. That's blown. Do you have any ideas?"

"Oh yes," said Liam Doyle, priest, spy, platonic suitor — discarded. "I have other ideas." He ordered two more coffees. "You see," he told Anderson, "I work for the Papal Assistance Board, the PCA at the Villa Bonaparte. There's a lot of activity there and a priest who was also a German paratrooper has been installed. I've seen him in the company of Bishop Hudal and Heinrich Brandt. I think the ultimate destination of this particular refugee will be The Vatican. But I think they'll take him to the Villa Bonaparte first because Bishop Hudal's church is too obvious. As it is the place is swarming with refugees, no one will notice one more. They can issue him with documents there and, when the time is ripe, smuggle him into The Vatican where no one will be able to touch him."

Anderson consulted his watch. "Christ! — sorry, Father. I've kept a General waiting for fifteen minutes. Can we meet again here tomorrow?"

Liam nodded. "Of course."

"Meanwhile I'm going to arrange a round-the-clock watch on the Villa Bonaparte." He stood up. "Thank you." He hesitated. "Don't take it too hard. About Maria, I mean. She'll come round."

Liam said: "May I ask you a question?"

"Fire away."

"Are you fond of her?"

"Yes, Liam, I am."

"I thought as much. In fact I'm glad," said Liam who liked the tall, rangy American. "But may I give you some advice?" Without waiting for a reply he said: "Never take her away from Rome. It would kill her."

Anderson nodded. "I'm afraid things haven't reached that stage yet. I don't even know if she likes me."

He walked away down the street watched by Liam. For Liam there had never been any hope of anything beyond friendship. *And even that has been taken away from me.*

XXIX

In the early hours of April 16th the Russians launched their long-awaited attack on Berlin from the banks of the Oder less than forty miles east of the city.

By the 18th they had made a break-through but, by and large, the German IX Army still held firm.

On the 19th the Soviet Belorussian Front fought its way to Muncheberg only twenty miles from Berlin and the 2nd Guards Tank Army broke through near Wriezen to the north of Muncheberg.

By April 20th it was virtually all over. Armoured spearheads were driving towards the heart of Berlin while other units were fanning north and south to encircle the city.

One man buried beneath the stricken city refused to accept that it was all over. It was Adolf Hitler's fifty-sixth birthday.

Among those who celebrated his birthday was Eva Braun, the pretty but insipid companion of the Führer — no one ever ascertained whether there was a sexual relationship — who had arrived from Munich on April 15th determined to share the last days with Hitler.

Hitler, attended by his valet, Artur Kannenberg, rose at 11 am that day and at midday began to receive his guests, among them Göring, Goebbels, Himmler, Bormann, Foreign Minister Joachim von Ribbentrop, and Grand Admiral Karl Doenitz, Commander-in-Chief of the Navy.

After the reception Hitler emerged into the daylight and, in the Reich Chancellery gardens, inspected a detachment from

S.P.P.—R

the SS Frundsberg Division and a pathetic group of boys from the Hitler Youth. He seemed oblivious to the sound of gunfire and crack of exploding rockets. But, as he presented medals to the schoolboy soldiers, his hands shook and he stooped like a cripple in need of a stick.

At the subsequent conference it was agreed to evacuate most of the remaining Government agencies to the Bavarian stronghold. Hitler gave no indication whether he intended to join them but, standing in the background, Wolff thought, or perhaps imagined, that Hitler glanced significantly his way.

Hitler told the assembled advisers that the only hope for Germany lay in the battle for Berlin. No one believed him.

Germany was almost bisected by the Americans. In the north the British were at the gates of Hamburg and Bremen. In the south the French had reached the upper Danube. In Italy Bologna had fallen and the Allies were swarming up the Po Valley. And now Lieutenant-General George Patton was storming through Bavaria towards the last bastions of Nazism.

That evening the exodus to Bavaria got under way. One of the first to leave was Hermann Göring — he had previously loaded twenty-four Luftwaffe trucks with the contents of his castle at Karinhall before blowing up the castle — but his farewell to Hitler was a curt affair. The Luftwaffe had failed!

Heinrich Himmler also left with the intention of negotiating a secret peace with the head of the Swedish Red Cross, Count Folk Bernadotte.

*   *   *

That night Kurt Wolff had two important meetings — one with Hitler, one with Harzer and von Geissel.

Hitler was eating his usual vegetarian meal in his quarters; Eva Braun had retired to the bedroom.

Hitler told Wolff to sit at the end of the dining table while he toyed with his vegetables and some sort of cutlet made from nuts.

He looked totally exhausted, although he would probably

work far into the night as was his custom.

He said: "I have been thinking about your suggestion. It is a good one because it enables me to stay here to the very end" — no talk of winning the battle for Berlin now — "and then to reach Berchtesgaden in secret." He chewed a morsel of cutlet, then pushed the plate aside. "How exactly do you propose to carry this out?"

Wolff told him as much as he knew without giving the impression that the project had been planned for a long time.

"And what about the body that is to be left behind?"

"It will be burned beyond recognition but certain items identifying you will be left on the corpse. The announcement of your death will be broadcast on the radio."

Hitler managed a wintry smile. "I would like to see Churchill's face when he hears it." (The American President, Franklin D. Roosevelt, had died eight days earlier and been replaced by Harry S. Truman).

Wolff said: "I should also like to see Churchill's face, *mein Führer*, when he learns that you are still alive."

Hitler nodded. "You're sure it will work?" Suddenly a querulous old man again, seeking comfort.

"I am certain."

"Very well, I will give it further consideration," dismissing Wolff with a wave of his hand.

At 11.30 pm Wolff knocked on the door of von Geissel's apartment, having picked his way through the centre of a city which was dying chaotically. Looting was rife, communications had broken down, refugees wandered the streets defying the air-raids in search of food and bedding. The Russians were rumoured to be advancing through the underground railway tunnels.

Harzer was lying on a sofa and it was apparent to Wolff that he was dying. His face was yellow, his eyes sunken, his features twisted in pain.

Von Geissel whispered to Wolff: "Apparently a growth formed round the piece of metal."

"How long has he got?"

Von Geissel shrugged. "How long have any of us got?" He pulled up a small table to the side of the sofa. Harzer managed to raise himself into a sitting position.

"So," Harzer said in a weak voice, "how is it progressing?"

"We need to know a date," von Geissel said.

"I can't give you one. It depends on the Russians. May I suggest that you bring his twin to Berlin before they cut the approaches from the south?"

Von Geissel nodded. "He's arriving tomorrow." He tapped manicured nails on the table. "My estimate is that Berlin will fall in the early days of May — if, that is, the people think the Führer is dead. With his indomitable will he could persuade them to fight to the last man. I was listening to some soldiers talking the other day," von Geissel said. "They would still throw down their lives for him."

Speaking with an effort, Harzer said slowly: "It depends on the Russians — and the Führer. He will stay until even he realises it is utterly hopeless. Judging by the rate of the Soviet advance they should have closed in on the centre of the city by May 1st. I suggest that we provisionally put Grey Fox into operation on April 30th."

Von Geissel nodded. "We must also take into consideration that the Führer may refuse to go at the last moment. He has been a little, ah, capricious lately." He looked at Wolff. "His behaviour hasn't affected your determination?"

Wolff regarded the two men steadily. "To be honest I have been disgusted."

Von Geissel said: "I warned you what he would be like. But," passion thickening his cold voice, "you must remember that he is a sick man. You must remember him as he was in the old days. As he will be again."

Harzer put a frail hand on Wolff's arm. "You aren't deserting us, are you, Kurt?"

Wolff smiled at the dying man. "I took my oath to the Führer. That is the answer to your question."

Harzer sighed with relief and slumped back on the cushions.

Von Geissel relaxed, his voice cold again. "If the Fuhrer

refuses to go at the last moment then you will have to use this," fetching a small cardboard box from the top of the book-shelves. Inside was a hypodermic syringe and an ampoule of colourless liquid. "It will put him out for at least an hour. You will have to carry him. But you are strong and these days the Führer is very light."

"Sometimes," Wolff said, "he is like a child. I suppose Frau-lein Braun and I are the only people who have ever seen him like that."

At the mention of Eva Braun's name von Geissel's lips com-pressed with distaste.

Harzer said: "Tell Kurt about the final arrangements."

Von Geissel took a plan of the Führerbunker from his pocket, and a small map of the centre of Berlin stretching from Charlottenburg in the west to Friedrichshain in the east and from Wedding in the north to Tempelhof in the south.

He prodded an area of green, the Tiergarten. "The Stork is at present located in an underground garage off Charlotten-burger Chaussee. The Volkssturm are keeping a strip of grass cleared in the park. You will fly south. The Russians haven't bothered to bring up any anti-aircraft guns there because the Luftwaffe is no longer in the skies — and they've destroyed all ours. The only danger is Russian fighter planes." He shrugged. "It's a risk you'll have to take. I suggest you fly in the day-time — even the Russians might respect the Red Cross."

"Where will Ziemann be?" Wolff asked.

"Here. At the agreed time he will be brought to the emerg-ency exit from the bunker to the garden. He will then be shot" — no emotion in von Geissel's voice — "in such a way that his features are mutilated. A phial of cyanide will then be broken in his mouth — the conventional way out these days. The dou-ble-death is essential to damage the features so that any discre-pancies are destroyed."

"Why the cyanide?" Wolff asked.

"To satisfy the investigators. It is known that the woman Braun has gabbled about some sort of suicide pact. It's just the sort of melodramatic rubbish that a woman like that would concoct. It will appear," said von Geissel, massaging his cold white hands, "that the Führer shot himself in the head but didn't die immediately. Eva Braun then crushed a cyanide ampoule in his mouth and did the same to herself."

"You mean Eva Braun will be killed?" Wolff looked at the mortician in horror.

Von Geissel nodded. "Of course."

Harzer, noticing Wolff's reaction, said: "You must remember, Kurt, that this is the way she wants it. If she sees what she presumes to be the body of the Führer then she will probably take the cyanide herself."

Von Geissel ignored the sentimentality. Pushing the sketch of the bunker across the table he pointed at the emergency exit. "Ziemann's body, wrapped in a blanket, will be brought through the ante-room and cloakroom, along the conference passage. It will then be taken into the Führer's suite, into his study," pointing at the cubicle in the south corner of the bunker between Hitler's bedroom and bathroom.

"And where will I be?" Wolff asked.

"You will be in the drawing room on the opposite side of the Conference Passage. A shot will be fired in the study by the man who has taken Ziemann's corpse there. He will have time to get away before anyone reaches the study. They will burst in and see the man they assume to be the Führer lying dead, blood pouring from his head, a 7.65 Walther pistol lying beside him. The woman Braun will be there too — dead. In the ensuing confusion you will escape with the Führer through the emergency exit. Then, wearing civilian clothes — no one will take any notice of you because the centre of Berlin will be a holocaust by then — you will make your way to the Stork which will be waiting, engine running, in the Tiergarten. When you reach Merano —"

"If I reach Merano."

"You have, I should say, a fifty-fifty chance." Von Geissel tapped his fingers on the table in annoyance. "When you reach Merano, Deussman will provide you with documents, new identities. The Führer," von Geissel added, "will be a priest, just as the unfortunate Otto Witt was."

"Which reminds me," Harzer said, struggling to sit up again, "we have just received a belated message from Brandt. It seems a woman was involved in the shooting. You didn't tell us about that."

"Someone had tipped off American intelligence," Wolff told him.

Von Geissel asked: "Why didn't you kill her?"

"There was a priest there."

"So?"

"You don't go shooting priests in Rome. In any case the police, American agents ... they would all have been there within seconds. We had to get Witt's body away and dispose of it."

Von Geissel looked unconvinced. "Anyway we must concentrate on the present. You are now easily identifiable in Rome as an SS officer. You will have to have a completely different identity."

Harzer said: "Brandt points out quite rightly that you can't use the same entry into The Vatican ..." His voice died away. He cleared his throat and said to von Geissel: "Tell him."

Von Geissel went to a dust-covered desk and produced a map of Rome which he spread on the table. "When you get to Rome you must go to this building," pointing at the Villa Bonaparte, the Papal Assistance premises.

*　　*　　*

On the following day Ziemann was taken from the Munich cellar by Steiner and Wenck and piled into a nondescript grey van. Steiner took the wheel, Wenck sat in the back with Ziemann. He held a Luger in one hand.

They headed for Berlin avoiding the main roads. To the south of the city the Russians had reached Schoneberg and were poised to capture Tempelhof airport. But it was still just possible to reach the centre if you knew your back streets.

Around them the suburbs blazed. The weapons known as

Stalin Organs pumped phosphorous shells indiscriminately into peaceful back-waters, the Soviet gunners remembering the scorched earth that the Germans had left behind them in Russia. Once the van was strafed by a *Yak* fighter-bomber; once the crew of a T-34 tank resting at the roadside yelled to them to stop, but Steiner put his foot down and they careered down a side-street to safety.

By 4 pm they were inside von Geissel's apartment. There they gave Ziemann, now frightened to the point of insanity, another vegetarian meal. "Not that you can get meat anyway," Wenck said cheerfully, rubbing his broken nose.

"No tablets?" Steiner asked, pouring himself a brandy.

Out of Ziemann's ear-shot von Geissel said: "No more tablets. Apparently Hitler has at last dismissed Morell. So he won't be having any more of Dr. Koester's Anti-Gas Pills."

Wenck said: "And now a little barbering. You know, I've always fancied myself as a barber. I suppose it's all those old gangster movies when Al Capone and his henchmen discussed their business while they were having a shave."

"You would have made a better gangster," Steiner told him.

Wenck fetched a shaving brush, soap and a cut-throat razor from the bathroom. He lathered Ziemann's straggling moustache and then shaved both ends so that Ziemann was left with a neat, tooth-brush moustache.

Wenck stood back to survey his work. "Excellent." And in a whisper to Steiner: "I almost saluted the poor bastard."

Ziemann submitted to the shave passively. He didn't question any more. He wanted only to die.

*   *   *

On the way to Berlin the grey van had passed a tattered refugee. Steiner paid no attention to him: what was left of Germany was crawling with refugees.

But there was a difference about this particular refugee, a difference which didn't occur to Steiner: he was walking in the

271

opposite direction to the others: he was heading towards Berlin.

In his home village Landau had obtained the information he wanted. Now he was on the last lap of his personal crusade: his bid to salvage one decency from the horror that had been his life.

He had hitched a lift across most of Bavaria in a stolen truck, driven by an Army deserter desperate to reach his family in a small town to the south east of Berlin before the Russians got there.

Then Landau continued by foot. When he reached the battle area he hid in a garden hut at the back of a small house devastated by a shell. In a house across the street Soviet soldiers were celebrating. Crouching in the hut, Landau heard the crash of breaking glass and the screams of women as they were repeatedly raped by wild men from the *steppes*.

One hour after nightfall he climbed on a bicycle he had found in the hut and pedalled north through the flames and carnage.

At some time during the night he crossed into what passed for the German lines. But there was no real demarcation, only a vague division between victory and defeat.

No one took any notice of the lone figure on a bicycle.

When he reached the centre of Berlin he was exhausted. He drank some milk and ate some cheese that he had found in the kitchen of a shattered house. Then he headed for the Charite hospital in the Mitte district of central Berlin. There was nowhere else he could go. It was his last hope.

*   *   *

One evening between April 20th and 30th — he could never isolate the exact date in his mind — Wolff heard a report that sickened him more than any single event inside the Führerbunker.

Assailed by mild claustrophobia in his own room in the Führerbunker he had wandered into the dining-passage area for a meal.

There he was joined as he ate a corned-beef salad by two of Hitler's Reichssicherheitsdienst bodyguards who had been in sole charge of Hitler's safety until the arrival of Wolff. Although they weren't surprised by it, they bitterly resented Wolff's presence; they were both tough, expert in unarmed combat and crack shots; they were also — like many of the inhabitants of the concrete caves beneath the Chancellery — a little drunk.

One of the guards named Schmidt said: "And how is our Leibstandarte friend and Führer's favourite tonight?"

"Fine," Wolff said, and went on eating.

The other guard, whose name was Rokker, said: "I'm surprised the Führer still retains your services in view of his action regarding the Leibstandarte."

Wolff put down his knife and fork. "What the hell are you talking about?"

"Surely you know," Schmidt remarked. "After all you do have the Führer's ear."

Dust fell on the table as a shell scored a direct hit on the Chancellery above.

Wolff dusted his jacket. "Please enlighten me."

"But it happened ages ago," Rokker said. "Do you really mean you don't know?"

Schmidt grinned. "Obviously a diplomatic omission on the Führer's part."

Wolff said tautly: "Tell me."

"Well," Rokker said, "it seems that the Fuhrer was displeased with Sepp Dietrich and his Leibstandarte fighting with the 6th SS. He attacked the upper Danube in the pouring rain and his men were massacred."

Wolff lowered his head and stared at the table. And then: "But what has that got to do with the Führer? And me for that matter?"

Schmidt said: "The attack was ordered by Hitler. That's why they didn't wait until the rain had stopped. When the Führer heard that the attack had failed he ordered them to take off their Leibstandarte armbands in disgrace."

A nerve in Wolff's jaw twitched. "I don't believe it."

Rokker said: "They sent their armbands to Berlin in a chamberpot — or so the story goes." He shrugged. "Ask anyone. Everybody knows about it. Everybody except you, that is."

Schmidt grinned at Wolff. "I see you're still wearing your armband, Sturmbannführer."

Abruptly Wolff stood up. He went into the Vorbunker and spoke to a Wehrmacht Colonel whom he trusted. The Colonel confirmed the guards' story.

Wolff stared at him incredulously. "But they are the bravest soldiers who have ever fought for Hitler."

"They were brave, certainly," the Colonel agreed.

"And they have been decimated. Thousands of them have given their lives for Hitler. Thrown themselves onto tanks clutching live grenades. How could Hitler do this?"

"You will have to ask him that yourself," the Colonel replied.

That night Wolff dreamed again about the parade long ago when 60,000 boys had raised daggers to the skies. But this time there was no blinding flash of light; and blood was dripping from the blades of the daggers.

*　　*　　*

On April 28th Wolff visited the Charite hospital where Frieda worked. He went in civilian clothes because he knew his uniform upset her.

The fighting was only a few hundred yards away. Bodies littered the streets; men and women lay in the gutters bleeding to death. Behind the hospital different calibre guns spat and barked, chattered and thundered.

The wounded overflowed from the wards into the corridors, into the hospital foyer itself. When Frieda came to the foyer to see Wolff her appearance shocked him. Her hair was unkempt, her uniform creased, the stamp of exhaustion on her face; only her hands were clean.

She kissed him and leaned heavily against him. "When's it

going to end, Kurt?"

"Soon," he said. "Very soon. But now you've got to come with me. The Russians will be here within hours."

"No, Kurt. My place is here. I know it sounds trite. But you understand, don't you?"

He tried once more but she was right — he understood. He kissed her. "Very soon it will be over. And then ..."

"And then?" She looked up at him.

He thought of what lay ahead of him. "We'll be together," he said. "Don't worry, everything will be all right," wondering at the inadequacy of the words.

He kissed her once more and was gone leaving her standing among the sick and the dead and the dying.

Outside the hospital a man in a shabby suit with a patchy stubble of hair and gaunt features ran up to him.

"Hauptsturmführer Wolff?"

"Sturmbannführer. Who the hell are you?"

"My name doesn't matter. But I must speak to you."

"I'm sorry," Wolff said, "I haven't the time."

"Please," hand grabbing at Wolff's sleeve, "I've waited years, a lifetime ..."

A Katyusha rocket exploded close by showering them with dirt. Wolff wiped the dirt from his face and sighed. "Do you know where we can get a coffee and a brandy?"

"I should do," the man said. "I've been waiting here for nearly a week."

They went to a cellar where a group of men and women were huddled round a small, marble bar. Wolff tossed some marks onto the bar. "Coffee and cognac," he said, shrugging as the barman pocketed enough marks to have bought a whole bottle of brandy six months ago.

They sat at a table and he turned to the gaunt man beside him. "Now what do you want? Food, documents, information? I must warn you I have none of these things."

"On the contrary," Landau said, "I want to give you something." From a shoe-box he carried under his arm he brought out a sheaf of papers and photographs.

One hour later Wolff emerged from the cellar-bar too stunned even to think.

XXX

Two blows finally broke Hitler.

The first was the revelation from a news agency that Heinrich Himmler, whose loyalty he had never doubted, was trying to negotiate a secret peace with the Allies. Himmler's liaison officer at the Führerbunker, Gruppenführer Hermann Fegelein, was promptly court-martialled and shot.

The second blow was the news that Benito Mussolini, whom he had both championed and despised, had been caught by partisans trying to escape to Switzerland disguised as a German petty officer.

His mistress, Claretta Petacci, had been captured with him. They were both shot against the wall of a villa and their bodies hung upside-down from the roof of a petrol station in Milan. On April 29th the Germans in Italy agreed to an unconditional surrender as the Allies — aided by the partisans who had attacked in force earlier in the month — swarmed towards the Swiss and Austrian borders.

On the night of the 28th-29th Hitler granted Eva Braun her dearest wish: he married her. The ceremony was performed by a civil servant, Walter Wagner, in the smaller of the two conference rooms. The couple retired for a wedding breakfast and then drank champagne with Bormann, Goebbels and his wife and a couple of secretaries.

Two hours after the ceremony Hitler retired briefly to his study and summoned Wolff.

He said simply: "It is all over. We leave tomorrow."

"*Ja, mein Führer.*"

"Is everything ready?"

"Everything. I suggest we leave at about 3.30 in the afternoon when Russian air activity is at its lightest."

"Very well," Hitler said. "I will be ready. Now I have to prepare them for my *suicide* . . ."

Hitler then dictated his two testaments — political and personal — to his secretary, Frau Junge. In the political testament he expelled from the Nazi Party Himmler and Göring, who, in a telegram, had proposed taking over the leadership of the Reich, while Hitler was trapped in Berlin. He appointed Grand Admiral Karl Doenitz as his successor.

In his personal testament Hitler said: "My wife and I choose to die in order to escape the shame of overthrow or capitulation. It is our wish that our bodies be burnt immediately in the place where I have performed the greater part of my daily work during the course of my twelve years of service to my people."

Just before dawn Hitler signed the documents.

He saw Wolff once more and asked: "Is there a possibility that my wife can come?"

Wolff shook his head. "The aircraft only carries two people."

Hitler nodded. "I understand." He retired to rest.

* * *

Just after dawn on April 29th, Wolff visited Harzer and von Geissel at the apartment.

It was apparent that Harzer was only just clinging on to life. His eyes were closed, his breathing barely perceptible.

Wolff said to von Geissel: "Does his daughter know it's the end?"

Von Geissel shook his head. "It seemed pointless to tell her."

"Is his mind lucid?"

"Not really. He's back in his childhood."

"We must let him die believing Grey Fox has succeeded."

"Believing?"

"There are many hazards ahead." Wolff no longer bothered with rank: they were merely fellow conspirators. "May I suggest that you tell him the mission has succeeded? I'll keep out of the way."

Von Geissel went back into the bedroom where Harzer lay propped up against two pillows. He bent over the bed while Wolff watched from the doorway.

Harzer's eyes flickered open and he stared uncomprehendingly in front of him.

Von Geissel said: "Listen to me, Werner. Grey Fox has succeeded. The Führer is safe inside The Vatican."

Harzer looked at von Geissel, recognition in his eyes. Momentarily his features lit up; he smiled, then his eyes closed again.

Von Geissel put his head close to Harzer's chest. He stood up shaking his head. "He's dead."

They went into the living room. With its dark drapes and empty fireplace it was like a funeral chamber.

"So," von Geissel said, "the stage is set for the last act."

Wolff told him that he wanted Ziemann brought to the emergency exit of the bunker at 3.10 pm the following day. "I will be waiting inside with the Führer as arranged. Do you have an appropriate uniform for Ziemann?"

"Of course."

"Can you contact Brandt to tell him?"

"I'll try and reach him by radio."

"Until tomorrow," Wolff said.

Von Geissel raised one arm. "Heil Hitler."

"Heil Hitler," said Wolff.

During the 29th Hitler held two conferences. At the second he was told that the Russians were expected to reach the Chancellery by May 1st.

That afternoon Hitler had his favourite dog, an Alsatian named Blondi, killed — with an ampoule of cyanide.

At 2.30 on the morning of the 30th Hitler summoned the staff of twenty women who worked in the underground com-

279

plex to the dining passage. He shook them all by the hand, murmuring a few words here and there.

The ceremony was interpreted as a farewell: the Führer was going to commit suicide. A bizarre euphoria spread through the bunker: men and women sang and danced and drank.

Later in the morning Hitler's military advisers reported to him for the last time. Wolff heard to his alarm that the Russians had taken the Tiergarten.

Afterwards Wolff spoke to one of the aides and asked if the Tiergarten was completely in Soviet hands. The aide told him that the situation was fluid; Russian troops were in the park but fighting was still in progress; parts of it were still in German hands.

Meanwhile cans containing 180 litres of petrol had been deposited at the emergency exit to the Führerbunker and all the guards dismissed.

Between 2 and 2.30 pm Hitler ate his lunch — spaghetti with sauce. Afterwards he and Eva Braun bid their farewells to Goebbels and Bormann and members of his military and domestic staff.

Hitler and his wife then adjourned to their suite. It was 3.20 pm.

While Eva Braun was in the bathroom, Hitler crossed the conference passage and went into the drawing room where he was to change from his uniform into civilian clothes and shave off his moustache. Wolff was waiting for him.

*   *   *

Wolff led the way through the holocaust that was central Berlin. Already the Soviet flag fluttered over the Reichstag, although fighting for the ruined building — its destruction by fire in 1933 had been used by Hitler as evidence of a Communist sabotage — was still in progress.

Snipers' bullets spattered the walls as they ducked and weaved in the direction of the Tiergarten. A mortar shell exploded behind them; a machine-gun chattered from behind a swaying wall of masonry.

Fighting was also in progress in the green, shell-pocked acres of the Tiergarten. Ahead, beneath camouflage netting, and guarded by a couple of dozen Volkssturm Wolff could see the Stork. He practically pulled his sweating, ashen-faced companion across the grass and bundled him into the passenger seat of the aircraft.

Wenck, whom he recognised, was pulling the netting off the plane. The engine fired. And the little plane was hurtling across the grass; then it was airborne, undercarriage brushing the branches of a leafless shell-blasted tree.

Wolff never knew whether they were fired at. At first, at roof-top level, there was just smoke and flames and shell-bursts.

As they gained altitude the noise of battle receded. Beneath them, bisected by the silver ribbon of the River Spree and, cloaked in grey, fire-tongued smoke, lay a city in its death agony.

Wolff banked and headed south.

XXXI

It was on May 3rd that Liam Doyle discerned unusual tension in the Villa Bonaparte.

He also spotted Brandt in conversation with the German priest who had been installed in the premises. He telephoned Anderson and told him that he thought the arrival they had been expecting was imminent — even though the death of Hitler had been announced on Hamburg Radio at 10.25 pm on May 1st.

Anderson posted men all around the villa and its gardens. He himself took up a position in a shop doorway on the Via Piave opposite the yellowing walls of the Villa. The agents were told to watch for a man answering the description of Hans Doppler, probably in the company of one other man who might be masquerading as a priest.

At 2.33 pm on the afternoon on May 3rd, a Volkswagen with red crosses painted on its roof and doors pulled up outside the Via Piave entrance to the villa. Two agents from either side closed in as Anderson ran across the street.

A man answering Doppler's description climbed from the driving seat, walked round the small car and opened the door for his passenger.

The passenger wore clerical clothes. His face was almost hidden by the brim of a black hat and the up-turned collar of a coat several sizes too big for him.

As the passenger climbed out of the car the agents grabbed his arms. One of them held the man known as Doppler, but all the interest was centred on his companion.

As Anderson moved to snatch away the black hat, Wolff tore himself free and raced down the Via Piave in the direction of the Via XX Settembre.

One of the agents snatched a Colt .38 from his shoulder holster and fired after the fleeing figure. Another gave chase.

Anderson removed the black hat, uttered an exclamation of surprise and said: "And who the hell are you?"

"My name," said the man in the black coat with dignity, "is Landau."

*　　*　　*

In the Via XX Settembre Wolff hailed a taxi, jumped into it before it had stopped and told the driver to take him to The Vatican and put his foot down — an order beloved by the cab drivers of Rome.

Through the rear window he saw his pursuer stop, look around wildly for another taxi, then drop his arms to his sides in defeat.

Wolff paid off the taxi at St. Peter's Square and walked through the Arch of the Bells, showing the Swiss Guards The Vatican pass he had picked up in Merano.

Once inside the walls he made his way to the post office in the north east of The Vatican City and asked if they knew where a priest named Liam Doyle lived. After the shooting in the Piazza Pia he had asked Brandt about the priest who had stopped Maria Reubeni from shooting Otto Witt. Brandt had provided his name. The post office official told him where Doyle lived.

Wolff had to wait three hours before Liam arrived. He approached him as he was about to enter the block where he lived.

Liam gazed at him in astonishment. "You!"

"I need your help," Wolff said.

"What are you doing here?"

"If you will invite me into your room I will tell you. If you still want me to go after that I'll go." He put his hand on Liam's sleeve. "Please."

Liam hesitated. This was the man who had betrayed Maria, the man who had committed murder in front of his eyes . . .

Wolff said again: "Please. In God's name listen to me."

"Very well. Follow me."

Inside Liam's room Wolff collapsed into the easy chair. "I suppose you don't have a drink?"

"I can make you a cup of tea."

Wolff smiled faintly. "You know, I think that's just what I would like."

Liam made the tea and handed Wolff a cup, watching him curiously. Finally he said: "And now perhaps an explanation."

"It's a long story," Wolff said.

"I have plenty of time."

"It begins many, many years ago . . ."

Liam sat on the edge of the bed, hardly moving as Wolff told him the story of his life. Three quarters of an hour, five cigarettes and three cups of tea later Wolff had reached the day he made his last visit to Frieda in the Charite hospital.

He paused. His face had grown pale and there were beads of sweat on his forehead.

"Would you like to lie down?"

Wolff shook his head. "I'll be all right." He opened the window and stood there breathing in fresh air. Then he sat down again and told Liam about the last days in Berlin.

* * *

In the cellar-bar near the hospital Landau had described how he had escaped from Dachau and told Wolff a story about a childless couple who used to visit his village in Bavaria in the '20's.

The name of the couple was Wolff. They had been well liked in the village and twice a year they had gone there on holiday, staying in the local inn, walking in the mountains. Their only sorrow seemed to be that they had no children.

The inn-keeper and his wife were Jewish. One day, long before the purges began in earnest, a gang of bully-boys stormed through the village looking for trouble.

They went into the inn where they got drunk. They identified the landlord and his wife as Jewish despite the inn-keeper's blond hair and blue eyes. They started to bait him but, aided by other customers, the inn-keeper threw them out.

That night they returned and set fire to the inn. The landlord and his wife were trapped in their bedroom where they suffocated to death. But before they died the wife managed to throw their baby son out of the window.

"Into my arms," Landau told Wolff in the cellar-bar.

"What happened then?" Wolff demanded as the shock waves began to hit him.

"The Wolffs were sleeping in a downstairs room and they had managed to escape. They took the baby from me. Who was I to argue? A peasant, a bachelor, a Jew . . . They spent the night in a rooming-house in the village. Next morning, after they had bought clothes, they came to see me.

"They said they were going to take the baby with them. No one else had seen the inn-keeper's wife throw the baby from the bedroom. I was the only one who knew. They gave me some money and swore me to secrecy. They said they were saving the life of one Jewish boy. I took their money and at the time I believed I was doing right."

"Are you trying to tell me I'm a Jew?"

"I'm telling you the truth."

"I don't believe you," although already he did and his life was crumbling around him.

Landau told him that the Wolff home was fairly isolated — as Kurt Wolff knew it was. Months later a premature birth was announced. The husand, a wealthy wine-producer and ex-Cavalry officer in the First World War, wasn't without influence. A birth certificate was made out with the connivance of the family doctor. The baby was named Kurt.

"I suppose you have proof of this ridiculous story," Kurt Wolff said.

"Oh yes, I have proof."

"Did this man Wolff still pay you well to keep the secret?"

"From time to time he gave me money, yes."

"So you were blackmailing him."

"I know I shouldn't have taken the money," Landau said. "Don't you think I've tortured myself with that in the years I was in Dachau?"

"I'm surprised you went to Dachau," Wolff said. "I should have thought you would have avoided that. You were smart enough — or so you claim."

Landau smote the table with his fist. "Don't you think I've suffered enough? Don't you realise I'm trying to save you?"

"I think you're trying to destroy me," Wolff said. "Anyway, finish your story."

Landau told Wolff that when the Nazis' anti-Semitic policies swung into action in full force the Gestapo came to the village and rounded up five Jews there. He was one of them.

He was imprisoned and beaten-up; charges of illicitly dealing in foreign currency were concocted against him. He was shifted from prison to prison until he ended up at Dachau. There he determined to find the baby who had been thrown into his arms and tell him about his true birthright. "I owed it to him. I didn't want him to spend the rest of his life glorifying the filth who perpetrated this ..." From the cardboard-box Landau took a bundle of photographs and threw them on the table. They showed the skeletal figures of the inmates of Dachau ... the gas-chambers ... the burial pits ... two small boys watching their parents dig their own grave ...

"The guards took those photographs," Landau said. "They were rather proud of them."

Wolff grabbed the photographs and threw them back in the box. His knuckles gleamed white on his clenched fists. "I don't want to see them." He swallowed his brandy but the liquor seemed to brand his stomach. "I asked for proof, where is it?"

Landau produced a faded document from the box. "First, proof that I am who I say I am."

Wolff picked up the sheet of paper. It was a prison admission form confirming Landau's name, race, birthplace and age. "What else?"

Landau said that after he had escaped from Dachau he had returned to his home village. There he had recovered the original birth certificate of the innkeeper's son; it had been salvaged from the wreckage of the inn, and Landau had buried it in a biscuit tin in a yard behind the farmhouse where he had once worked. He showed Wolff the birth-certificate. "You see," he said softly, "your name is Kaufman."

"This proves nothing," Wolff said.

"There were letters too from the Wolffs. I have those if you want to read them. You see I kept in touch until the Gestapo came for me. But there is one photograph that will convince you. A photograph taken of the new-born baby. The baby had a birthmark on its chest shaped like a comma." Landau searched in the box and produced a cracked, yellowing photograph of a baby; on its chest the birth-mark was clearly visible.

Slowly, as though in a trance, Wolff undid his jacket and lifted his shirt. They both stared at the birth-mark shaped like a comma on his chest.

* * *

The only sound in Liam Doyle's room was the tapping of rain against the window. Liam sat motionless on the side of the bed while Wolff buried his head in his hands, fingers pushing through his blond hair.

Liam had no idea what to say. He felt deeply compassionate towards this man with the ravages of war printed indelibly on his face. But Wolff was SS; Wolff had killed; Wolff was the enemy.

He had no idea what Wolff wanted of him. But first he had to finish his story, to purge himself. Gently, Liam questioned him. "What I don't understand," he said, "is how Landau contacted you."

Wolff raised his hands and looked at Liam through bloodshot eyes. "It wasn't difficult. He managed to telephone the house where I had once lived with my . . . with my foster-parents. I had unwittingly helped Landau by visiting the house with . . . with my fiancée, a girl named Frieda Harzer. Frieda told the new owner that she worked at the Charite hospital. That was all Landau had and he took full advantage of it. He guessed, hoped, that I would visit Frieda at the hospital and, of course, I did."

Outside it had begun to rain harder. Thunder grumbled in the distance and lightning flickered on the horizon over the rooftops of The Vatican City. The clock on Liam's mantelpiece chimed seven.

They were nearing the end of the story. Liam said: "And what happened then? Why didn't you bring Hitler to Rome?"

Wolff stood up and, staring through the rain streaming down the window, told him.

*　*　*

After Landau's revelations, after Hitler's treatment of the brave and loyal Leibstandarte, Wolff had determined not to implement Grey Fox.

On the afternoon of the 30th he had stationed himself at the exit to the Führerbunker, now unguarded. He had hoped to prevent the murder of Ziemann but, when Steiner arrived, he was already dead, covered with a blanket in Steiner's arms.

Wolff recognised Steiner and another fragment of his past slotted into place. Steiner smiled at him cheerfully. "Yes, it's me. I hope we didn't shock you too much that day with our treasonable talk. However, you had your revenge as I recall it."

Wolff noticed that Ziemann's socks were darned. That was an oversight that they would have had to correct — if he had been going through with Grey Fox.

"Give me a hand," Steiner said. "He's a skinny little runt but he's heavy enough."

Wolff walked behind Steiner as though to examine Ziemann's face which was lolling over the back of his arm. Then he pulled the Walther from his holster and clubbed Steiner on the back of the head. Steiner collapsed on the ground with the corpse. Wolff pulled the unconscious body and the dead body behind some rubble at the edge of the garden. He knew he should kill Steiner but ... Steiner was merely doing what he himself had sworn to do.

He threw himself to the ground instinctively as he heard the whoosh of a Katyusha rocket. When he got to his feet there was no need to worry about Steiner: a jagged piece of metal was protruding from between his pouched eyes.

Wolff ran down the stairs and the emergency exit and into the drawing room. A couple of minutes later Hitler came in. By this time Wolff had fitted a silencer onto the barrel of the Walther.

No words were exchanged. Wolff took one step forward, produced the pistol from behind his back and shot Hitler in the head. The mad genius who had raised Germany from the ruins of one world war and deposited it in the ashes of a second lay dying at his feet.

Wolff picked up Hitler and carried him across the conference passage into the ante-room of his suite. There was no one about because Hitler had earlier taken precautions to ensure that he had no visitors. From the ante-room he took him to the study and threw his body on the sofa. Then he took a cyanide ampoule from his pocket and crushed it between Hitler's jaws.

At that moment he heard the sound of running water from the bathroom adjoining the study. He let himself out of the study and waited. He heard a woman's scream. He peered round the door and saw Eva Braun biting on another ampoule.

She died while he cleaned the blood and fragments of bone from the drawing room. When he returned he fired Hitler's own Walther at the concrete wall, wrapped Hitler's hands round the butt of the still smoking gun and let it fall.

Then he raced out of the bunker through the emergency exit, collected Landau who was waiting round the corner and headed for the Tiergarten.

* * *

The storm was overhead now, rain lashing the window, the sharp crack of thunder following flashes of forked lightning.

Wearily Wolff returned to the chair and sat down. "I ask only three things, Father."

"And those are?"

"One that you tell no one else what I have told you. It is a confession after all. Do you agree?"

Liam thought for a moment, then nodded. "The second?"

"That you forgive me."

"Only God can do that."

"As I understand the Roman Catholic faith you can forgive me if I perform a penance."

"I think you've done that already," Liam said softly.

"Then you forgive me?"

"I forgive you," Liam said. "And the third?"

"I want you to take a message to Maria Reubeni. Tell her what I have told you, no one else. Ask her if she will see me."

Thunder crashed over The Vatican.

Liam stood up. "That is the hardest of all," he said. "She won't even see me." He turned away so that Wolff couldn't see the pain in his eyes.

"Try," Wolff urged him.

"Very well I will try. But I am not hopeful. Now lie down and get some sleep."

Wolff lay down on the bed and was instantly asleep. Liam waited until the rain had dwindled to a drizzle before leaving the block and heading through the streets that smelled of wet dust towards Maria Reubeni's apartment.

But Liam was wrong. Anderson's words had penetrated the numb area of unforgiveness. She remembered what Liam had done for her and the Jews of Rome; she remembered his devotion, his torment. And when she heard his footsteps on the stairs she flung open the door. And then she was in his arms.

Happiness suffused Liam Doyle. He stayed close to her for a moment before gently pushing her away.

She was crying now and he let her. And when she had finished she said: "I'm sorry, Liam, so sorry. Will you forgive me?"

Liam smiled at her. "Everyone wants forgiveness today."

And he led her to the sofa and told her about Kurt Wolff. When he had finished he said: "Well?"

Slowly she said: "No, Liam. Tell him it's too late." She paused. "Tell him it was always too late. He will understand."

When Liam returned to his room Wolff was still lying on the bed. He opened his eyes as Liam walked in. "Well?"

Liam shook his head.

Wolff said: "I knew, but I had to try. It is for the best. Maria and I . . ." He spread wide his hands. "It was something no man or woman has the right to expect. We will now live our lives as others live them."

Liam opened the window and fresh moist air smelling of dust and blossom poured into the room.

Wolff sat up on the bed. "Two more favours, Father," rasping his hand across his unshaven cheeks. "Can I stay here for a little while?"

"You won't be the first Jew who has been given sanctuary in The Vatican."

"And secondly, can I have some writing paper and an envelope?"

Wolff rested the paper on a folded copy of The Vatican newspaper. It might take months for the letter to reach its destination, maybe it never would — although Wolff had an intuitive feeling that it might. Just as he had an intuitive feeling that one day he would be able to return to Germany and live as it had been intended when he had been born to the wife of a Bavarian inn-keeper. He thought for a moment and then began the letter:

Dearest Frieda, I want you to become the wife of a Jew.

*   *   *

On May 8th, the day the Germans unconditionally surrendered, Liam Doyle packed his bags and left Kurt Wolff in his room. Wolff had said that he would deal with Brandt. Liam didn't encourage or dissuade him: his period of indecision was over.

He went by taxi to Maria Reubeni's flat. She told him that she was going to marry Anderson and Liam was happy for her. He thought she would probably have five children and grow pasta-plump.

She kissed him and, for the first and last time, he kissed her back and he knew he would always feel the kiss on his lips. Then he told her that he was going back to the Bronx 'where I belong.'

She opened the window and watched him climb into the waiting taxi. She waved as the taxi accelerated down the street. After the taxi had disappeared, she stayed at the window for several minutes staring through her tears at the glimpse of the river from her apartment which the estate agents had so preposterously described as 'overlooking the Tiber.'

EPILOGUE

Although the bodies of Adolf Hitler and Eva Braun were almost certainly burned in the garden of the Chancellery during the afternoon and evening of April 30th, 1945, controversy has surrounded two aspects of the death of the Führer.

(1) After the discovery of the bodies of Goebbels, his wife and their six children, who had presumably been killed by their mother, the Russians found the remains of two bodies resembling Hitler. The charred remains of one were, according to the guarded submissions of the Russians, identified as those of Hitler on the basis of dental evidence. Any possibility that the other corpse was Hitler was finally rejected, a contributory factor being that the dead man wore darned socks. Surely the Führer wasn't reduced to wearing patched hosiery.

(2) Despite eye-witness accounts that Hitler had suffered a gun-shot wound to the head there has always been debate as to whether a bullet or cyanide killed him.